ACCLAIM FOR KATHLEEN FULLER

"A warm romance that will tug at the hearts of readers, this is a new favorite."

—*THE PARKERSBURG NEWS & SENTINEL*
ON *THE TEACHER'S BRIDE*

"Fuller's appealing Amish romance deals with some serious issues, including depression, yet it also offers funny and endearing moments."

—*BOOKLIST* ON *THE TEACHER'S BRIDE*

"Kathleen Fuller's *The Teacher's Bride* is a heartwarming story of unexpected romance woven with fun and engaging characters who come to life on every page. Once you open the book, you won't put it down until you've reached the end."

—AMY CLIPSTON, BESTSELLING AUTHOR
OF *A SEAT BY THE HEARTH*

"Kathy Fuller's characters leap off the page with subtle power as she uses both wit and wisdom to entertain! Refreshingly honest and charming, Kathy's writing reflects a master's touch when it comes to intricate plotting and a satisfying and inspirational ending full of good cheer!"

—KELLY LONG, NATIONAL BESTSELLING
AUTHOR, ON *THE TEACHER'S BRIDE*

"Kathleen Fuller is a master storyteller and fans will absolutely fall in love with Ruby and Christian in *The Teacher's Bride*."

—RUTH REID, BESTSELLING AUTHOR OF *A MIRACLE OF HOPE*

"*The Teacher's Bride* features characters who know what it's like to be different, to not fit in. What they don't know is that's what makes them so loveable. Kathleen Fuller has written a sweet, oftentimes humorous, romance that reminds readers that the perfect match might be right in front of their noses. She handles the difficult topic of depression with a deft touch. Readers of Amish fiction won't want to miss this delightful story."

—KELLY IRVIN, BESTSELLING AUTHOR OF
THE EVERY AMISH SEASON SERIES

"Kathleen Fuller is a talented and a gifted author, and she doesn't disappoint in *The Teacher's Bride*. The story will captivate you from the first page to the last with Ruby, Christian, and engaging characters. You'll laugh, gasp, and wonder what will happen next. You won't want to miss reading this heartwarming Amish story of mishaps, faith, love, forgiveness, and friendship."

—MOLLY JEBBER, SPEAKER AND AWARD-WINNING
AUTHOR OF *GRACE'S FORGIVENESS* AND THE
AMISH KEEPSAKE POCKET QUILT SERIES

"Enthusiasts of Fuller's sweet Amish romances will savor this new anthology."

—*LIBRARY JOURNAL* ON *AN AMISH FAMILY*

"These four sweet stories are full of hope and promise along with misunderstandings and reconciliation. True love does prevail, but not without prayer, introspection, and humility. A must-read for fans of Amish romance."

—*RT BOOK REVIEWS*, 4 STARS, ON *AN AMISH FAMILY*

"The incredibly engaging Amish Letters series continues with a third story of perseverance and devotion, making it difficult to put down . . . Fuller skillfully knits together the lives within a changing, faithful community that has suffered its share of challenges."

"This compelling series continues with a serious story of forgiveness and redemption, as Fuller returns to Birch Creek to develop new relationships and revisit old friends."

"Fuller's refreshing portrayal of the Amish as complex, flawed children of God adds deeper dimension to a plot already filled with lovable characters and an artfully crafted world that draws readers in and invites them to stay. Passion and joy for God and the written word are evident throughout the book, woven into a heartwarming invitation to share the love."

"The first book in the Amish Letters series features a poignant love story made even sweeter by the humorous penpal exchange between Phoebe and Jalon at the start. These are standout characters with complicated emotional histories. Readers of Fuller's Birch Creek series will be happy to return to this community and discover new characters and new romantic possibilities."

"Evoking a simpler time, when letters were handwritten and partially narrated in an epistolary style, Fuller's . . . first volume in a new series introduces two charismatic protagonists and an appealing, heartwarming story line. With elegantly clear prose and evocative settings, the author delivers another captivating read fans will relish."

—*LIBRARY JOURNAL* ON *WRITTEN IN LOVE*

"Fuller's inspirational tale portrays complex characters facing real-world problems and finding love where they least expected or wanted it to be."

—*BOOKLIST*, STARRED REVIEW, ON *A RELUCTANT BRIDE*

"Fuller has an amazing capacity for creating damaged characters and giving insights into their brokenness. One of the better voices in the Amish fiction genre."

—*CBA RETAILERS + RESOURCES* ON *A RELUCTANT BRIDE*

"This promising series debut from Fuller is edgier than most Amish novels, dealing with difficult and dark issues and featuring well-drawn characters who are tougher than the usual gentle souls found in this genre. Recommended for Amish fiction fans who might like a different flavor."

—*LIBRARY JOURNAL* ON *A RELUCTANT BRIDE*

"Sadie and Aden's love is both sweet and hard-won, and Aden's patience is touching as he wrestles not only with Sadie's dilemma, but his own abusive past. Birch Creek is weighed down by the Troyer family's dark secrets, and readers will be interested to see how secondary characters' lives unfold as the series continues."

—*RT BOOK REVIEWS*, 4 STARS, ON *A RELUCTANT BRIDE*

"Kathleen Fuller's *A Reluctant Bride* tells the story of two Amish families whose lives have collided through tragedy. Sadie Schrock's stoic resolve will touch and inspire Fuller's fans, as will the story's concluding triumph of redemption."

—Suzanne Woods Fisher, bestselling author of *Anna's Crossing*

"Kathleen Fuller's *A Reluctant Bride* is a beautiful story of faith, hope, and second chances. Her characters and descriptions are captivating, bringing the story to life with the turn of every page."

—Amy Clipston, bestselling author of *A Simple Prayer* and the Kauffman Amish Bakery series

"The latest offering in the Middlefield Family series is a sweet love story, with perfectly crafted characters. Fuller's Amish novels are written with the utmost respect for their way of living. Readers are given a glimpse of what it is like to live the simple life."

—RT Book Reviews, 4 stars, on *Letters to Katie*

"Fuller's second Amish series entry is a sweet romance with a strong sense of place that will attract readers of Wanda Brunstetter and Cindy Woodsmall."

—Library Journal on *Faithful to Laura*

"Well-drawn characters and a homespun feel will make this Amish romance a sure bet for fans of Beverly Lewis and Jerry S. Eicher."

—Library Journal on *Treasuring Emma*

"*Treasuring Emma* is a heartwarming story filled with real-life situations and well-developed characters. I rooted for Emma and Adam until the very last page. Fans of Amish fiction and those seeking an endearing romance will enjoy this love story. Highly recommended."

—BETH WISEMAN, BESTSELLING AUTHOR OF *HER BROTHER'S KEEPER* AND THE DAUGHTERS OF THE PROMISE SERIES

"*Treasuring Emma* is a charming, emotionally layered story of the value of friendship in love and discovering the truth of the heart. A true treasure of a read!"

—KELLY LONG, AUTHOR OF THE PATCH OF HEAVEN SERIES

THE PROMISE
OF A LETTER

OTHER BOOKS BY KATHLEEN FULLER

THE AMISH BRIDES OF BIRCH CREEK NOVELS

The Teacher's Bride

The Farmer's Bride

The Innkeeper's Bride

THE AMISH LETTERS NOVELS

Written in Love

The Promise of a Letter

Words from the Heart

THE AMISH OF BIRCH CREEK NOVELS

A Reluctant Bride

An Unbroken Heart

A Love Made New

THE MIDDLEFIELD AMISH NOVELS

A Faith of Her Own

THE MIDDLEFIELD FAMILY NOVELS

Treasuring Emma

Faithful to Laura

Letters to Katie

The Hearts of Middlefield Novels

A Man of His Word

An Honest Love

A Hand to Hold

Story Collection

An Amish Family

Amish Generations (available June 2020)

Stories

A Miracle for Miriam included
in *An Amish Christmas*

A Place of His Own included
in *An Amish Gathering*

What the Heart Sees included in *An Amish Love*

A Perfect Match included in *An Amish Wedding*

Flowers for Rachael included
in *An Amish Garden*

A Gift for Anne Marie included in
An Amish Second Christmas

A Heart Full of Love included
in *An Amish Cradle*

A Bid for Love included in *An Amish Market*

A Quiet Love included in *An Amish Harvest*

Building Faith included in *An Amish Home*

THE PROMISE
OF A LETTER

AN AMISH LETTERS NOVEL

Kathleen Fuller

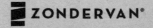

ZONDERVAN

The Promise of a Letter

© 2017 by Kathleen Fuller

This title is also available as an ebook.

Requests for information should be addressed to:
Zondervan, *3900 Sparks Dr. SE, Grand Rapids, Michigan 49546*

ISBN 978-0-7180-8254-3 (trade paper)
ISBN 978-0-7180-8255-0 (e-book)
ISBN 978-0-310-36000-1 (mass market)

Library of Congress Cataloging-in-Publication Data
CIP data is available upon request.

Printed in the United States of America

20 21 22 23 24   QG   10 9 8 7 6 5 4 3 2 1

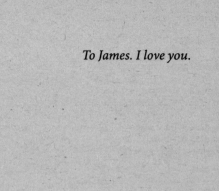

To James. I love you.

Glossary

ab im kopp: crazy, crazy in the head
ach: oh
aenti: aunt
appeditlich: delicious
bann: temporary or permanent excommunication
    from the Amish church
bruder: brother
bu/buwe: boy/boys
daag/daags: day/days
daed: father
danki: thank you
dawdi haus: smaller home, attached to or near the
    main house
Dietsch: Amish language
dochder: daughter
dumm: dumb
dummkopf: idiot
Englisch: non-Amish
familye: family
frau: woman, Mrs.
geh: go
grossmammi: grandmother
grossdaadi: grandfather

gut: good

gute nacht: good night

haus: house

kaffee: coffee

kapp: white hat worn by Amish women

kinn/kinner: child/children

maed/maedel: girl/young woman

mamm: mom

mann: Amish man

mei: my

mudder/mutter: mother

nee: no

nix: nothing

onkel: uncle

Ordnung: the set of rules, written and unwritten, by which the Amish live

schee: pretty/handsome

schwesters: sisters

seltsam: weird

sohn: son

vatter: father

ya: yes

yer: your

yerself: yourself

CHAPTER 1

Leanna Chupp clasped her hands behind her back as her Rollerblades glided against asphalt. She smoothly avoided ruts and small rocks as she skated along her street, perspiration running down her back and beading across her forehead. *Nothing wrong with a little sweat, especially on a hot August day.*

She'd left work well after five tonight, the second day in a row she stayed late. Although she was tired, the skating invigorated her. After spending over twelve hours inside the small engine repair shop, being out in the open and inhaling the sweet scents of hay and flowers and freshly mown grass brought a smile to her face. A slightly weary smile, but still a smile.

She dodged another rock and glanced over her shoulder. Her street was fairly isolated, and there usually wasn't much traffic, buggy or otherwise. But that was changing. Her brother, Jalon, married last year, and the Bontragers—his wife Phoebe's parents and her eleven younger brothers—all moved to Birch Creek after the wedding.

Leanna skated to the middle of the street and waved at the Yoders' house, home to her best friend, Ivy, and Ivy's parents and siblings. A couple of the Yoder boys were outside playing tag in the front yard, too busy with their game to notice her. If she wasn't late for supper, not to mention being tired, she might stop and join their game. It wouldn't be the first time.

She skated past the brand-new house that belonged to Phoebe's family. It was a large house that easily fit thirteen people, with a neatly mown yard and pretty flower baskets hanging from the front porch eave. A lovely home, but still plain and in keeping with the *Ordnung*.

After a few more blade strokes she braked to a stop in front of her own house. Well, not exactly her house, but her brother Jalon's. Leanna had moved to the finished *dawdi haus* behind the main house just before Jalon and Phoebe got married.

She stopped and looked at the main house. A little over a year ago she and Jalon had lived there after their parents moved to Mesopotamia to be near extended family. While they were growing up, the house had been big enough for a family of four, and the structure itself hadn't changed over the years. But everything else had. In addition to the *dawdi haus*, there was a large farm, twice the size of the one her father had struggled to make successful.

An expanded barn and a huge fenced-in pasture were recent additions. Colorful flowers bloomed in the flower beds and pots on the front porch, and a large garden thrived behind the house. Phoebe was not only a fantastic cook, but she also had ten green thumbs. In a short period of time, Leanna's family and living arrangements had blossomed stronger than the overflowing tomato plants in the garden.

Leanna stopped in front of the mailbox and opened it. If there was any mail for her, Phoebe or Jalon always left it in the box for her to retrieve after she got off work. She pulled out a postcard, smiled at the picture on the front, and then turned it over.

Dear Leanna,

I saw this card in a bookstore near my cousin's house and thought of you. See you when I get back.

Ivy

Leanna turned the card back over and examined the stunning photo of tall, majestic sunflowers wide open to the sun. Sunflowers were her favorite flower, especially the giant ones. Leave it to Ivy to send her a thoughtful card.

Ivy had left only a week ago to stay with her cousin in Michigan who was on bed rest. Leanna took off her backpack, put the card in it, and made a mental note to write to Ivy as soon as she could. "Mutt and Jeff," their mothers used to call them. Until she finally asked, Leanna had no idea who Mutt or Jeff were, but she assumed one was tall and one was short, just like her and Ivy. At six feet, Leanna was the tallest woman in Birch Creek, while Ivy was the shortest.

Leanna tromped through the neatly shorn grass toward the front porch. Although she lived separately from her brother and his family, she joined them for meals as often as she could, and not only because she enjoyed their company. Her cooking skills were limited to making peanut butter and jelly sandwiches, along with the occasional boiled egg, so she was happy to take her meals at Jalon's.

As she sat down on the porch steps and removed one of her skates, Blue, her Maine Coon cat, strolled up to her. "Hey *bu*," she said, leaning forward to scratch him under the chin. "Miss me?"

Blue sat down just out of Leanna's reach and looked at her. He sniffed the air and then walked off.

"Humph. Be that way." She chuckled. Blue used to be her closest companion until Malachi, Phoebe's young son, had won his heart. Now Blue rarely left Malachi's side, and Leanna loved seeing them together. She didn't have enough time to spend with the cat anyway, considering how busy she was at work, and she was glad the two of them had bonded.

She stripped off her other skate and put both her skates and the backpack near the front door, then slipped off her socks. Her shoes were inside the pack, but she didn't bother to put them on. It was summer, after all. The perfect time of the year to go barefoot.

The moment she walked into the house, she breathed in the aroma of food cooking. That surprised her since she figured she'd missed supper. Usually Phoebe set aside a plate for her when Leanna worked late. She headed for the kitchen and saw Phoebe standing at the stove, scooping mashed potatoes into a bowl.

"*Aenti* Leanna!" Malachi got up from the table and hugged her. He was an affectionate kid, another quality Leanna loved. She returned his hug and he dashed back to his seat. She walked over to Phoebe. "Anything I can do to help?"

Phoebe shook her head. "Supper's almost ready." She looked a little sheepish as she put her hand on her lower back. "I took a nap today and that set me behind schedule. But Jalon and Adam are working late on the barn addition, so it turned out okay."

Leanna nodded. Phoebe was eight months pregnant, and although she never complained, Leanna had noticed she was favoring her back a lot more lately. She also looked tired. Knowing how Jalon hovered over her, Leanna believed it wouldn't have mattered to him if Phoebe had slept completely through suppertime . . . as long as his wife had been able to rest.

"I'm hungry," Malachi griped.

Phoebe looked over her shoulder. "You'll have to wait on everyone else."

Malachi slumped in his chair and then reached out and started pushing his plate forward, a tiny bit at a time, with his index finger. The plate clanked against his cup of milk, making the liquid slosh.

"Don't play at the table," Phoebe reprimanded.

Malachi nodded, but Leanna kept her eye on him, and sure enough, he started pushing the plate again. She went to him. "That's not going to get you *yer* supper any earlier," she said, then leaned forward and added, "Trust me. I know. I used to do the same thing when I was little."

"I'm not little. I turned five two months ago."

"Excuse me, then. You're practically a grown-up." She gave him a sly grin and ruffled his pale blond hair before sitting down across from him.

Jalon came into the kitchen, followed by their cousin

Adam, who wheeled his chair over to his place next to Malachi at the table. Adam put the brakes on his wheelchair, then slipped off his fingerless leather gloves and placed them in his lap. He and Jalon had obviously already washed up, since this pair of gloves was his household pair. He used another beat-up, dirty pair when he was working outside.

Phoebe put the bowl of potatoes on the table and sat down. After silent prayer, she passed a plate heaped with perfectly browned steaks.

Leanna's stomach grumbled in anticipation as she filled her plate with two pieces of meat, a huge spoonful of mashed potatoes, an extra helping of cream gravy, buttered corn off the cob, and a slice of bread slathered with homemade blueberry jelly. "Hollow Legs," her father had called her growing up. Leanna didn't complain about the nickname. She didn't have to worry about food or her figure, something Ivy had admitted envying. "You never have to watch what you eat," Ivy had said over the years. "I have to watch all the time. Any extra calories *geh* right to *mei* hips."

Unlike Ivy, Leanna didn't have hips—or any curves to speak of. When she was younger, she had sometimes envied Ivy's petite, curvy figure, although she never admitted it out loud. Having a boyish frame had bothered her a little bit growing up. But now she was past such superficial concerns. People had to accept her the way she was—tall, boyish, and a good mechanic. If they didn't, that wasn't her problem.

As she wiped her mouth with her napkin, she smiled. Delicious food, her happy family, a steady job she loved

. . . Life was good. Her heart swelled with gratitude. *Thank you, Lord.*

"You worked late again," Jalon said to her, then took a drink of ice tea.

Leanna swallowed a bite of mashed potatoes. "*Ya.* We've been busy this week."

"When's Daniel coming back?" he asked.

"Tomorrow. Maybe the next day." Her boss, Daniel Raber, owned Raber's Small Engine Repair. He and his wife had returned to his hometown of Draperville, Kentucky, a few days ago to attend his grandmother's funeral. Draperville was such a small and insular Amish settlement that Leanna had never heard of it until Daniel and his wife moved to Birch Creek. Even then, he rarely talked about his former community. But she had seen how hard the news of his grandmother's death hit him. Obviously, they had been close, despite his never mentioning her.

Leanna had told him not to worry about the shop and to go to Draperville immediately.

"I'll hold down the fort," she'd said.

"I know you will."

She didn't take his confidence in her for granted. Daniel had been the first—actually, the only—person who had given her a chance as a mechanic. She thought the world of him and Barbara.

Before he left for Kentucky, Daniel glanced around the small shop, filled with engines and appliances that needed repairing and maintenance, and blew out a breath. "I'll have to hire someone when I get back," he said and then turned to her. "We're starting to get more business than we can handle. Not that I'm complaining." His tone turned stern. "Promise me you won't work too late in the evenings while I'm gone."

"I promise. But only if you promise me you won't rush back here because you're worried about work. Take time to be with *yer familye*."

"You wouldn't say that if you knew *mei familye*," he muttered. He'd left after that, but the words had stuck with Leanna. She did know part of his family—Barbara especially, who had become a friend. She also knew his brother, Roman. That man had definitely *not* become a friend.

"Why are you frowning, *Aenti*?"

"What?" She looked at Malachi, who had a froth of milk above his lip. "I'm not frowning."

"You were," Adam said.

"Humph." Leanna scraped the last bit of potatoes off her plate. "You're both mistaken. I wasn't frowning. I was just thinking."

"About something bad?" Malachi said.

Roman's image popped into her mind—serious blue-gray eyes, wide nose, a constant cold and distant expression—and she shook her head. "*Nee*. Just something annoying." *Someone* annoying, she mentally corrected. "Anyway, Daniel will be back soon, and I won't have to work as late." She looked at Malachi. "How was school today?"

Now it was Malachi's turn to frown. "I don't like it."

"What's not to like? You get to color, play with *yer* friends . . ." Leanna tapped her fork against the table and tried to remember her kindergarten days. "Uh, color . . ."

"We have to write the alphabet."

"You already know how to write the alphabet," Phoebe said. "That should be easy for you."

"It is." Malachi lifted his chin with confidence. "It's boring."

"School just started," Adam said. He reached for a slice of bread. "It will get more challenging as the year goes on."

"I don't want more challin . . . challinga . . ."

"Challenging," Phoebe supplied.

"*Ya*, that." Malachi started to pout. "I want to be here with you and Jalon and work on the farm."

"There will be time for that, *sohn*," Jalon said. "Right now you have to focus on learning as much as you can in school. That includes behaving *yerself*. Understood?"

"*Ya*." But the pout didn't leave his face.

Leanna sympathized. She hadn't liked school either. Sitting still, doing worksheets, keeping quiet—she had struggled to behave in class. Now that she was an adult she realized the importance of an education, especially math, which she excelled in and used every single day. But she never cared for reading or writing or learning High German, although she did enjoy the little bit of geography and history her teacher had insisted they learn. Still, she'd spent her school days counting the minutes between recess and going home, which was sometimes delayed because of her misbehavior. "You have to mind the teacher," she said to Malachi. "You don't want to stay after class." She leaned forward. "They make you write sentences on the board, and then you have to wash the boards and clean the classroom."

"Ugh," Malachi said.

"And you definitely don't want to scrape old gum from underneath the desks. That was gross."

"Gross," he repeated. "I don't wanna do that."

"Then mind *yer* teacher." Jalon put his fork on the table and looked at Phoebe. "Delicious supper, as always."

Phoebe, who had glowed throughout her pregnancy, now beamed as she took in Jalon's compliment. Her blue eyes, clear and bright, sparkled as she acknowledged Jalon's words with a small nod. Jalon always made sure to praise her cooking, which was easy since Phoebe's meals were always mouthwateringly good. Leanna had to admit that her brother, who had struggled with problems in the past, was a good husband and father.

"*Mei* night to do the dishes." Adam pushed back from the table, then chucked Malachi under the chin. "I could use an assistant."

"Okay." Malachi scrambled down from his chair and got out the small stool, placing it under the sink.

Adam began to clear the table, starting with his plate and utensils. He piled a few more dishes into his lap, then rolled his chair to the sink. His being a paraplegic hadn't stopped him and Jalon from becoming partners last year. Not only had the farm become successful in a short time, but they were making plans to expand, starting with the barn so they could raise cattle to sell.

Phoebe stood and arched her back. "I need to work on some sewing tonight."

"Not if you're too tired," Jalon said, his brow furrowing.

"I'm fine. The nap helped."

He nodded but didn't look too convinced.

Leanna took her plate and silverware to the sink. Phoebe didn't bother asking her to help with the sewing, and Leanna didn't volunteer. Everyone knew her gift was working with machinery, not sewing. Or cooking. Or cleaning. Which reminded her that she probably should go clean her house. Or at least pick it up a little.

After telling everyone good night and retrieving her skates and backpack, she headed for her house. She stopped when she saw a firefly dance in front of her. She reached to catch it, missed, and then chased it a few steps. When she caught it, she peeked at it through her fingers and then let it fly free. When she looked up, she realized she was standing in front of the yard's large tree stump and stared at it. Jalon had cut down the tree last year. The magnificent oak had stood there long before her family moved from Mesopotamia to Birch Creek, when she and Jalon were barely teenagers. Leanna had always loved that tree. Jalon had too . . . until that day.

Jalon had been fourteen, Adam twelve. They were playing a game, just as they always had whenever he and Adam visited each other. Jalon had shimmied up the tree, Adam close on his heels. Then Adam fell.

Leanna closed her eyes at the memory. Jalon and Adam had been more like friends than cousins. Now they were more like brothers, but it hadn't always been that way. For years Jalon blamed himself for the accident. And when Jalon found Malachi up in the tree one day, he'd been terrified that the little boy would fall, just like Adam had. After getting Malachi out of it, Jalon cut down the giant oak.

"Miss it?"

Leanna turned around to see Jalon standing behind her. She could see the tension lining his face in the fading sunlight. She was surprised he brought up the subject. He hadn't mentioned the tree since it had been chopped up for firewood. Before that, he ignored the tree for years, until Malachi climbed it. "*Nee*. I don't. It represented too much pain."

He nodded. "*Ya*. It did." Then he rubbed the back of his neck.

Uh-oh. Leanna knew that gesture. Her brother always rubbed the back of his neck when he had something important on his mind.

"Can I talk to you for a minute?" he asked.

"What did I do now?" she said, heaving a sigh.

"You didn't do anything,"

"I find that hard to believe," she muttered.

"Believe it." He put down his hand. "I was thinking about the future, that's all."

"What do you mean?"

"With the *boppli* coming and the farm expansion, it's been on *mei* mind a lot. I asked Phoebe's father to be a full-time partner."

Another surprise, although she should have seen that one coming. Phoebe's father, Thomas, had been a farmer when her family lived in Fredericktown. "What will *Daed* think about that?"

"I talked it over with him and he's fine with it. He really did wash his hands of this place when he left. He's much happier now."

Leanna nodded, ignoring another firefly flitting by.

"He definitely is. It's *gut* to see him and *Mamm* so content." She made a note to pay them another visit when things settled down at work. She'd gone to see them last year, but hadn't been back since because of her work schedule. She loved to travel and visit family whenever she could, and in the past she'd been able to leave her visits open-ended because she only worked part-time for Daniel. But then Roman left. Now she worked full-time, which she didn't mind. She did hope Daniel really would hire someone new, though, so she could have a few days off to visit Mespo.

She blinked, forcing herself back to the topic at hand. "Why are you running *yer* future plans past me?" she asked Jalon. "You know I'll support you in whatever you do."

"Not everything," he said, looking away from her as he spoke.

They both knew what he was referring to—his alcoholism, which had plagued him for a long time. But he had been sober for two years, and she was proud of him for that. Not wanting to turn this into a mushy sibling moment, she said, "You've shown *yerself* to be pretty levelheaded this past year, so I'm going to keep trusting you."

"Then since you trust me, will you believe me when I say I have the best of intentions?"

Uh-oh. Again. "Depends on what they are."

"I'm offering you a job."

This time she was so surprised she burst into laughter. When she saw Jalon's stone-faced expression, she quit laughing. "You're serious, aren't you?"

"Absolutely serious."

That made her even more wary. "What exactly would I do as *yer* employee?"

"You wouldn't have to look at it that way—"

"Oh *nee*," she said, holding up her hand. "If I'm going to work for you, I don't want any special favors."

"Don't worry," he said with a smirk. "You won't get any. As far as what you'll be doing, I was thinking you could do a little repair work."

"Like what? It's not like you have a lot of machines around here."

"There's the Weed Eater, the washing machine . . ." Jalon ticked off on his fingers. "Uh, Phoebe's sewing machine—"

"All of which are in perfect working order."

"They could break down."

"When they do, I'll repair them. For free." Her eyes narrowed. "Why would I leave a busy, satisfying, full-time job to do a few odd chores for you?"

"It's not just those. You could help Phoebe with the household stuff. And there's always the farm chores."

"Jalon, Phoebe has eleven *bruders*. Plus her father, who is a farmer. And of course Adam too. You have plenty of farmhands here." She crossed her arms over her chest. "What is this really about?"

He sighed. "I'm worried about you."

She should have known he wasn't really talking about hiring her. "Not this again."

"Leanna—"

"Everything is going great. *Mei* life is the best it's been in a long time. You don't have to worry about me."

"You're working a lot of hours."

"Temporarily. When Daniel gets back, that will change. Besides, look who's talking. You're an expert when it comes to overwork, and you were even before you started the farm up again."

"And remember how many times you told me to take a break? To *geh* on vacation? To not work so hard?"

"Um, yeah." She'd done that more than once. "But that was because you were mopey."

"Mopey?" His brow shot up.

"Mopey. Forlorn. Pining for *yer* true love—"

"All right." He laughed. "I get it."

"I'm not pining for a true love, or any love," she said, straightening her shoulders.

"I know."

They were close in height, so she didn't have a problem looking him in the eye, which she needed to do at the moment since he couldn't get it into his thick head that she didn't need him hovering over her. "Or any *mann*."

"Everyone in Birch Creek knows," he added under his breath.

"And if you're trying to steer this conversation into when-is-Leanna-going-to-get-married territory, don't bother. I can take care of myself. I *am* taking care of myself. You should be focused on *yer* own growing *familye*. Not me." She chuckled. "Are you and Phoebe going to have twelve *kinner* too?"

Jalon paled. "Only if God wills it."

Leanna's smile widened. She loved teasing her brother about kids. He already had Malachi, who would soon be his adopted son. Jalon had decided to make it official after the baby was born. Since Malachi's biological father was out of the picture, there was nothing stopping Jalon from being Malachi's legal father. Her brother was a terrific father to Malachi, and he would be whether he had three more children or ten. "I couldn't imagine having even one *kind*, much less eleven *buwe*. Sheesh."

"Hey, *buwe* aren't bad. Look at Malachi. He reminds me a lot of you when you were young," he said, his grin returning. "You turned out okay. I think."

Her nephew was a handful, and Leanna didn't mind that one bit. He was a fun kid, very inquisitive, and not afraid to speak his mind, something she identified with and appreciated. She enjoyed spending time with him, playing games, jumping around in the sprinkler on hot summer days, teaching him how to fish. In winter she planned to give him ice-skating lessons. She was also showing his uncles how to ice skate. With the exception of two, the boys weren't much older than Malachi. Phoebe was the eldest child in the family.

"Let's get back to *mei* job offer," Jalon said.

Not this again. "Which isn't an offer at all. I'm a *gut* mechanic, Jalon."

"I know. I'm not questioning *yer* skills."

"Then why do you want me to quit *mei* job?"

"Because . . ." He rubbed his hand over his neck again. "It's not . . . traditional."

"So?"

"I want what's best for you, Leanna."

"And you think being a wife and having a passel of kids is what's best for me."

"It's our way, isn't it?"

That stopped her, because he wasn't wrong. In Mesopotamia she'd known only three single women who had never married. They mostly lived with a family member, and as far as she knew they were content. But in Birch Creek everyone was either paired up, pairing up, or going outside the district to find someone to pair up with. This included Adam, who, Leanna suspected, was going to propose to Karen, Ivy's sister, any day now. The only two women who weren't dating or looking to date were Leanna and Ivy. Leanna wondered if her friend was getting the same pressure from her family to marry. They didn't talk about it too much, other than they agreed men weren't worth the trouble. "I expected this kind of conversation from *Mamm*. Not you."

He threw up his hands. "All right. I give. You're settled in *yer* life. You don't want to marry, you don't want kids, you're happy living in the *dawdi haus*, and you don't want to work for me. Got it."

Leanna nodded, but instead of feeling satisfied that Jalon had surrendered, she was suspicious. His reasoning behind this conversation—that he was worried about her—was faulty. She was a grown, capable woman. She didn't need him to worry about her or offer her a so-called job that was really nothing more than her doing a bunch of household chores, which she disliked intensely.

Was there something else going on, something he wasn't coming right out and saying?

"I've got to finish the chores." He turned and headed toward the barn.

The slight slump of his shoulders triggered a bit of

guilt in her. She was thankful Jalon cared enough about her to be so concerned. "Wait." She caught up with him. When he faced her, she said, "I appreciate that you want to look out for me. And I'm glad you have the life you want."

Jalon shook his head. "I didn't always think I wanted this. For a long time I wasn't sure what I wanted."

"That's where you and I differ. I know what I want, and I have it." She held up her hands and grinned, needing to lighten up the mood. "Why mess with perfection?"

He chuckled, his features finally relaxing. "You're something else." Then his expression sobered. "Just know that I love you, little *schwester*."

"I'm hardly little." She stood on her tiptoes, which put her at six foot one, the same height as Jalon.

"You always will be to me."

She watched as he walked toward the barn, the pale colors of the sunset a beautiful backdrop that clashed with her suspicious mood. At twenty-five Jalon was only a year older than Leanna. It wasn't as if she had been a pesky younger sibling—okay, she had definitely been pesky—but they had been more like twins than older and younger siblings.

Maybe now that he was a husband and father he felt as though he had to take on all the responsibility for his family, including her. He'd spent so many years shirking family duty, arguing with their father, and drinking in secret, that he was overcompensating. That had to be it. Leanna could forgive him, but hopefully this was the last time he butted into her personal business.

When she stepped into her house and turned on the

gas lamp, she sighed. Clutter was everywhere—a few mechanics magazines were on the end table, several pairs of socks from the previous week were by the front door, and she didn't even want to think about the dust. Her intention to pick up tonight went by the wayside as she yawned. The mess wasn't going anywhere. She'd deal with it tomorrow.

As she made herself a glass of ice tea—ignoring the dirty dishes in the sink, because those could wait too— she reminded herself that life was good. Very good. Jalon didn't need to worry about her future, because she wasn't worried about it. Everything was going right for her, and she wasn't going to let anyone spoil that . . . including her suddenly overprotective, overly nosy brother.

. . .

Everything was going wrong for Roman Raber.

He crumpled the letter he'd just opened and tossed it into the nearby trash can. He missed. He plopped down in the chair near the window and looked outside. It was nearly seven, but there was still plenty of summer daylight for him to watch a few cars pull in and out of the small parking lot in front of his dumpy motel. He'd been here a few days, mostly because it was within walking distance from work. So was the apartment he'd shared with his friend who was now English, Matt. But the money he made working in the convenience store wasn't enough to cover his living expenses and rent.

"Sorry, dude," Matt had said, running his hand through

his shoulder-length, dirty-blond hair. "I hate telling you this, but I don't have a choice. I need a roommate who can pay the bills."

Roman clenched his fist at the memory. He understood Matt's point of view, and he'd been grateful that the guy, who had left their small community of Draperville five years earlier, had given him a place to stay. Roman hadn't known much about him when he lived there, mostly because Matt was a couple of years older and Roman always kept his distance . . . from everyone. But when he decided to leave Draperville nine months ago, Matt was the first person he sought out. Luckily, Matt had been eager to help him, at least until now. Again, Roman didn't blame him.

He'd thought he'd have found his bearings by now. He'd left Draperville with only his journal, his clothes, a little savings, and hope for his future—one that didn't involve living in a claustrophobic Amish community. Problem was, he was still adrift. Living in the motel was temporary—he could barely afford to be here either. He'd have to get a second job, which was tough to do when he didn't have a car or even a bicycle.

Now he was stuck in a dank motel room, reading his third scholarship rejection letter. It had been hard enough getting accepted into the engineering program at Dupree University, a small college near Akron. He'd spent almost all his savings getting his GED, taking the SAT and ACT, paying for the college application fee, and then taking another test to prove he could handle the college coursework. Just in case, he sent a personal letter to the dean, along with copies of some sketches of his engineering ideas from his journal. After he was finally accepted, his advisor had assured him he wouldn't have a problem getting financial aid. "You just have to fill out the forms," he'd said, giving him a sheet with all the information. "Here's a few scholarships you could apply for too."

So he applied for everything. And so far he'd been rejected for it all, except for the government financial aid. He was saving that as a last resort—and now it looked like it would be.

He drummed his fingers against the windowsill. He couldn't stay in this room and stew.

He got up and walked to the library a few blocks down the street. When he arrived, he went to the front desk and signed up to use the computer. When he sat down, he stared at the screen, barely noticing the icons at the bottom. This wasn't the first time he'd felt a nagging doubt about going to college. He'd had it drilled into him that higher education, along with almost everything else in the "world," was to be avoided.

Yet did he have a choice? Life in Draperville was not only stifling, it was a dead end. He wasn't like his brother, Daniel, a talented mechanic with a drive to match. He wasn't a farmer like his father, even though at age ten Roman had designed a cistern system that would have made it easier to water the crops and the few livestock his father possessed. When he'd shown it to his father, his idea had been rejected before he could thoroughly explain it. "We don't need something like that," *Daed* had said.

"Even if it made the work easier?"

"Life isn't easy."

Roman crossed his arms over his chest. "It doesn't have to be hard either."

"You should focus on working hard, not on pie-in-the-sky ideas."

"They're not pie in the sky. Cisterns have been used for centuries—"

"The bishop won't allow it. I won't allow it." His father turned away and walked to the barn, never saying another word about the cistern.

Roman didn't either. He never showed his father another drawing or spoke about any of the ideas that popped into his head. He sketched them out in his journal, along with his other private thoughts.

Instead of going to the financial aid website, he clicked on a search engine and typed the word *mountains* in the search box. He scrolled through beautiful images of different mountain ranges from all over the world. The Rockies. The Himalayas. The T'aebaek Mountains in Korea. The Swiss Alps. When he was a kid, he used to run off and spend hours in the library, poring over books filled with photographs of mountains, beaches, cathedrals, state parks. He imagined himself visiting those places . . . sometimes even living there. Anywhere was better than home.

That familiar draw pulled at him again. "One day I'll get there," he said, staring at a gorgeous image of the Rocky Mountains.

"Shh."

He turned to see an older woman sitting next to him, her finger pressed against her pursed, wrinkled lips. He glanced at her screen. A Facebook page was splashed across it.

He clicked off the images. He couldn't travel, or do anything, without an education. He was learning that the hard way. *Life isn't easy.* His father was right about that.

He'd filled out only part of the online application when he felt a tap on his shoulder. He looked up to see the librarian standing behind him.

She tugged her light-purple cardigan around her slim body, as if she was cold even though it was August and hot as blazes outside. "We have a waiting list for the computers," she said, then pointed at the watch on her wrist. "Your time is up."

He nodded, then logged out of the website, making a mental note to come back after work tomorrow and finish the form. As he walked back to the motel, he thought about his family again. His father was a stern man, and his mother was a cold woman. He'd spent most of his life feeling like an outsider, even in his own home. The only person who hadn't made him feel like a burden was his grandmother, who had moved in with their family when Roman was seven and Daniel was nine. Even before she lived with them, she had given him the acceptance he didn't get from his parents. Just thinking about her now brought an ache to his heart.

The noisy sound of the freeway filled his ears, and he saw the bright lights of the gas station and convenience store where he worked come into view. When he walked into his motel room, he pulled the curtain closed and then sat down on the edge of the bed. His gaze landed on his journal lying on the table near the window.

He stared at the thick, leather-bound book that had to be held closed with a rubber band. He should get a new one, but he couldn't part with this one. His grandmother had given it to him when he was ten, along with one of her many letters to him over the years. Even though they lived in the same house, she had written letters to both him and Daniel. Sometimes she mailed them, and when he was younger, Roman enjoyed getting the letters, even if he knew she could have handed them to him. When he was older, she stopped mailing them, choosing to leave them on the dresser in the bedroom he shared with Daniel. When she'd given him the journal, he remembered the letter that had been inside.

Dear Roman,

Here is a place for you to draw your designs, write down your dreams, and give your prayers to God. Remember, he has promised to teach and guide us, and he will always be with you. Never forget that.

Love,
Grossmammi

Roman went to the journal and touched the cracked leather cover. He missed her. He saw the disappointment in her eyes as he was leaving and felt the guilt burrow into his heart. It wasn't the first time he'd left over the years, sometimes for a few days, the longest was the time he went to live with Daniel. That had been a mistake, one he should have realized.

But this time he had left for good. "There's *nix* for me here," he'd told her. He still remembered how the tears shone in the corners of her creased gray eyes.

"*Yer familye* is here." But she didn't look at him when she said the words, and she didn't have to speak the truth. His parents hadn't even told him good-bye when he walked out the door with his duffel bag. "We can't stop you," *Daed* had said, while *Mamm* continued with her knitting, not looking up at Roman even once.

He hugged his grandmother quickly and then took off on foot, walking for the next three hours until he reached the bus station. He spent the entire time convincing himself this was the right thing to do. He had to do something with his life. He was tired of feeling aimless and disconnected. And while he didn't get along with his brother, he did admire that Daniel had found his niche—he owned a machine repair business and had married a wonderful woman. Even Daniel had moved away, to a small community called Birch Creek, near Canton, Ohio. There had been nothing in Draperville for Daniel either.

Roman had tried the Amish way. He had even tried his brother's way, at least the working part. Now he had to find his own way. Maybe getting an education would be the first step.

The motel room phone rang. He frowned. No one had called him there before, and Matt was the only other person who knew how to reach him. His boss at the convenience store didn't even know where he was staying.

He walked to the bedside table and picked up the receiver. "Hello?"

"Hey," Matt said.

Roman sat back down on the bed. "What's up?" A pause, and Roman's belly filled with dread. "Matt?"

Another pause. Roman gripped the receiver. Finally Matt spoke. "I checked the Draperville paper today. I don't do it very often, but sometimes I look at the obituary section because . . . you know."

Matt didn't have to explain his reasoning. It was morbid, but it was also a way to stay connected to their hometown. Roman had avoided looking at the paper on the internet. He wanted to make a clean break of things. A sudden unease filled him. There was only one reason Matt would call him and bring this up. "What happened?"

Matt let out a heavy sigh. "Dude . . . I hate to tell you this."

"Just say it."

"Your grandmother passed away."

The receiver almost fell through his fingers. He was just thinking about her. How could she be gone? "When?" he somehow managed to ask.

"Five days ago."

Five days? "They've buried her by now," Roman said, his voice barely above a whisper. *If you hadn't left, you would have been there.*

"Man, I'm so sorry. I know how close you two were. You need anything?"

Roman shook his head, then remembering he was still on the phone said, "No."

"You sure? You need a ride back to Draperville? I can take you if you want."

Roman knew what Matt would be risking. He hadn't always been English. He'd left the Amish too, and, like Roman, he was in the *bann*, which the district in Draperville took very seriously. If Matt ran into any of his family members, he would be rejected on sight, as would Roman. "Thanks for the offer, but I'll figure it out."

"I understand. Just let me know if you change your mind."

"I will." He put the receiver in its cradle and looked at the journal still on the table, his shoulders suddenly feeling like a pile of bricks had been dropped on them. *Grossmammi* was gone. He couldn't believe she was gone. If he'd been there, he would have seen she was sick. He would have convinced her to go to a doctor, even though that was discouraged in their community. Natural medicine was the only medicine allowed, and if it didn't work and someone died? That was God's will. Her image came to his mind—her kind smile, the wrinkles that deepened around the corners of her eyes when she smiled, the way she always reminded him and Daniel of God's love. God's promises.

He looked up at the stained ceiling. "What kind of promise is this? She was the one person who had faith in me." At least she used to.

He hung his head. *I should have been there . . . I shouldn't have left.*

It was dark by the time he stood. He didn't know how long he'd stayed there on the lumpy bed, guilt pulling him under. His eyes dry but his throat clogged with grief, he lifted his duffel bag from the floor and packed his few belongings. He'd take the bus back to Draperville first thing in the morning. Matt had done enough for him, and he couldn't ask him to take him there.

His eyes filled with tears. Instinctively he put his fists to his eyes and pressed down, something he'd done as a child whenever he cried. Tears weren't accepted in his family. Only his grandmother had worn her heart on her sleeve. When he removed his fists and opened his eyes, the tears were gone, replaced by hazy dots as his vision cleared. He had to see his grandmother's grave, and he wouldn't let his parents, or the fact he was in the *bann*, stop him.

CHAPTER 2

A re you okay, Daniel?"

Daniel Raber placed a mug of tea in front of his wife and tried to muster a smile. He didn't want to worry Barbara, and he knew she'd been concerned for him ever since he'd received the news of his grandmother's death. They'd returned from Draperville a couple of hours ago, after spending a few days there for the funeral. She took a sip of the chamomile, flavored with a sprig of fresh mint. It was the same tea his grandmother used to give him at night when he had trouble sleeping, which had been often. His insomnia wasn't any better as an adult, and he made himself a cup of tea before sitting down across from his wife. He'd rather have coffee, but it was late, and the caffeine would keep him up for sure.

"I'm still waiting," she said, peering over her mug.

"For what?"

"For an answer to *mei* question."

He gripped the hot mug in his hand, ignoring the heat seeping into his skin. "Sorry. I was distracted."

"I know." She reached over and touched his hand. "That's why I'm worried."

"You don't have to be."

"I'm *yer* wife, Daniel. That's *mei* job."

He gave her a small smile. This wasn't the first time he realized how blessed he was that Barbara was his wife. She was from a larger, less-strict community, and her family was the exact opposite of his—close, affectionate, and supportive. When he was considering leaving Kentucky for the growing community of Birch Creek to start his business—and a new life—he'd been reluctant to ask Barbara to leave her friends and family in the state. She was so close to them all. "Where you *geh*, I *geh*," she'd said, and without hesitation his wife made plans for the move. He didn't know what he did to deserve her.

"I thought worrying about you was *mei* job," he said. One that he took seriously, considering what had happened during the past four years.

The teasing glint in her eyes faded. "Daniel, we won't lose this one."

His grip tightened. She couldn't say that. Only God knew if this pregnancy, their sixth, would be viable. Although he knew he shouldn't worry, that God had everything in control, it didn't stop the anxiety that continually chased him. He wouldn't relax until the baby was born. But Barbara didn't need to know that. She needed him to be strong, the way she was. He took her hand and kissed her knuckles. She had such soft, pretty hands. Hands that should hold and care for a baby. "I know we won't," he said. "Drink *yer* tea. It's getting late."

"It's not that late." She sat back in her chair, her dark-brown, deep-set eyes becoming apprehensive. "I wanted to talk to you about working at Schrock—"

"We've already discussed it." He looked away and took another drink of the tea he didn't want anymore.

"You made a decision, you mean."

He put down the mug. "Am I being that unreasonable? We don't need the money, and you don't need the extra work."

"But I enjoy working there."

Barbara's family owned a small grocery store, and he knew working at Schrock Grocery reminded her of home. He didn't want to take that away from her, but he also couldn't risk her working in addition to everything she did at home.

"The women could use *mei* help," she added, referring to the three Schrock sisters. "Joanna just had her second *boppli*, Abigail is expecting her second, and Sadie will be having her first in a few months."

If there was one thing to be said about Birch Creek, it was a fertile community. *Except for us.* He shook his head. "I'm sure they can find someone else to work in the store."

Barbara looked at him for a long, tense moment. He hated disappointing her, but he wouldn't budge. Not on this.

Finally she cupped her mug with her hands and glanced down. "We should talk about something else."

Relieved she was dropping the subject, he said, "I'm all ears. What do you want to talk about?"

"Roman."

He froze. This was the last subject he wanted to discuss. "There's *nix* to talk about."

"You're not worried that he didn't show up for the funeral?"

"*Nee.* I'm not. And you shouldn't be either."

"Daniel—"

"He made the decision to leave."

"You left too."

"That's different and you know it." He tempered his tone. "I left Draperville, not the Amish. There's a big difference."

"Are you sure he left the Amish? Maybe he was just thinking about it—"

"He's in the *bann.* Even if he didn't officially leave, he's officially out. Until he changes his mind and confesses."

"You don't think he will."

"I know he won't. He's never been happy in Draperville." He held up his hand. "And before you point out that I wasn't happy either, I wasn't the one running off all the time. I'm not the one who left without telling anyone where to find me. I didn't turn *mei* back on *mei grossmammi.*" He sat back in his chair, his lips pressed together.

"I'm sorry," Barbara said quietly. "I shouldn't have brought it up."

She shouldn't have, but he couldn't stand to see her upset. "It's okay." He reached over and took her hand. "You look tired."

She gave him a weary smile and released his hand. "I always look tired." She pushed away from the table. "But you're right. I am feeling weary from the trip home. I'm ready for bed."

Daniel shot up from his chair. "I'll *geh* with you."

"To sleep?"

He had been planning to just tuck her in, but when he saw the expectation in her eyes, he nodded. "*Ya*. To sleep."

When they both got into bed, Daniel put his arm around his wife, tucking her close against him. She rested her cheek against his chest, and for the first time since the news that his grandmother had died, he felt his body relax a little. He stroked her shoulder until he felt her breathing deeply next to him, and then he kissed her temple before removing his arm from behind her head. She snuggled into the pillows without waking up.

Daniel reached for the folded paper on his nightstand, slipped out of bed, and went downstairs. He turned on the gas lamp and sat down at the kitchen table. He looked at the paper, and then with pain in his heart he unfolded it.

Dear Daniel,

If you're reading this, I have passed on into heaven. Don't mourn for me, but rejoice. I've lived a good life, and I'm ready to see your grandfather. Twenty years a widow is too long. Although to the family my death might seem sudden, I've felt it coming for a while. A pain in the heart, some shortness of breath . . . I knew awhile ago that the end was coming. I'm ready for it. Perhaps it's selfish of me not to tell anyone about my troubles. But my time here on earth is done, and I pray God welcomes me home with open arms.

Of all the joys I've had in my long life, being grandmother to you and watching you grow up has been a

special blessing. You were always the serious one. The
one who took his responsibilities to heart, sometimes
too deeply. You married a special woman. Barbara is
your perfect match, the same way Moses was mine. Care
for her deeply and nurture the love you share. Remember God's teaching: "Husbands, love your wives, even
as Christ also loved the church and gave himself for
it." Knowing the man you are, I believe you will do just
that. And although God hasn't blessed you with children yet, don't lose hope. Never lose hope.

I had hoped to see one thing before I passed, and
that was you and Roman reconciled. He hasn't made it
easy on any of us, but who says life should be easy? God
promises to make our paths straighter and our loads
lighter. One day Roman will realize this. And when he
does, you need to be there to help him along. Forgive
him, Daniel, not just for leaving our family and community, but for any slights he's done against you. No
one is perfect, even though you strive to be. Promise
me, if the opportunity comes, you will reconcile with
your brother.

Daniel dropped the letter on the table. He leaned
on his elbows and squeezed the bridge of his nose. His
grandmother had written him lots of letters over the
years, especially reminding him of God's promise for
this and his promise for that. And he'd taken those
promises to heart. But it was hard to believe during the
nights he held Barbara in his arms as they mourned
the loss of another baby. And now he was mourning the
loss of a woman he loved and respected. His father had

been a stern man, his mother even sterner. Nurturing had come from his grandmother.

He stared at the half-full mugs of tea still on the table. He'd told Barbara he would take care of washing the mugs in the morning, but there was no reason to wait until then. He picked them up and went to the sink, throwing out the limp mint leaves along the way. For once his mind wasn't on Barbara or the baby, but on his grandmother's letter.

Daniel didn't have to worry about keeping a promise to her. Roman wouldn't be back. As he filled the sink, he felt the familiar resentment growing inside him. He'd given Roman a chance, and his brother squandered it. Even when he was here working in the shop, he hadn't taken the job seriously. He spent more time writing in that journal of his than improving his skills as a mechanic, which he needed to do. Roman wasn't stupid or inept—he was smart, which was why Daniel was so frustrated with him. His brother could design a complex cistern system, but when it came to fixing a lawn mower, he barely bothered to try.

At least Daniel hadn't been left high and dry at the shop when Roman took off. He had Leanna, who was as loyal as Roman was unreliable. She and Roman hadn't gotten along the few months they'd worked together in Daniel's shop. From what Daniel could tell, she'd been relieved when Roman left.

If he were honest with himself, he'd have to admit he'd been relieved too. He was tired of worrying about his brother. About feeling responsible for him. Roman was a grown man, and he had made his decision. Daniel was glad his grandmother wasn't alive to see his rejection of everything she cared about and valued.

He finished washing and drying the mugs, put them up in the cabinet, and then scooped coffee into the percolator so it would be ready when he got up in the morning. He'd let his wife sleep in tomorrow. And even though he knew she was disappointed about not working for the Schrocks, Daniel wouldn't change his mind. He'd do anything he could to keep her and their baby safe.

He started to turn off the light, but then noticed the letter again. He picked it up, his eyes prickling with tears he thought he'd already shed. In private, of course. His family, other than his grandmother, never showed emotion. But she deserved to have tears shed over her. She deserved that and so much more.

. . .

The next morning Leanna settled her conversation with Jalon in her mind. He was being overprotective because of Phoebe and impending fatherhood. She could understand that. She could also ignore his meddling in her life—and she intended to do just that.

Satisfied, she placed an orange and an apple in her backpack, then shoved on her skates and left for work. She waved to Phoebe's father and four of her brothers, who were headed to work with Jalon and Adam on the farm. Phoebe's mother came out on the front porch, a toddler on her hip and two little boys flying past her at full speed into the yard. They ran straight for Leanna.

She braked to a stop and waited for them on the side of the road.

"When are we going to skate again?" they asked in unison, looking up at her.

"Soon," she promised.

"When?" seven-year-old Perry asked. His blue eyes, similar in color to his sister Phoebe's, looked at her with reproach. "You said you were going to show us how to skate backward."

She had said that—a month ago. Trying to save a little face in the presence of the young boys, she said, "You two are smart *buwe*. I thought you would have figured out how to skate backward by now."

"It's funner when you show us how to do it," five-year-old Perry said.

"Yeah," Jesse added, rubbing his nose with his palm. "It's funner."

Perry poked out his bottom lip. "Malachi said you're too busy for us. That's why you haven't come over."

Uh-oh. Guilt slammed into her. She didn't like to go back on her promises, whether or not she intended to. "He's right. I have been busy." She balanced on the inline skates as she crouched in front of them. "Tell you what. I promise this Saturday I'll come over and we'll practice skating."

"*Buwe*, Leanna has to *geh* to work," Phoebe's mom called from the porch. The youngest twins, Moses and Mahlon, were standing in front of the screen door, Mahlon's nose pressed against it. "Don't bother her."

"Okay." As she straightened, they added, "You promise we'll skate on Saturday?"

"*Ya*. Saturday evening, after I finish up with work." She put her hand over her heart. "I promise."

They waved to her and ran back to the house.

Relieved that placating Jesse and Perry hadn't been too difficult, she skated past the Yoders' house, not surprised to see Ivy's father, Freemont, working in the field along with his sons. He was also the district's bishop. She waved, but Judah was the only one who saw her and waved back. She started to skate away, knowing she couldn't loiter any longer. At this rate she would be late for work. Assuming Daniel wouldn't be back yet, she didn't want to leave customers waiting for her outside before she opened up the shop.

She was a few feet past the Yoders' house when she heard Karen, Ivy's younger sister, call her name. She spun around, continuing to skate backward. "Can't talk. Got to get to work!"

"But—"

"We'll talk soon. I promise." She spun around again, but not before she caught Karen's crestfallen expression. Another pulse of guilt went through her. Although Ivy was her best friend, Leanna was also close to Karen. Leanna didn't want to disappoint her, but she couldn't be late. Not today. Not ever, really. Punctuality was important.

She picked up her speed and raced to Daniel's, whizzing past Timothy Glick's buggy. "Slow down," he called out, sounding only half-serious.

"*Nee* time!"

When she reached the repair shop, her chest heaved as she gasped for breath, her face damp with perspiration. She glanced at the empty parking lot and smiled. Made it just in time.

She took off her skates, shoved on her shoes, stuck her key into the lock, and opened the door. The gas lights were already on, and she could smell the scent of coffee brewing. Coffee? Daniel, the caffeine fanatic, must be back. She was a little surprised he had returned so soon.

She hurried to the back of the store, where Daniel was seated at his desk. "Welcome home," she said as she hung her backpack on one of the pegs on the board behind him. As an afterthought, she pulled out the apple and took a bite.

"You were busy while I was gone," he said, sorting out orders and receipts on his desk. "Looks like we got several new customers."

"*Ya*," she said around a bite of the apple. "We've probably got enough business to last us the next two months."

"*Gut* to hear." He turned in his chair and looked up at her and then frowned. "Don't tell me you worked late while I was gone."

"A smidge." She held up her thumb and forefinger. "Just a smidge."

"I told you not to."

"I know. I know. But I didn't want you to be overwhelmed when you got back."

His expression softened. "Don't worry about me. I can handle the extra work."

Leanna nodded, but lately she wasn't so sure. The past two months or so he'd been a little agitated, and the shadows underneath his eyes never fully went away.

Good thing he was going to hire extra help. "You should probably cut back on the caffeine," she said, looking at the half-full coffee mug.

"What?"

"The caffeine. You'd sleep better if you didn't drink so much *kaffee*."

He squinted at her. "Who told you I wasn't sleeping?"

Uh-oh. She'd put her foot in her mouth . . . again. *"Nee* one. I promise. You just seem . . . tired."

"I'm fine." He turned and faced his desk.

Subject closed, and Leanna was glad for it. She admired her boss and appreciated him giving her this job, but she didn't want to upset him. She also didn't want to cross the line from professional to personal, which she'd just done. It wasn't any of Leanna's business how much coffee Daniel drank or if he wasn't sleeping well. "I'm breaking *mei* own rule," she muttered.

"What did you say?" Daniel asked, not looking up from his desk.

"Nix." She started to go to her workstation before she said something else she shouldn't.

"Leanna?"

She turned and looked at him. *"Ya?"*

"Danki." He glanced up from his paperwork. "I don't know what I'd do without you." He turned his focus back to the orders on the desk.

She couldn't hide her grin. Daniel didn't give compliments freely. He rarely gave them at all. It was nice to be wanted. To be *needed.*

Leanna went to her workstation, eager to get started. Her first job was to finish the generator Asa Bontrager dropped off two days ago. Asa wasn't related to Phoebe Bontrager's family. But even if he wasn't, she certainly wouldn't make him wait on a repair any longer than necessary. Every customer was as important to her as to Daniel. She had taken it halfway apart, and she was pretty sure she knew what the problem was. She finished the last bite of her apple and then tossed the core in the trash can, where it easily landed. Two points.

The morning went quickly, with only two customers coming into the shop, each dropping off two more repair jobs. At noon Barbara showed up with their lunch inside a wicker picnic basket slung over one arm. Leanna had packed a lunch when she first started working at Daniel's shop, only to stop after Barbara insisted on making her and Daniel lunch every day.

Leanna put down her screwdriver, took off her safety goggles, and went to the front door, where Barbara stood. "Smells yummy," she said when Barbara opened the basket.

"Meat loaf." Barbara pulled out two sandwiches neatly wrapped in wax paper. Daniel suddenly appeared behind her.

"You shouldn't have gone to the trouble," he said, his voice more brusque than usual.

Barbara turned and looked at him. "Making meat loaf isn't any trouble. Besides," she said, smiling, "it's *yer* favorite sandwich."

Daniel nodded, but he didn't return Barbara's smile. Sensing the tension, Leanna took the sandwich and said, "I'll wash up outside," only to realize neither one of them was listening to her. Instead they stared at each other, as if engaged in some sort of odd standoff. *None of your business, remember?*

Outside, Leanna set her sandwich on the small plastic table behind the shop. Against the building there was a tall, round cooler filled with water on a wooden bench and a soap dispenser next to it. She washed her hands, wiped them on the front of her dress because no one was around and she didn't care if her dress had a few wet spots, and then sat down on the plastic chair near the table.

It was a nice little picnic area. She knew Daniel set it up when he first opened the shop, but he rarely sat out here. He usually ate his lunch at his desk. But Leanna enjoyed sitting in the quiet, looking out over the large, lush field that butted up against Daniel's property.

She looked at the oil well in the distance, a reminder that out of the numerous oil-rich properties in the Birch Creek area, her family's property had been one of the few that didn't have an oil deposit. Her father had never talked about that. She had to wonder, though, if when farming was the most difficult, he resented that his land was empty. Many families in Birch Creek had leased their oil rights, which brought them a good amount of money. Much of it went to the community fund Bishop Yoder oversaw. Asa, who had his own accounting business, also helped manage the fund and gave the bishop financial accountability, something that had been lacking when Bishop Troyer was here. Emmanuel Troyer had insisted on managing the fund himself, and unknown to everyone, he had hoarded the money instead of sharing it with the community. When Emmanuel fled Birch

Creek two years ago, Bishop Yoder had insisted on doing things differently, especially when it came to the community fund.

"Sorry about that."

Drawn out of her thoughts, Leanna watched as Barbara sat down in the chair next to her. She set a glass of tea for Leanna on the table.

Leanna unwrapped the sandwich, brought it to her nose, and sniffed. "I can't wait to taste this," she said, her stomach already growling. "Let's pray." She bowed her head, and when she finished, she took a bite. Barbara's cooking rivaled Phoebe's sometimes. "This is delicious," she said around a mouthful. "And what are you sorry about?"

"That." She pointed her thumb toward the shop. "Daniel."

"What did he do?" She took another big bite of the sandwich.

"He . . . never mind." Barbara folded her hands in her lap. "I hope he at least thanked you for minding the shop while we were gone."

Leanna swallowed. "He did."

"*Gut.*" Barbara sighed. "He's been preoccupied lately."

Leanna focused on the sandwich. She was never sure what to do in these situations, when Barbara seemed in the mood to talk about her and Daniel. It didn't happen often, but Leanna never wanted to say anything that might offend either one of them—or worse, put her in the middle of something. But she and Barbara were friends, and if Barbara wanted to talk, she would listen and hopefully not say anything she shouldn't.

"We've both had a lot on our minds," Barbara continued.

When Barbara didn't say anything else, Leanna looked at her. Really looked at her this time. There was a glow about her, similar to Phoebe's. Then she knew, and now Daniel's over-caffeinated binging made sense. Barbara was pregnant. She glowed, but she also looked tired. She'd had that same look when she was pregnant last summer.

"Don't tell Daniel I told you," Barbara had said then, pulling Leanna aside before she went home after work. Daniel had left early to pick up some tools in Holmes County. Barbara's eyes shone as she spoke. "I'm almost three months along. He doesn't want me to say anything until I'm showing, but I can't help it. I know this time will be it."

Leanna couldn't help but grin. She was happy for her—happy for them both.

A week later the glow was gone. So was the joy. But the weariness remained, with Barbara trying to hide it behind her pretty smile. She hadn't said anything about the pregnancy or the apparent miscarriage since.

And now that Leanna knew Barbara was pregnant again, it took everything she had not to say anything. *Don't pry . . . Don't pry . . .*

Barbara asked, "Anything exciting happen while we were gone?"

"Nope." Leanna stared at the tea in her glass. "Just boring old Birch Creek."

"Sometimes boring is nice," Barbara said, looking straight ahead.

Leanna nodded, focusing on the topic at hand instead

of on Barbara's pregnancy. "True. And if I had to be someplace boring, it would be Birch Creek. Although I'm hoping that I'll be able to visit Mespo soon. Maybe later in the fall when we get caught up with work."

"Daniel's been talking about hiring someone. I hope he'll do that soon." She let out a sigh. "I wish things had worked out with him and Roman."

Leanna tensed at Roman's name, and the memories that came with it. But she didn't respond.

"I'm not happy with what Roman did," Barbara said. "I can't explain it, either."

Taking a sip of tea made it even easier to keep her mouth shut. But that didn't stop the thoughts in her mind. She couldn't imagine doing what Roman did— taking a job, then abandoning it without an explanation and leaving without saying good-bye. What kind of work ethic was that? What kind of brother did such a thing?

"He and Daniel have a complicated relationship," Barbara said.

"I gathered." The words slipped out before Leanna could stop them. She waved away a fly trying to get near her sandwich, making sure to keep her face noncommittal. She didn't like what Roman did, but it wasn't her place to judge him, either. She would do well to remember that.

"The funeral was hard," Barbara continued. "Daniel was very close with his grandmother, so having her pass away so suddenly was difficult. Roman not being there made it that much harder." She turned to Leanna. "You knew he left the church, right?"

Leanna's brow lifted. *"Nee."* He'd left the church?

"I think Daniel was hoping Roman would be home. That he somehow knew their grandmother had passed away and decided to come back to see her one last time, even though he's in the *bann*." She let out another long sigh. "Anyway, what happened with Roman shouldn't keep Daniel from finding another employee. He depends too much on you as it is. But it's his business. He'll do what he sees fit. He always does," she added quietly, as if her words were an afterthought. Barbara rose from her chair. "Do you need anything else?"

"You didn't eat," Leanna said, shaking her head.

"I'm not very hungry. I'll have something a little later." She smiled. "I'm sure I'll be starving by then."

Especially if you're eating for two. The suspense was driving her nuts, but if Barbara didn't want to talk about it, Leanna would respect that.

After Barbara left, Leanna finished her lunch, washed her hands again, and went back inside the shop, propping the door open since the heat of the day made the air inside stifling.

"Where's Barbara?" Daniel asked, wiping his grease-covered hands on an old clean rag.

"She went inside the *haus*."

"Did she have lunch?"

"She said she'd eat later."

He frowned, concern filling his eyes.

Leanna didn't need the confirmation, but now she was a hundred percent certain Barbara was expecting, and Daniel knew about it.

"I'll be back in a minute," he said suddenly, and then dashed out the door.

Leanna poked her head out the back door and watched him hurry to the house, obviously to check on Barbara. She shook her head. She would lose her mind if someone hovered over her like that, like Jalon also hovered over Phoebe—even though her sister-in-law didn't seem to mind the attention. "Just one more reason not to get married," she mumbled, going back to her workstation.

As she walked past Daniel's desk, she picked up a folded piece of paper on the floor near his chair. She opened it, scanned the words, and saw that it was a personal letter and not business-related. She was about to fold it and put it back on his desk when she spied a familiar name written in the center paragraph on the paper. Roman.

She looked around the shop, which was still empty. She glanced at the letter in her hand again. She should put it on Daniel's desk. But questions filled her mind, which they usually did when her curiosity got the best of her. Was Roman still in the *bann*? Had he gone back to Draperville after all? Was he coming to Birch Creek? Did he want his job back?

No. I can't read this. I shouldn't read it . . . She started to put the letter back on the desk. Paused. *Just a quick peek . . . just to find out about Roman . . .*

A minute later she set the paper on Daniel's desk. Her face heated with shame. She'd read the whole letter, despite knowing better. She'd read personal correspondence from Daniel's grandmother, and she'd done it because she wanted to find out about Roman. Roman Raber, a man she not only disliked, but also resented for what he'd done to Daniel. It didn't make sense.

She went back to her workstation and tried to focus on the generator, but all she could think about was the letter, especially what Daniel's grandmother had said about Roman. *God promises to make our paths straighter and our loads lighter. One day Roman will realize this.*

She was confused by that. If anything, Roman's load was easy, at least when he worked here. He'd spent more time writing in what she assumed was a journal than fixing anything, and even when he did work on a machine he was uninterested. At lunchtime he would take off, sometimes longer than the time allowed, only to return annoyed, as if he couldn't be bothered to be there. She'd never met an Amish person who was lazy, but Roman came very, very close.

However, there was something else she noticed, something she hadn't told anyone, and something she tried not to think about. When Roman hadn't been annoying her with his laziness and daydreaming, she'd found herself watching him. Even worse, she would sometimes think about him. Which was stupid, since he was everything she disliked in a person, never mind a man. Then there had been the weird feeling in her stomach when she was around him. "Probably indigestion," she said to the empty workshop. Maybe a small dose of fascination too. She'd never met anyone like him before. Aloof. A little cold sometimes, and definitely distant. He wasn't rude, but he wasn't the least bit friendly either. Not with Daniel, not with her, and not with anyone else in the community.

Yet he did talk sometimes, like with the English customers. He'd been more open to them, and even engaged in a bit of small talk occasionally. That hadn't made sense to her at the time, but now that she knew he'd left the Amish, his friendliness with English people wasn't that surprising.

And one more weird thing happened when he was working there. A couple of times she caught him staring. *At her.* Of course, she was used to being stared at, not only because of her height but also because of her profession. But the way he looked at her . . . It made butterflies flit in her stomach. Or bats. He never stared at her for long, and the only reason she knew he was staring was because she had been sneaking glances at him. She couldn't help herself—Roman was a mystery wrapped up in an enigma and tied with a baffling bow. That had to be the reason she paid any kind of attention to him in her mind.

Now it didn't matter anymore. Daniel's grandmother might have wanted the brothers to reconcile, but Leanna couldn't see it happening, especially since Roman left the Amish. She did feel sympathy for their grandmother, imagining the ache of having her grandchildren, whom she clearly loved and adored, being at odds and separated. She also felt for Daniel. Although he hadn't said anything about Roman after he left, she knew it bothered him.

"Stepped out for a minute," Daniel said, coming back inside through the front door. "Had to *geh* to the *haus* for . . . something."

Leanna nodded and tried to focus on her work again. She really needed to finish this generator. She also needed to get Roman out of her mind. But she had only herself to blame. If she'd gone with her first—and correct—instinct, she wouldn't have read the letter. She wouldn't be thinking about him right now, wondering if he was okay, and then wondering why she cared.

Instead she shifted her thoughts to praying for Daniel and Barbara, and the baby. She asked God to bless them with a healthy child. "If anyone deserves happiness, it's them," she whispered. Then she forced herself to stop thinking about the Rabers and to focus on what she did best—repair engines.

CHAPTER 3

Roman took a late bus from Laketown and arrived at the bus station nearest Draperville hours before dawn. The walk was a long one, but he didn't mind it. He'd forgotten how quiet it was here at night. Quiet, and totally dark. But he'd know his way around this area blindfolded.

More than once he'd taken off from home at night, heading for the station, even though he often didn't have the fare to get to the next town, much less any decent distance. He'd always come to his senses a few hours later and return home. Daniel had met him halfway a couple of times. He never said anything, but the anger on his face told him all he needed to know. Roman knew his grandmother was the one who sent Daniel after him. He couldn't blame Daniel for being resentful.

Dawn broke just as he arrived at the small Amish graveyard. Sparse, flat clouds streaked above, lit with pink, orange, and lavender. He breathed in the warm August morning air and gazed at the sky. A quick emotion flashed through his heart and soul. Peace. How long had it been since he'd felt contentment in any form? The feeling was so fleeting he wasn't sure he actually experienced it. On second thought, he was sure he hadn't. Draperville wasn't a place of peace, not for him. And with his grandmother now gone . . .

He glanced at a patch of sunflowers near the cemetery, their large heads drooping, as if dipped in deference to the souls buried in the graveyard. Once sunlight hit them, they would stand up, seeking more of the light and warmth. *Grossmammi* had loved sunflowers. He couldn't help but smile a tiny bit when he saw she was buried near them.

He opened the gate, the creak echoing in the quiet of the morning, and went to the graveside. He knew she'd be buried next to his grandfather, a man Roman barely remembered from his childhood. He died when Roman was three, and soon after that *Grossmammi* had moved in with them. She would often come here to visit him, and when Roman and Daniel were younger, she brought them along. "I don't want you to forget him," she would say as she pulled a few weeds away from the base of his plain headstone. Despite her efforts, Roman had forgotten him anyway.

Would that happen with her? A lump formed in his throat as he brushed away a stray blade of grass from the top of the small square headstone. Twenty years from now, would he remember her smile, her kind words, the loving way she hugged him when his own mother kept him and Daniel at arm's length?

God, please don't let me forget.

He didn't believe in sentimentality. He was like his parents in that respect. But his heart ached as he moved to his knees, the grassy dew seeping through his jeans.

He didn't know what to do . . . what to say. Sorry wasn't enough, and it meant nothing now. She wasn't alive to hear his apologies.

"You there."

Roman shot up to his feet at the familiar voice. He turned and saw his father standing at the gate, his grizzled face stern, an uncharacteristic flash of anger in his eyes. He wasn't a cruel or angry man. Emotionless described him best. He obviously didn't recognize Roman, who was wearing not only jeans, but a red T-shirt and a ball cap over his short hair. "*Daed*," he said, clearing his throat and moving forward. "It's me."

The anger disappeared, and his father's face turned to stone. His normal expression. Obviously that hadn't changed since Roman left. "You're not supposed to be here," he said in his usual flat tone.

Roman walked toward his father with tentative steps. "I couldn't stay away."

His father didn't respond. He didn't move either. Just stared into the distance as if Roman weren't there.

Something inside Roman had hoped for a different reaction. That *Grossmammi*'s death would have meant something to his father. *Daed* was her son. Couldn't he at least feel pain over her absence?

"*Daed* . . ." Roman hated the pleading in his voice. Why did he want what his father couldn't give? His father had never understood him or Daniel. Roman never understood him either. He'd seen other fathers and sons together and knew from an early age that something was wrong in his family. Only his grandmother's love and outward affection had kept him from blaming himself for his parents' distance. "You're a wonderful *bu*," she would say to him. "Smart and clever. God has a bright future in store for you. Believe that."

She was wrong, though. His future looked bleak, especially now that she was gone. And how pathetic was it that at the age of twenty-three and being away from his family for almost a year, he still wanted a kind word from his father. A pat on the back, literally. Even a half smile would be enough. His aching heart would take anything.

Daed continued to stare straight ahead.

Roman glanced over his shoulder, looking at *Grossmammi*'s grave one last time. There was no reason to stay any longer. He'd done what he set out to do—see her for the last time. His father's rejection only cemented what he already knew—he didn't belong here. *I have no idea where I belong.* He'd head back to Laketown, and figure it out, though . . . somehow.

Roman walked past his father, following his cue and keeping his distance. Roman didn't look at him. Didn't speak. He was nearly to the gate when his father touched his arm, stopping him. Roman stiffened.

Still not looking at him, *Daed* reached into the pocket of his pants and pulled out a folded piece of paper. He handed it to Roman.

"What's this?" Roman asked, taking the paper.

Without saying a word, *Daed* walked into the cemetery.

Roman turned to see his father standing at the end of the grave, his hands in his pockets, staring at the headstone with an empty look. Roman waited a few minutes and then blindly left the graveyard. He started to jog, turning down roads he'd known since birth but not paying attention to where he was going. He should be going back to the bus station. Instead he ran faster.

He finally stopped, out of breath, the paper burning a hole in his pocket. He pulled it out and stared at it, afraid of what it might contain. Finally, he opened it and started to read.

Dear Roman,

It's been nearly a year since you left us. I haven't stopped praying every day, every hour, since. I hoped you would have returned to us by now. If you're reading this letter, then you haven't. Because if you had, I would have told you this in person.

He read about how she knew something wasn't right with her health, about how she probably should have said something but she was ready to be with his *grossdaadi*.

Always remember this, Roman. God loves you, and I love you. No matter your path in life, those things will always be true. Even as a young boy you were your own person. Smart, stubborn, always trying to find ways to make things better. Easier. But God never promised us an easy life. Struggle and pain is what makes us grow, and it also shows how we need the Lord in our lives. Escaping isn't the answer. Facing things is. You can be the person God created you to be and still be part of the community and family that loves you. It breaks my heart that you have isolated yourself from us. And even though they can't show it, it breaks your parents' hearts too.

I've always felt it was my place to provide what your parents couldn't, and not ask for what you couldn't give. But you still told me more than once that if I needed anything, you would do what you could to give it me. I'm reminding you of that promise. I've never asked you for anything, not even to return to us. But I'm asking you for something now.

Please, Roman, promise me you will reconcile with your brother. You and Daniel are more alike than you think. I'm not asking you to seek out your parents, or even to come back to the church. But reach out to Daniel, at least. You don't realize it now, but you need each other.

With love,

Grossmammi

Roman's shoulders slumped as he absorbed his grandmother's words. She had prayed for him. He wasn't surprised. Looking back, he remembered times he had felt those prayers. When he felt especially low. And while reading her past letters, which were filled with encouragement and promises and acceptance. They had been the only thing that sustained him.

But this last request seemed impossible. How could he reach out to Daniel after all this time? Roman had left without a word, something he'd known would anger his brother, but he had done it anyway. Daniel had given him a job and a place to live, and Roman had repaid him by disappearing in the middle of the night. He'd been a coward, avoiding confrontation, not wanting Daniel to talk him out of leaving. Or worse, not care if he left at all. It would be better for them both if Roman stayed away. Daniel probably didn't want to see him anyway.

Yet how could he refuse his grandmother? He remembered his promise to her, but he hadn't realized she had. Why hadn't she asked him to stay in Draperville, then? Why was she calling in that promise now? Did the reason matter? He still left with a choice—go back to Laketown, or be true to his word.

His grand plan seemed so pointless in light of his grandmother's death and her request. What had he accomplished since he left? Absolutely nothing other than getting his GED and passing a few tests. He could keep trying, keep striving to get a scholarship while working minimum-wage jobs and barely keeping his head above water.

Or he could do something more difficult. He could swallow his pride and go see Daniel.

He looked up and finally noticed the building in front of him. He hadn't realized he was standing in a church parking lot, a tiny church tucked in the back roads of Draperville. He hadn't attended church since he left here. He'd felt that nudge every Sunday, but couldn't bring himself to attend. He didn't want to field the questions, or even meet new people. Just like he always did, he kept his distance.

When was the last time he'd even prayed? He'd questioned God plenty of times, especially when things weren't going his way. He had no idea what denomination the church in front of him was, since he'd rarely paid attention to the building when he used to live in Draperville. Now he kept staring at it, his mind and heart filled with guilt and regrets. He'd let his grandmother down, and if her letter was to be believed, he let his parents down too—although he doubted that part.

And Daniel. He couldn't forget his older brother, the one who always seemed to know his own path and what his life was about. How Roman had always envied that.

If he decided to return to Birch Creek, he'd first have to get out of the *bann*. That meant confession and rejoining the church. Could he do that when he wasn't sure? When his heart wasn't truly committed?

The choice lay in front of him. *Lord, show me what to do.*

. . .

Barbara yawned as she climbed out of the buggy, which she'd parked in front of Schrock Grocery. Daniel tried to convince her not to go shopping, but she had finally prevailed, telling him they would both starve if she didn't get food in the house. An exaggeration, of course, but at least he'd relented.

She looped the horse's reins over the hitching post, then paused and touched her belly, something she had been doing a lot of lately. She knew it was a nervous habit, and a fruitless one. It wasn't as if touching there made their baby safe. But it calmed her anxiety, which had been in full swing since she realized she was pregnant again. "Please," she whispered. "Please let this *boppli* be okay."

She walked into the grocery and stifled another yawn. She'd been so tired lately, and traveling to Kentucky had made it worse. She hadn't slept well, and trying to keep up good spirits during the funeral had been difficult. In the years she'd known Daniel, she'd rarely seen his father crack a smile, and his mother had rarely showed one either. Of course she wouldn't expect that while they were dealing with a death in the family, but they weren't outwardly grieving either. When Barbara's parents met them before the wedding, her father had remarked to her, "They are two peas in a very serious pod."

Daniel was a serious man too. But he had a light-hearted side, and she had fallen for him the moment she saw it. She was visiting a distant cousin in Draperville for a couple of weeks, and she had seen Daniel at church, playing around with some of the older children. His smile, his laugh, his ease with the children—all that had drawn her to him. Her visit stretched out to more than a month after they started courting, and eventually she'd returned home and told her parents she was marrying him. She didn't hesitate to move to Draperville, even though the district was extremely conservative. And when she later told her husband she would go anywhere he went, she meant it.

She walked into the store and greeted Sadie Troyer, who was working behind the counter helping customers. "Hi," she said.

Sadie smiled back as she gave one of the customers their change. When the customer left, she said to Barbara, "When did you get back?"

"Yesterday."

"You're not here to work, are you?" Sadie asked, her cheeks slightly pink from the heat of the day. "You don't have to come back so soon."

Barbara took a deep breath. "About that." She fidgeted with the strap of her purse. She didn't want to tell Sadie, but she didn't have a choice. She wouldn't go against Daniel's wishes, even if she thought they were misguided. And yes, a little unfair. "I can't work for you anymore."

Sadie's brow lifted. "Oh? If you need more time—"

"It's not that." She shielded her middle with her purse. "Daniel needs me at home." Hopefully, in seven months a baby would too.

Sadie's expression relaxed. "I understand."

"I hope I'm not causing a problem for you."

"Of course not. We'll find someone to fill the position soon. Maybe two people, since Abigail says she's not going to work after the *boppli* is born. At least not for a long while." She smiled. "Her *familye* needs her at home too."

Relieved, Barbara returned her smile. "*Danki* for understanding."

With a nod, Sadie asked, "How are you and Daniel doing?"

"We're fine," she said. "Glad to be home. I just stopped by to pick up a few things."

"*Gut* timing. We're having a sale on flour this week."

"I'll pick up some, then."

Another English customer came to the counter, and Sadie began checking out her groceries. Barbara pushed a small, gray shopping cart down the baking supply aisle and decided she would get some butterscotch chips too. She'd make Daniel some oatmeal scotchies tonight, his favorite. After what he'd been through this past week, he deserved the treat.

"I don't know why she allows it to keep going on," a female voice from the next aisle said.

"It's not like she has much of a choice," another female voice said. Both were speaking *Dietsch*. "Her husband makes the decisions, obviously."

"As it should be. But I wonder if he's making this one for his own benefit."

Barbara put the chips in her shopping cart and frowned. She recognized the voices as belonging to Tabitha Smucker and Melva Miller, widowed sisters who loved to gossip. Even after Bishop Yoder gave a sermon on the evil of gossip several months ago, she'd overheard them whispering about whether his daughter Ivy would ever get married, especially since she was so short and as plain in the face as Leanna, and no wonder they were best friends since both of them would probably be spinsters for the rest of their lives. Barbara had been upset on both girls' behalf. Leanna had become a good friend since she started working for Daniel, and Ivy was a sweet woman. Melva and Tabitha were truly unpleasant people.

Barbara tuned the women out and was almost to the end of the aisle when Melva's words stopped her.

"Mark *mei* words, Tabitha. Daniel Raber is having an affair."

Barbara froze, a chill running down her spine.

"You don't know that for sure," Tabitha said.

"*Nee mann* of any character would hire a single woman,

much less work with her day in and day out alone with *nee* chaperone, *unless* there was something going on. I'm sure I'm not the only one who thinks so."

Barbara brought her fingertips to her lips. Daniel and Leanna? No, that wasn't possible. Daniel would never stray. She trusted both him and Leanna completely. Taking a deep breath, she finished her shopping and went to the counter. She ended up having to stand behind Melva and Tabitha, who smiled at her sweetly and made small talk as if they'd never gossiped about her husband's and her friend's characters.

On the way home, she tried to stay calm. Logical. But Melva's words kept echoing in her mind. An affair. It wasn't possible . . . Was it? And as for Leanna, Barbara knew she had no interest in anyone in the community or in getting married, because she liked being independent.

But what if she didn't like anyone else because she already had Daniel?

Barbara thought of all the hours Daniel and Leanna spent in the workshop. Late hours a few times, especially when they were trying to complete a difficult repair for a customer, or when business was busy. Barbara had even gone to bed, perfectly at peace with the two of them working into the night. Alone. With each other.

A car horn blasted as it sped by, jarring her out of her thoughts. She gripped the horse's reins. She was being ridiculous, letting her imagination run roughshod on the basis of cruel gossip. She was also hormonal. She knew that, too, having read as much as she could about pregnancy since her first miscarriage. But the logical thoughts didn't keep the assumptions at bay. What if those women were right? What if she'd been stupid and oblivious all this time?

As she pulled into her driveway, she settled her mind. Daniel was not having an affair, and Leanna would never betray her. It wasn't in either of their characters, regardless of what Melva and Tabitha said.

She'd planned to quickly put up the horse and buggy, but Daniel met her right away, as if he'd been waiting for her to return. It was nearly five, and Leanna came outside, too, waving at Barbara. "He's making me leave," she called out, hopping on one foot as she put on a skate. "He said I was working too much."

Daniel leaned forward and took the groceries from her. "You were gone awhile. I was starting to worry."

"See you both tomorrow!" Leanna shoved on the other skate and made her way down the gravel driveway. Barbara had always been impressed with Leanna's athleticism. Barbara could barely hit a volleyball over the net. Was Daniel impressed with Leanna's skill too? Sharp thoughts of suspicion and jealousy jabbed at her.

"What's wrong?" Daniel frowned, worry clear on his face. His dark-blue gaze didn't move from her as he held the groceries.

"Nix." She pushed the ridiculous and unfounded thoughts out of her mind and smiled at her husband. She touched his cheek, feeling the soft hair of his beard against her palm. His hair was a medium blond color, but his beard was darker, almost a dirty blond. He was kind, he was handsome, and he was hers till death parted them. That was the truth, not the gossip she'd heard.

He leaned into her palm for a brief moment, but the

concern didn't leave his face. "You're upset," he said in a low voice.

"And you're overly worried." She started to get out of the buggy and he took a step back. But he stayed close behind her as they went into the house.

He set the groceries on the kitchen counter, looked at her for a long moment, and then said, "I have a few more things to do in the shop, but they can wait until tomorrow."

"*Geh* ahead and finish them." She started unpacking the groceries, determined to put the negative thoughts out of her mind. "I'll have supper ready before too long."

"Meat loaf sandwiches are fine," he said. "I don't mind eating leftovers, you know."

"And you will, for lunch tomorrow." She'd already cut individual slices of the leftover meat loaf for sandwiches for him and Leanna. She turned to him with a smile. "Don't worry, I won't make you a fancy meal. Just one of *yer* favorites."

A grin formed on his face. "I wonder what that could be?"

"You'll have to see."

She let out a relieved sigh as he left, glad to see that he relaxed a bit. She'd be glad when she hit the three-month mark. That would be the furthest along she'd been in a pregnancy, and he wouldn't hover over her so much by then. A part of her warmed at his attentiveness, knowing it was because he loved her and their child, but it was also stressful to be around.

She put the groceries away quickly and then whipped up the oatmeal scotchies batter. While the cookies were baking, she prepared hamburger casserole. It was a simple dish and quick to make, but one Daniel really liked. By the time he came back the cookies were cooling on a rack and the casserole was about to come out of the oven. She felt his strong arms go around her waist as she washed a few dishes in the sink. "You sure you're okay?" he whispered in her ear.

She leaned against his back, finding comfort and surety in his embrace. She glanced up at him with a smile. "I'm perfectly fine. Now *geh* wash up. Supper will be ready in a few minutes."

After prayer at the table, they dug into their meal. As expected, Daniel was appreciative of the casserole, even though she'd made it so many times during their marriage. She'd stood up to get him two of the oatmeal cookies when he said, "Leanna did an excellent job while we were gone. I don't know what I'd do without her."

Barbara's hand hovered over the cookies, another stab of jealousy going through her. Melva and Tabitha's gossip came back to her mind, along with seesawing feelings. *Stop. There's* nix *going on between them. Don't be foolish. Don't be desperate.*

"Barbara?"

She snatched up the cookies, breaking one of them. "Oh *nee*," she said, bringing her hand to her mouth. Suddenly tears came to her eyes.

Daniel was at her side in a flash. "I knew it. There *is* something wrong."

Barbara moved away from him, wiping her eyes with the back of her hand. "It's hormones," she said. "That's all." Which was the truth. She wouldn't have this irrational reaction if her hormones weren't all messed up.

"It's more than hormones." He gently put his hands on her shoulders and turned her to face him. "Tell me," he said with soft pleading. "Remember, we promised not to have any secrets between us."

But maybe you do. Her eyes widened as the thought came unbidden.

"Is it the *boppli*?"

She shook her head. "*Nee*. If it was, I'd tell you."

"So there is something."

She felt trapped. He wouldn't leave her alone until she told him, and she couldn't lie to him. Taking a deep breath she said, "It really is nothing. Just some idle gossip I overheard while I was at the store. You know Melva and Tabitha. They can never keep their mouths shut."

"What gossip?"

"It's *nix*—"

"What gossip?"

Her face heating, Barbara said, "They think you and Leanna are having an affair."

Daniel's brow shot up, his blue eyes filling with shock. He dropped his hands from her shoulders. "What?"

"Like I said, it's ridiculous."

"Where did they get that idea?" His voice was low. Hard. Angrier than she'd ever heard.

"Probably because you and Leanna work alone together. But where else are you supposed to work? It is a mechanic shop." She let out a small chuckle, but it fell flat. "I don't believe them," she said.

"You shouldn't." He cradled her face in his hands and

kissed her deeply, allaying her fears. "I would never, ever stray."

He loved her, and only her. That's what she had to cling to. "I know. That's why I didn't want to say anything."

He searched her face. "But hearing that upset you."

Again, she couldn't lie. "*Ya.* Not because I don't trust you, or Leanna. Because I do."

He let go of her face, took a few steps back, and ran his hand through his hair. "I'll fix this right now." He went to the mudroom and retrieved his straw hat.

"Where are you going?" Surely he wasn't going to confront one of the women.

"To talk to Leanna."

"Daniel, *nee.*" She went to his side as his hand covered the back door's knob. "She doesn't need to know about this."

"I'm not going to tell her. But I am going to let her *geh.*"

"You can't fire her."

"I can." He faced her. "She's *mei* employee."

"And like you said, you don't know what you would do without her."

"I'll handle that." His expression softened. "What I can't handle is you being upset, especially while . . ." He touched her abdomen possessively. "We can't lose this one," he said, his voice thick as if he was almost choking on the words.

"We won't. I'm upset, but not that much, and a lot of it *is* hormones. Besides, I don't take stock in gossip." At least not until now, and even then, she didn't believe it. She believed in Daniel.

"Still, if Melva and Tabitha have come to this conclusion, then others might come to the same conclusion." He gave a curt nod, as if he was convincing himself at the same time he was convincing her. "I have to let her *geh*. I'll hire someone else."

"Who? There aren't any other mechanics in Birch Creek. That's why business has been so *gut*."

"I'll figure something out." He kissed her cheek. "It's the right thing to do."

But Barbara could see he didn't want to do the right thing. Yet did he really have another choice? "It's not fair," she said, tears coming again. She tried to force them back. She didn't want to cry in front of him and worry him further. She knew how much Leanna loved her job. She was a gifted mechanic. Daniel had recognized that, which was why he'd hired her right away. Replacing her wouldn't be easy, for so many reasons. "I'm sorry," she whispered.

"This isn't *yer* fault," he said as he turned to leave. His eyes became haunted. "It's mine."

CHAPTER 4

Leanna made it home in time to help out with supper, but as usual she didn't offer to help with the cooking, especially since Karen was staying for the meal. She was also an excellent cook and already helping Phoebe tonight. Which was good, because Leanna could think of a thousand things she'd rather do than stand over the stove, stirring a pot of chocolate pie filling to make sure it didn't burn.

Instead she quickly set the table, poured the tea into the adult glasses and milk into Malachi's, and then finished up washing the extra dishes in the sink.

Since Malachi liked fried chicken and potatoes, he ate contentedly while everyone else visited and enjoyed the food. Leanna had purposely guided Karen to sit down next to Adam, and she didn't miss the looks between them. She also suspected they were probably holding hands under the table, although she wouldn't embarrass Karen or Adam by making a joke of it. That didn't mean she wasn't tempted, though.

After supper, she and Malachi washed the dishes while Jalon, Phoebe, Karen, and Adam relaxed in the living room.

"What are they doing in there?" Malachi asked as he dried his plastic cup and set it on the counter. He had grown a little in the past year, and when he stood on the stool, the counter was at his waist.

"Talking." She dipped her hands into the soapsuds and washed a plate, rinsed it, then handed it to Malachi. "Boring grown-up talk."

"You don't like grown-up talk?" he asked.

She stifled a chuckle. "I do. I am a grown-up, you know."

"I know." Malachi lifted his chin indignantly. "But you like to play with us *kinner* too."

"Because all work and *nee* play is very, very dull."

"Then why do you work so much?"

Pausing, she became serious. "Because I have to. We have a lot of things to repair, and Daniel can't repair them all by himself." Everyone's machines seemed to be breaking down at once lately.

"Wanna see a new yo-yo trick after we're finished?" Malachi asked. "I learned this one myself. Jalon didn't have to teach me."

"Sure, you can show me. Maybe you can teach it to me too." She wasn't as good at using a yo-yo as her brother was. When Phoebe and Jalon first met, Jalon bonded with Malachi by teaching him yo-yo tricks. Malachi used to bug Jalon to learn more tricks, but during the past couple of months the pestering had diminished. His enthusiasm for yo-yo'ing hadn't, though. All his uncles had received yo-yo's for Christmas, including the older ones, and Malachi enjoyed showing them his arsenal of tricks.

"That would be fun." He peered into the sink. "Are we almost done?"

"Almost." She quickly washed and rinsed the rest of the dishes, and by the time Malachi was drying the last one the bubbles gurgled in the drain.

"Leanna?"

She looked over her shoulder to see Jalon standing in the kitchen doorway. Once again he had a serious look on his face, and she had to stifle a sigh. Was she in for another *talk*? "Whatever you have to say, it can wait. Malachi promised to teach me a yo-yo trick."

"I can show you, too, Jalon." Malachi jumped down from the stool and ran over to him.

Jalon put his hand on Malachi's blond head. "Why don't you show me right now?"

"What about Leanna?"

Jalon met her gaze. "Daniel is here to talk to her."

"Why didn't you tell me?" Leanna hung the damp kitchen towel on the ring near the sink. Ugh, leave it to her brother to act weird about nothing. "Is he in the living room?"

"*Ya.*" Jalon put his hand on Malachi's shoulder. "Come outside and show me the trick."

Jalon and Malachi left through the mudroom as Leanna went into the living room. She was surprised to see Daniel was the only one there, and he wasn't seated. He'd been over to the house a couple of times before, not including the Sundays after service when her family had hosted church. Usually he looked relaxed and at home here, since he and Jalon and Adam got along well. Now he looked tense. No, worse than tense. He looked upset.

"What's wrong?" she said as she hurried to him. A horrible thought occurred to her. "Did the shop burn down?"

Surprise flickered across his face, but then he shook his head. "*Nee*. The shop is fine."

She let out a relieved breath, a little annoyed with herself that she had jumped to such an extreme conclusion. If something had happened to the shop, he definitely wouldn't be here. "*Gut*." She waited for him to speak, but he kept turning his hat in his hands as he stared at the floor. Another thread of alarm went through her. "Daniel, what's wrong?"

He finally met her gaze. "There's *nee* easy way to say this." He paused again. "I have to let you *geh*."

At first she thought her hearing was off, because certainly he didn't say he was terminating her employment. Not after he'd thanked her earlier that morning for keeping the shop open while he was away and then before she left for the day said he'd see her tomorrow. No, he wouldn't say those things if he was planning to fire her. She had to be misunderstanding him. "What?" was the only word she could say.

"I have to let you *geh*."

Her mind refused to register his words. "Let me *geh* where?"

"You're fired, Leanna," he said, more sternly this time. "I don't need you to work at the shop anymore."

The words sank in. "I don't understand," she said, shocked. "Why are you firing me?"

"Because I have to. I'll make sure you get your tools

tomorrow." He put his hat on his head and headed for the door.

"Daniel . . ."

But he didn't turn around. He didn't say anything else. He opened the door and left.

She sank onto the couch. Fired? How was that possible?

"Leanna?"

Phoebe's gentle voice reached her ears, but she didn't respond. Her sister-in-law came in the room and sat down next to her. "Are you okay?"

Leanna looked up at her. Phoebe didn't look one bit surprised. "You knew he was going to fire me?"

"We weren't sure . . ."

Leanna looked at her. "What do you mean 'we'?"

Phoebe blanched, as if she'd been caught with her hand in the cookie jar. "He looked upset when he got here."

"I could see that. But it doesn't explain why you suspected he was going to fire me."

"Why else would he be upset?" She put her hand on Leanna's shoulder. "Is there anything I can do?"

Leanna sighed. It wasn't fair to quiz Phoebe on something she didn't know about. "Can you get me *mei* job back?" A lump formed in her throat and she felt stupid. Had she missed the signs that she'd done something wrong? "I don't understand," she whispered. "I thought everything was great—"

"Are you ready to learn the trick now?" Malachi said as he burst into the living room.

Phoebe glanced at Malachi and frowned. Oblivious

to the tension in the room, he came over and leaned against her, rolling the yo-yo in his hand. He'd learned long ago that he couldn't throw it in the house.

"He's excited to show Leanna his trick," Jalon said, coming around the couch.

Leanna didn't look at him, or Malachi, but she sensed all their eyes on her. She had to regain her composure. People were let go from their jobs all the time. Jalon had even lost his construction job before he and Adam reestablished the farm. But to be fired? That meant she'd done something wrong. She searched her mind, but she couldn't think of a single thing. Daniel couldn't even complain about her workstation, because unlike her house, she kept it tidy and organized. But she must have done something to make him do this . . . to come out to her house in the evening and fire her.

Her stomach lurched. "Excuse me," she said, jumping up from the couch. She had to think, and she couldn't do that with everyone looking at her. She started for the front door.

Malachi went after her. "But I'm supposed to show you *mei* trick—"

"Another time," Jalon said, holding him back.

Leanna barely heard Malachi or her brother. She ran to the *dawdi haus*, threw open the door, and walked inside. She paused, glancing around her home, remembering that less than an hour ago her heart had been filled with contentment. Now her world was upside down, and she had no idea why it had happened.

She paced the length of the living room, going over everything she could think of—the jobs she'd been working on for the past few weeks, the way she'd organized the orders that had come in while Daniel was gone, how she made sure to keep the shop clean and neat, even sweeping the floor before Daniel had to ask—

Oh *nee*. She halted, her stomach knotting up. Had he seen her reading his grandmother's letter, the one he'd dropped on the floor? "I knew I shouldn't have done that," she said, pacing again and chewing on her bottom lip. She'd thought she'd been alone in the shop. But if Daniel had seen her, why hadn't he said anything to her before she left this afternoon? If he was mad, why did he pretend everything was okay? Daniel was as straightforward as a person could get. He didn't play games, which was why none of this made sense. And even if he had seen her read the letter, he should have reprimanded her. That's what she deserved.

Reprimanded. Not fired.

She stopped pacing again. "I have to do something," she said. "Apologize, beg for *mei* job back . . ." She put on her shoes, then hurried to the front door and yanked it open. She froze when she saw Jalon standing on the front stoop, his hand raised to knock.

"I came to check on you," he said, warily taking a step back.

"I'm fine." She tried to move past him. Dusk was descending, and she'd have just enough time to get to Daniel's, apologize and get her job back, then get home before it was completely dark. She didn't like to skate or drive the buggy after the sun went down.

"You're not fine." He blocked her path.

She glared at him. "Get out of *mei* way."

"Not until you tell me where you're going."

"It's none of *yer* business."

He frowned, but he didn't move. "You're upset, so it's *mei* business."

That was the last straw. She was finished with Jalon's hovering. "I'm not a *kind*! I don't need you watching and managing *mei* every move."

"I'm not." But a guilty look crossed his face. "If you weren't so unreasonable—"

"I just got fired." She stomped her foot, which didn't help her case any, but she didn't care. "You expect me to accept that without an explanation?"

"You have to."

She put her hand on his shoulder and pushed. "I don't have to do anything. Now, let me by." She pushed him again, but it was like shoving a brick wall. He stood his ground.

"You're not going to see Daniel," he said, glancing at her hand as though it were a pesky fly. She half expected him to shoo it away. "You'll just make it worse."

"By apologizing and asking for *mei* job back?"

A puzzled look crossed his face. "What are you apologizing for?"

Her cheeks grew red and she turned away. She wasn't about to tell him that she'd read Daniel's personal mail. "None of *yer* business."

Now his baffled expression turned serious. "Leanna, tell me what you're apologizing for."

Her frustration level hit an all-time high. Before she could stop herself she yelled, "For reading his *grossmammi*'s letter. Satisfied? Now will you let me leave?"

He didn't move, but he tilted his head as he regarded her. Was that relief she saw on his face? She didn't have the time or interest to try to figure it out. "I've got to get to Daniel's—"

"So he fired you over reading his *grossmammi*'s letter?" Jalon asked, continuing to block her way.

"I don't know. He didn't give me a reason. But that's the only thing I can think of that I've done wrong."

Jalon paused. "Maybe you should wait until morning to talk to him. Let both of you settle down a bit."

She lifted her chin. "I'm perfectly settled."

"You're wearing two different shoes."

She glanced down at her feet and saw that she had on one white tennis shoe and one black. She quickly took off the white one and reached for the black one lying on its side near the front door beside the other white tennis shoe. Hopping on one foot, she put the matching shoe on.

"Leanna, will you listen to me for once? You're upset—"

"*Ya*. I am. And I'm going to get angrier if you don't move."

"Hold on a minute." His voice was low and calm. Soothing almost, except she wasn't in the mood to be soothed. "Do you think Daniel would hire you back when you're like this?"

Leanna stilled, her chest heaving from hopping on one foot and putting on her shoe, not to mention being a few words away from hopping mad. A long breath escaped her lungs. Although she didn't want to admit it, she knew her brother was right. He always was, something that usually irked her but outright annoyed her right now. "Fine," she said, taking a step back. "But first thing in the morning I'm going over there and getting *mei* job back."

"If you still feel the need to do that, then do it."

"Feel the need? Jalon, I'm this close to—"

"Twisting *mei* ear?" His mouth tilted up in a smirk.

She hadn't thought about twisting his ear in years. When they were in their early teens, Jalon hadn't had his growth spurt yet, and for a few years Leanna was taller than him, something she took full advantage of. Twisting his ear was a favorite way to put him in his place. There wasn't much of a height difference between them now, but he did outweigh her by more than fifty pounds, and all of it was muscle. "I was going to say slamming the door in *yer* face, but either one would be equally satisfying."

The smirk fell from his face. "Would it?"

Her shoulders slumped. "*Nee.*"

Jalon put his hand on her shoulder. "I understand how you feel."

"You can't." She pressed her lips together, refusing to look at him. "You've never been fired."

"True. But that was only by God's grace because there were more than a few times that I showed up for work hungover. I should have been fired."

"Are you saying Daniel firing me is God's will?"

"What? *Nee.* That's not what I mean." He looked up at the sky, then at her again. "Why is it so difficult to make a point with you?"

Leanna knew that when it came to sparring, she was an expert, and Jalon an amateur. Right now she was too tired to engage in this argument anymore. "What is *yer* point, Jalon?"

"Promise me you'll wait until morning to *geh* see Daniel."

"I already said I would."

He nodded. *"Danki."* He paused before his next question. "Want me to ask Karen to come over?"

"Karen? What for?"

"To keep you company."

Leanna scowled. "You mean to keep an eye on me."

"That too."

She shook her head. "I gave you *mei* promise. I don't need you or Karen to babysit me."

"All right. I'll see you in the morning, then. If you want, I can drive you over to Daniel's."

"Sure. Why not?" But she had no intention of being driven by her older brother to beg for her job back. She would do this herself. When Jalon hesitated to leave, Leanna said, "You can *geh* now."

"Are you sure you're okay?"

"I'm fine. You talked some sense into me. Appreciate it." She started to shut the door against him.

"Gute—"

"Night!" She pushed against the door, then turned and leaned her back against it. She loved her brother, but sometimes he was ridiculous. "At least he cares about me," she murmured. The reminder took away some of her annoyance with him.

She felt like a limp noodle as she walked over to the couch. She wasn't angry anymore, at least not much. She was devastated, though, to think that one little mistake—okay, maybe not so little and definitely not a mistake—would cost her her job. Reading the letter didn't have anything to do with her job performance, but this was a wake-up call. She was never, ever going to read anyone's personal correspondence again. She'd learned her lesson, and hopefully Daniel would accept her apology and hire her back. She prayed he would. She didn't know what she'd do if he didn't.

. . .

It was just before dawn by the time Roman arrived at Daniel's house. After reading his grandmother's letter two days earlier and deciding he would fulfill her request, he went straight to the bishop in Draperville and asked for forgiveness and reinstatement into the Amish. The bishop had agreed, although Roman could see the man doubted Roman's sincerity. Which made Roman wonder why he'd allowed him back in the community. The moment he was out of the *bann*, he sensed imaginary walls closing in on him. He was trapped, again. But for once, he had to stop thinking about himself. He was doing this for his grandmother, and he would deal with any anxiety for her sake.

That didn't mean he could deal with seeing his parents. After his encounter with his father at the graveyard, it was clear nothing had changed between them. The only warmth in his home had been from his grandmother, and he couldn't bring himself to face the coldness without her. Instead he spent the last of his money on a bus ticket to Birch Creek, then a taxi to Daniel's home.

The taxi dropped him off in the driveway, and Roman paid the driver, who didn't seem fazed by having to work so early in the morning. As he left, Roman looked at the house. It was as if the last year hadn't happened and he was arriving here for the first time, after his brother agreed to hire him on. It wasn't that Roman had wanted to work in a machine repair shop. But he had to get out of Draperville. He thought he could follow his brother's lead and make a new start. That hadn't worked out any better than moving to Laketown had. It didn't help that Daniel was exceptionally skilled at repair work. So was his employee, Leanna Chupp. She was actually better than Daniel, and being surrounded by two mechanical geniuses made Roman feel more like a failure than ever before.

Leanna had surprised him, and not just with her skill. He'd never met a woman like her. First was her appearance. She was taller than him, and at five ten he wasn't all that short. He'd guessed her to be close to six feet. She was definitely the tallest Amish woman he'd ever met. But after his initial surprise he hadn't thought much about her height. Her unique personality and bluntness, though . . . That quickly got under his skin.

He shook his head. Why was he thinking about her? He needed to focus on what he was going to say to Daniel, not muse over Leanna. If his reception when he'd arrived last year had been chilly, this one would be downright frigid. But as long as he had his promise to his grandmother to use as a bargaining chip, he knew he wouldn't be turned away completely.

Roman made his way up the driveway. He'd arrived this early on purpose—he wanted to talk to his brother before the shop opened and before Leanna and customers arrived. He slung his duffel bag over his shoulder, ran his hand through his shorn hair, realized he needed to buy a hat at some point—although he'd saved his Amish clothes—and went to the front door. He lifted his hand, hesitated, and then knocked. He expected to knock a second time, but the door immediately opened.

Daniel stood there, his figure shadowed by the streetlamp several yards away from the driveway. He didn't say anything for a long moment, and Roman was at a loss too. Finally he said the first thing that came to his mind. "You're up early."

"I never went to sleep."

The words were weary, and Roman noticed a slump in his brother's normally square shoulders. "Why not?"

"Long story." He pushed open the screen door. "You might as well come in."

That surprised Roman. He thought he'd at least get the third degree before he was allowed to walk inside. He deserved it. He followed Daniel through the darkened living room to the kitchen. A pot of coffee was on the stove, the rich scent filling the air. A mug was on the table. Roman glanced around the kitchen. "Where's Barbara?"

"Sleeping." Daniel went to the cabinet and got down another mug. Without asking him if he wanted coffee, he poured some into the mug and handed it to him. "Have a seat."

Roman sat down, setting his bag on the floor by his chair. He didn't touch the coffee.

Daniel sat down across from him and took a big swig of his coffee before setting the mug on the table. "Did you get a letter from her?"

Roman nodded, fingering the handle of the mug.

"Is that why you're here?"

"*Ya.*" There was no reason to pretend anything else. "You got one too?"

Daniel nodded, took another swig of coffee, and then got up and refilled his mug. "She wanted us to reconcile."

Roman nodded and moved his mug closer. He hated coffee, but maybe he should take a drink to show Daniel good faith. The scent of the brew reached his nose and he hid a frown. He wasn't ready to take that step yet. "Her last request." A lump formed in Roman's throat. "I should have been there," he whispered.

"*Ya.* You should have." Daniel went to the table and glared down at him. "Instead you were off doing God knows what."

Now, this was the Daniel he expected, and even though he'd prepared for the jabs and digs he was sure would come, that didn't stop him from being defensive. "I did what I had to do."

"You always do." He paused. "I didn't expect you to show up."

Roman deserved that, but it still stung. "I'm here. That's all that matters."

He didn't acknowledge the comment. Instead he looked Roman up and down. "You look thinner."

"I needed to lose weight."

"*Nee*, you didn't." He took another drink from the mug, stared at it, and then looked at Roman again. "What do you want from me?"

Roman paused, not expecting the question. "What do you want from me?" he countered.

"*Nix.* So you don't have to stick around. I forgive you. We're reconciled. Request fulfilled."

His brother's words should have made Roman feel better. Instead they made him angry. "You're not taking this seriously."

Daniel leveled his gaze. "I'm taking this very seriously. But I know how this is going to *geh*. You'll stay here until you get bored or tired or decide you want to leave the Amish again, and then you'll disappear and do *yer* own thing. So I'm saving us both the trouble. We're fine. Now you can be on *yer* way."

Daniel was giving him an easy way out, and Roman was tempted to take it. But on top of his desire to fulfill his promise, he had to face reality. He was broke. Dead broke, having spent almost his last dime getting here. He'd have to find a job right away, and a place to live. He had no choice but to throw himself on the mercy of his brother. "I can't leave," he said, grinding out the words.

"You always leave," Daniel sneered.

"This time I can't." He briefly relayed his circumstances, not going into much detail, and Daniel not asking any questions. "I promise I won't leave. Not this time." *Not until things are truly good between us.*

Daniel didn't answer for a long moment. Roman squirmed in his chair, and he saw a flash of satisfaction in Daniel's eyes. He'd never thought of his brother as cruel or vindictive. They'd gotten into their fair share of fights when they were younger, and more verbal sparring when they were older. By the time Daniel married Barbara, they were barely speaking to each other. It was Barbara who convinced Daniel to give Roman a chance and hire him. Now he was back at square one, but the situation was worse. His grandmother was dead, and Roman had been reduced to begging.

There was also something else, a desire that hadn't been there before. Roman wanted to prove Daniel wrong. He wanted to show Daniel he could be trusted. But he could do that only if his brother gave him another chance. And from the inscrutable look on Daniel's face, he wasn't so sure he would. "Please, Daniel. Hire me back."

His brother's brow lifted. "You're that desperate?"

"Not desperate." A lie, but he wasn't about to peel every layer of pride away. "I'm determined. And if you won't give me a job, I'll find one here in Birch Creek." He didn't know the first place to look, even though he'd lived here for nine months. He'd kept himself at double arm's length from everyone. His stomach turned into a knot, because the last thing he wanted to do was *geh* door-to-door and ask for work. "I'm not leaving, Daniel." *At least not until I keep my promise.*

Daniel rubbed his chin, and Roman could see his guard drop a tiny bit. Weariness started setting in, something Roman could identify with. He was near exhaustion himself, mostly from holding in his grief. But Roman kept his gaze on him, silently persuading his brother to give an answer. Finally, he got one.

"You can start this morning." Daniel grabbed his mug and went to the sink, rinsed out the mug, and then started to leave the kitchen.

Roman stood. "You're serious?"

Daniel paused in the doorway to the living room, not turning around. "You might as well stay here. Barbara wouldn't have it any other way. *Yer* room's the way you left it." Then he walked out of the kitchen. A moment later, Roman heard the front door open and close.

Roman stared at the empty doorway. His brother had actually agreed. A part of him couldn't believe it. Then he remembered that his grandmother had written to Daniel too. Her request was probably the only reason Daniel had hired him back. Roman frowned. It wasn't what he'd said to his brother that had convinced him. It was all because of their grandmother.

Did the reason matter? Roman now had a good job and a place to live, which was more than he'd had when he left Laketown. He should be grateful. *"Danki,"* he said to the empty room.

He picked up his bag and went upstairs, careful not to disturb Barbara. He was surprised she wasn't up by now. She usually got up pretty early. As he passed her and Daniel's bedroom, the door was ajar and he could see inside. She was still sleeping. Was she ill? That might be why Daniel looked so tired. Roman treaded quietly to the end of the hallway where his old room was. When he walked inside, he saw Daniel was right—the room hadn't changed at all. He wouldn't even have to buy a hat. One of his old ones was still on the dresser.

"Roman?"

He turned to see Barbara standing in the doorway. She was tying a housecoat over her nightgown, and her hair was in a long braid that trailed over her shoulder. Normally she wouldn't be seen without her hair up, which just added to Roman's worry that something was wrong. He went to her. "Are you okay?"

She looked surprised, the dusky daylight of the rising sun coming through the window and outlining her features. "I'm fine," she said, smiling. "What are you doing here?"

He hesitated before he answered, surprised that she didn't know. Maybe Daniel hadn't told her about their grandmother's letter. If he hadn't, Roman wasn't going to reveal it either. "I needed a job," he said, holding up his hands. "It's rough out there in the real world."

"So you're back with the Amish?"

At the pleased note in her voice he nodded, forcing a smile. "*Ya.*"

"I'm so glad to see you." She reached up and hugged him. Barbara was petite. Not overly small, but several inches shorter than both him and Daniel.

"It's *gut* to see you too," he said, hugging her more tightly than he'd expected to. It felt good to feel welcomed, and her embrace reminded him of his grandmother's—tight and filled with love. He held her at arm's length. "I'm surprised you're sleeping in."

A shadow passed over her face, but it went away as she smiled. "I was a little extra tired yesterday, that's all. The funeral . . ." Her smile faded. "It was hard."

Guilt stabbed at him. "I'm sorry I wasn't there."

"I'm sure she understood. What's important is that you're here now, and that you've found *yer* way back. I take it you talked to Daniel?"

"*Ya*. He told me to come up here and get settled in. Even gave me *mei* job back."

She looked surprised again, but said, "I'm glad he did. We can celebrate with buttermilk pancakes."

His stomach rumbled. He hadn't had homemade pancakes in over a year. "Sounds *gut*."

"I'll see you downstairs in a bit."

Roman nodded, and Barbara left. He went to the window and watched the pale light streaking across the sky. Once again he felt the walls closing in. One of the things that had bothered him so much about the last time he was here was the contrast between his and Daniel's lives. His brother, as usual, had it all together. A great wife, a nice home, a thriving business. Roman had . . . nothing. And while he should have been happy for Daniel, all he could see was what he lacked. Roman still had nothing, other than a long, uphill climb ahead of him.

His grandmother's favorite time of the day was dawn. "The promise of a new day," she always said. "More time to see what God has in store for us." As he gazed out the window, Roman wondered what God had in store for him here. Reconciliation? Or more failure? He didn't know how he would handle either of them. The only thing he did know was that when it came time to leave again—and he knew that time would come, because it always did—he would do it right this time, without leaving any hurt feelings or resentment in his wake.

CHAPTER 5

As soon as daylight streaked the sky the next morning, Leanna hit the road. She skated with purpose, going over and over her apology to Daniel in her mind. She had to make sure the words were right, and that Daniel would understand how sorry she was, that she'd learned her lesson, and how she was going to keep her nose out of other people's business from now on. That required a lot of swallowing of pride, but she was willing to do it. Not to mention that confessing and apologizing was the right thing to do.

When she reached Daniel's house, she saw the shop light was on. That wasn't unusual—lately, since business had picked up, Daniel had gone out to the shop early. She stopped at the front door, her palms slick with sweat as she removed her skates and took her shoes out of her backpack. She'd come here prepared to get her job back. Hopefully Daniel would see that too.

Leanna slipped on her shoes and opened the door. She expected the scent of coffee in the air, but all she smelled was motor oil and grease. She frowned. "Daniel?" she called out. When he didn't answer, she walked farther into the shop. Surely he hadn't left the light on and the door unlocked all night. "Daniel?" she called out again. She saw the back door was ajar and assumed he was outside. She headed for the back of the store and peeked out. He wasn't there. Turning around, she ran right into him.

"Oh!" Her eyes widened as she took a step back. "I'm sorry, Daniel. I didn't see you there—" Her eyes widened more as she realized who was standing in front of her. Not Daniel, but his brother, Roman.

"Uh . . . hi," he said, lifting his hand in an awkward wave. When she didn't respond, he let it fall.

Roman Raber was the last person she thought she'd ever see again. When she regained herself, she said, "What are you doing here?"

"Nice to see you too," he said, frowning.

Surprise pinned her in place, along with something else. He looked different than the last time she'd seen him. Thinner, for sure. Then there was his hair. He used to wear his hair long, longer than the men in Birch Creek did. She knew longer hair was part of his and Daniel's *Ordnung* from their prior district, which was a very strict one and had rules that she honestly didn't understand. It was even more strict than Birch Creek had been when Emmanuel Troyer had been the bishop. She never would have been able to work for Daniel if Emmanuel was still here. He not only hoarded all the community funds, but kept a tight rein on everything in the community. Leanna had always been wary of the man, and she had felt his disapproving gaze on her more than once. She'd been a little relieved when he disappeared from their community almost two years ago. However, she felt bad for his wife, Rhoda, who kept insisting he would come back.

Once Freemont became bishop, he relaxed several of the rules, including a lot of the ones Leanna thought were nitpicky, like about length of hair and hem. Daniel now kept his hair just below his ears, which was more in line with what Birch Creek men wore. But Roman had kept his loose ash-blond curls just above his shoulders. Now his hair was short on the sides and a bit longer on top, just enough that the ends curled. He also had several days of whiskers on his chin, which was definitely not appropriate for a strict district—or Birch Creek, for that matter. Although his clothes were Amish, everything else about him was from the English world, reminding her that he'd left his Amish faith behind.

She pulled her gaze from him, barely wondering why she had spent so much time staring at him in the first place. "I probably shouldn't be talking to you," she said, moving past him. Where was Daniel? And did he know his brother was here?

"I'm not in the *bann* anymore."

She turned around as he crossed his arms over his chest. He was thin, but she could still see the muscle of his bicep underneath the short sleeves of his yellow shirt. Why was she noticing his biceps anyway? "That's *gut*. You came to *yer* senses, then."

He scowled a bit. Now this was the Roman she remembered. Cranky. Scowly. With strong hands that probably would have been good working with the engines if he hadn't acted as though he was above working on them. The memory annoyed her, which helped turn her gaze from his angular jaw—something else she'd noticed when they worked together—to his face. "You didn't answer *mei* question. Why are you here?"

He hesitated. "To get *mei* job back."

She felt the color drain from her face. "You're working here?"

"*Ya.* Today's *mei* first day." His scowl turned into a smirk. "We'll be working together again."

"*Nee.* You won't."

They both turned to see Daniel walk through the front door. His gaze went to Leanna, and he looked angry. "Why are you here?" he snapped.

For a laughable moment, the irony that she'd been drilling Roman with the same question hit her, only to be replaced with dread. "I . . . I came to apologize. I'm sorry—"

"I don't want to hear it." His tone was icy, and very un-Daniel-like. "Get *yer* tools and leave, Leanna. I don't want to see you here again."

The dread turned to pain as her face burned like fire. She couldn't look at Roman. She took a step toward Daniel. "Please, I just want to explain—"

Daniel turned and went back to his desk. She waited to see if he would look at her. Or at least look up. He didn't. The room echoed with silence, except for the soft shuffling of papers as Daniel looked over the orders and receipts just as he did first thing each day.

"Okay," she said, squeaking like a mouse. She never squeaked. "I'll . . . I'll get *mei* tools." Humiliated, she didn't look at Roman as she went to her workstation, gathered the tools that belonged to her from the table, and then put them in her toolbox, which she'd stored underneath the table. She picked it up and, without a word, walked out the front door. She nearly had both skates on when she sensed someone behind her. *Don't turn around . . . Don't turn around . . .*

"What was that all about?" Roman asked.

"Nix." The hurt in her heart deepened, and she wondered if his ignorant act was just that, an act. Clearly Daniel had been planning to fire her for some time. How she'd been so clueless, she had no idea. And now Roman had quickly taken her spot. She hadn't known he and Daniel had been in contact with each other. And now he had the nerve to act as though he didn't know what was going on.

Her anger got the best of her and she whirled around. "You know exactly what's going on," she shot at him. Then she grabbed her toolbox and marched in her skates toward the road, which was cumbersome enough without carrying the heavy toolbox. Just as she was about to step on the curb, her skate caught on a divot in the yard and she went down. Her palms skidded on the gravel on the side of the road, and rocks dug into her knees as her chin slammed onto the asphalt road. Tears pricked her eyes, because she was sure Roman was right there, watching everything. Wasn't it bad enough he had to see her beg for her job and fail? Now he had to see her fall too?

. . .

As soon as he saw Leanna going down, Roman ran to her. He didn't reach her in time, but he was there to offer to help her up. "Here," he said, extending his hand.

She batted it away. "I'm fine." She pushed against the ground to get on her feet. When she stood, she brushed her palms together.

That's when he noticed the blood. "You're hurt," he said, glancing at her dress. There were blood spots there, too, and he saw some dripping down her legs. She had landed hard.

"I'm fine." Leanna wiped at the blood dripping from her chin. She bent over and picked up the toolbox, but before she could get her hand on it, Roman grabbed it.

"I'll take you home," he said.

"Forget it." She reached for the toolbox, wincing as she moved.

"Don't be stupid, Leanna. You're hurt, and it won't take long for me to get the buggy hitched up. Barbara can clean up *yer* face and hands and knees and . . ." He gave her a once-over, and only then did he realize her dress was hitched up by the backpack she'd slung over her shoulder. He not only saw her skinned knees, but he also noticed her legs a little above the knees. Long legs. Toned legs. He'd always thought Leanna had a boyish figure, but right now her legs didn't look boyish at all—

"Quit staring at me." She pulled the skirt of her dress back down.

She was right, he shouldn't have been staring. He had no idea *why* he was staring, either.

"And give me *mei* toolbox."

Good grief, she was stubborn. "You might need stitches, you know," he said as he handed her the toolbox.

She shrugged and took the box from him, then skated away at a slow, lumbering pace. This was ridiculous. He couldn't let her skate home looking like she'd been in a fight. He also didn't have time to get the horse hitched to the buggy. When he saw her almost stumble again, he ran and caught up with her. He'd seen Leanna skate plenty of times, and she was a natural athlete. The fall and whatever was going on with her and Daniel had her completely rattled.

"Let me carry the toolbox," he said, jogging alongside her.

"*Nee*." She sniffed and skated a little faster.

He easily kept up with her. The one thing he'd been successful at while he'd been living in the English world was jogging. He'd taken it up to get away from the confines of the small apartment he shared with Matt, and at some point walking among the city streets wasn't enough.

"You realize you're struggling for nothing," he said.

She glared at him. "I don't need *yer* help. *Geh* back to *yer new* job."

He ran in front of her and turned to face her, running backward. "I didn't know Daniel had let you *geh*."

"I don't care what you know." She tried to skate around him but he blocked her way.

Suddenly she stopped. An utter expression of defeat crossed her features, one he'd never thought he'd see on Leanna's face. "First Jalon, now you," she mumbled, the toolbox hitting the ground with a clattering thud.

He had no idea what her brother had to do with this, but he took the opportunity to grab the toolbox. The blood on her chin was beginning to dry, and he felt genuine sympathy for her. Something had gone terribly wrong while he was gone, and even though he didn't understand *why* he was concerned, it didn't stop him from *being* concerned. Knowing it was better to act than to argue, he turned and headed toward her house.

A few moments later she followed him, skating past him and looking a little steadier. Since he wasn't about to run carrying a heavy toolbox, by the time he reached the driveway she was in front of the Chupp house and had stripped off her skates and socks. Her bare toes dug into the green grass as she reached for the toolbox. He handed it to her without a word, and she turned around and went inside.

He jogged back to Daniel's. The front door was propped open, but there weren't any cars or buggies in the small parking area in front of the shop. He walked inside and saw Daniel still sitting at his desk, his head in the palm of one hand.

"What was all that about?" Roman asked as he approached his brother.

"None of *yer* business."

"But—"

"Get the broom and sweep the floor." Daniel stood and walked over to his workstation.

Roman glanced around the shop. Projects were everywhere. A couple of them looked as though they were finished, but most of them were only halfway done or waiting to be worked on. And with Leanna gone . . .

there was no way Daniel could do all this himself. Yet he was telling Roman to sweep the floor? Roman went to a lawn mower. The ticket said it was due tomorrow. "I'll work on this," he said, starting to pick up the mower.

"You'll do what I say or you're gone."

Roman turned and looked at his brother. The tone and expression brooked no argument, although Roman was tempted to give him one. He couldn't, though, knowing that all Daniel had to do was say the word and he would be without a job and a home. It would also slam the door shut on any reconciliation they might reach. "Fine," he muttered, unable to keep from sounding like a kid. Daniel sure was treating him like one. But Roman realized now wasn't the time to argue with him. Even as he stewed in his resentment, Roman could see Daniel was upset, and since his brother kept his emotions close to the vest, Roman knew whatever was going on was significant.

Still, he was confident that in a couple of hours, when things settled down and Daniel could think straight, his brother would give him one of the easier repair jobs to work on. In the meantime, Roman grabbed a broom and began sweeping the floor.

His mind went back to Leanna. He hoped she would be okay. The image of her bloody chin and palms came to mind and then her bloody knees, which led to him thinking about her legs . . .

He squeezed the broom handle and pushed the dirt harder. Good thing she wasn't working here anymore. He didn't need the distraction. The last thing he expected was to think of Leanna as a distraction. An annoyance, possibly. A work rival, more likely—especially since he planned to take this job seriously. But to be distracted by, of all things, her legs? Clearly he was more exhausted than he thought.

. . .

"You need stitches," Phoebe said as she held a damp cloth to Leanna's chin.

"I'll be fine." Leanna winced at the pain, not only from her chin but also from her skinned palms and knees. But more distressing than her physical pain was the humiliation, coupled with the way Daniel's harsh words and hard expression wouldn't leave her alone. He hadn't given her a chance to apologize or ask for her job back. He had cut her off, which not only saddened her but angered her. And then there was Roman. What right did he have to act nice toward her when he'd taken her job? She was more convinced now that he had something to do with her firing, and any kind gesture on his part was due to guilt, plain and simple. Although she didn't think he had a guilty bone in his body, since he'd had no trouble leaving his family and the Amish with little regard for anyone else. "Ouch!" she said as Phoebe pulled the cloth away.

"Sorry." Phoebe's brown eyebrows pulled above her blue eyes. "It won't stop bleeding."

"Here." She took the cloth and pressed it hard against her chin. Feeling the physical pain dulled the other pains. She got up from the chair, her palms and knees smarting. "I'm going home," she said, not wanting to see anyone. At least Phoebe hadn't asked her what happened, beyond Leanna telling her she'd fallen. Her sister-in-law had looked surprised, but hadn't pried further. Unlike Jalon, Phoebe knew when to mind her own business.

"Are you sure you don't want to stay here for a little bit?" Phoebe asked. "I made some biscuits and gravy for breakfast."

Even though Leanna loved Phoebe's biscuits and gravy, she didn't have an appetite. "I'm sure." Leanna gave her a half wave and left the house.

She walked across the lawn, the cool grass on her bare feet barely noticeable. She opened the door to the *dawdi haus* and went into the kitchen, turned on the cold tap, and rinsed out the bloody cloth, trying not to panic when she saw how red it was. She didn't want to go to a doctor or deal with stitches. Instead she sat down on the couch and pressed the cloth against her chin again. It would stop bleeding eventually, wouldn't it?

A few minutes later she heard a knock on the door. Certain it was Jalon, she ignored it.

Another knock. "Leanna?"

She closed her eyes at the sound of Adam's voice. She was tempted not to answer it, but Adam hadn't done anything to annoy her . . . at least so far. She got up and went to the door. "I'm not in the mood for company," she said to him.

"I'm not company." He tapped the first aid kit sitting in his lap.

"What, *yer mei* nurse?"

"If you want to look at it that way. Now let me in or I'll roll over you."

She rolled her eyes and let him in. When she sat down on the couch, he wheeled in front of her. "Let me see *yer* chin."

Too tired and hurting to resist, she pulled away the cloth. "I'm not going to the doctor."

He looked at the injury. "You don't have to."

"Phoebe thought I needed stitches."

"You do, but you don't have to get them." He opened the box and pulled out a smaller box, which turned out to hold thin white strips. "Steri strips," he said. "I always keep them around. Learned the hard way when I was getting used to the chair. It tips sometimes." He pointed to a long scar on his chin. "We'll be matching now."

Ordinarily she'd be joking back with Adam, since he was her favorite cousin and they did have the same sense of humor. But there was nothing funny about any of this. Adam must have sensed her mood because he went to work doctoring her chin without saying anything else.

After he'd cleaned and bandaged all her wounds, he went to the sink to wash his hands. "I'm sorry about *yer* job," he said after he turned off the tap.

She stared at the tiny wood-burning stove in front of her. *"Danki,"* she managed.

Adam wheeled himself in front of her again. "Maybe it's a *gut* thing this happened."

She rolled her eyes. "You're joking, *ya?*"

"Nee. Jalon said he offered you a job and you turned it down. Now you're free to reconsider."

"I'm not reconsidering."

"We could actually use *yer* help around here, Leanna. Not just with the mechanical stuff."

"I'm not a farmer," she said. Jalon wasn't the only one who'd disliked working on the farm when they were growing up, although that had less to do with the farm work than their father's frequent black moods when it came to working the land. She mostly helped her mother with the garden, and while she didn't mind the planting part of gardening, she disliked everything else—the weeding, harvesting, and canning. It was dull, repetitive work. There was nothing challenging, nothing that stimulated her mind. Putting pickles in a jar wasn't remotely as satisfying as figuring out what was wrong with a broken machine.

"I'm aware you don't like it. But if you try it again, you might change *yer* mind."

"There's a better chance of goats flying figure eights over the Eiffel Tower."

A glint of amusement showed in his brown eyes. "All right, forget the farming. We still have equipment here. We'll have more when we expand. Plus between Phoebe's *familye* and ours—"

"Wait." She sat up. "Define 'ours.'"

"You, Jalon, Phoebe, Malachi . . . me . . ." He averted his gaze.

"And?"

He shrugged. "There's *nee* 'and.'"

"Then why are you being cagey?" A smile suddenly formed on her lips, distracting her from her aching chin and humiliated heart. "You asked Karen to marry you."

"*Nee.* But I'm thinking about it."

"What's taking you so long? Just propose already."

"This coming from the confirmed bachelorette of Birch Creek."

"We're not talking about me." Thankfully. "What's holding you back?"

He glanced down at his lap. "There's this little thing called being a paraplegic."

She scoffed. "Don't be stupid. She loves you. You being in a wheelchair doesn't mean anything."

"It does." He looked at her, and his expression silenced her. "I manage okay—"

"You manage great," Leanna said, meaning every word. Adam had never needed pep talks, but she was prepared to give him one now. Forgetting the pain in her body and pride, she sat forward. "You're one of the most capable people I know."

He blushed a little at her praise. "That's all fine and *gut*, but I need help with things or accommodation normal men don't need. Like reaching for things on a shelf, or making sure there's a handicapped accessible way to get into a building . . . or a *haus*."

"Ivy can't reach everything either, and making the accommodations for a *haus* is simple. We've all done it here in our community, in one way or another. Remodeling an English *haus* by stripping out all the wire. Or building plain cabinets and replacing fancy ones. And everyone has a collapsible ramp for you, so you won't have any problems with attending church." She grinned. "See? There's *nix* to worry about."

"I appreciate all that. I really do. The community

quickly welcomed me as one of their own." He sighed. "I just . . ."

"Adam, what?"

"I just wonder if ten, twenty years down the line she'll wish she had a whole *mann*. There are things she'd have to deal with. Personal things." He stared at the kit in his lap. "I take care of all that myself. But if I get sick, or something happens and she has to deal with it . . ."

Leanna's heart ached for her cousin. She never thought Adam would be filled with doubt about this. The fact that he was hinting at such personal needs during their conversation meant it weighed heavily on his mind. She measured her words for once, something she rarely did. "Have you talked to Karen about this?"

He nodded. "She says she won't care. That she loves me the way I am."

"Then you have *yer* answer."

"She says that now, though." He rubbed the back of his neck. "But ten years from now—"

"She'll still love you. Give Karen some credit. You don't think she understands what she's getting with you? That *maedel* has been head over heels for you since you came here. Even before that. I'm positive she had a crush on you when we were kids and you used to visit."

"Before the accident," he said.

"*Ya*. That was before the accident. But her feelings haven't changed. If anything, they've grown stronger. I've known her for a long time, and Ivy is *mei* best friend. Trust me when I say the Yoder women don't give their hearts easily, and when they do, they do it completely."

She paused. "Don't be afraid. You've faced tougher things than proposing marriage."

"It doesn't seem like it." He looked at her, uncharacteristic doubt in his eyes. "What if she says *nee*?"

"You'll never know until you ask her." Leanna lifted her chin, the strips pulling on her skin a bit. "And if you don't ask her, I'll do it for you."

The doubt in his eyes disappeared, replaced with wariness. "*Nee*, you won't."

She crossed her arms over her chest. "You want to try me?"

Adam shook his head. "*Nee*. Absolutely not." He let out a sigh. "Fine. I'll ask her."

"Because I'm cornering you?" While she wanted to give him a nudge, she didn't want to force him into something he wasn't ready for. That wouldn't be fair to him or Karen. "Because I know I can be—"

"Demanding? Overwhelming? A bulldozer in a dress?"

"I'm not that bad."

He chuckled. "*Nee*. Not that bad." He sobered. "I'm asking her because I want to. I want to marry Karen."

"Yay!" Leanna pumped both her fists. "We can celebrate tonight after she says *ya*." She was excited about their engagement. Plus she needed something positive to focus on, and her favorite cousin and one of her closest friends getting married was definitely a positive thing.

"Whoa." He held up his hand. "I'm not asking her tonight. I'll do it in *mei* own time." At Leanna's look he added, "But it will be soon. I promise."

"*Gut*. That's all that matters then."

"Now, do you feel better?" He grinned. "About everything?"

His question made her realize that he'd led her down this conversational road to distract her. Not that what he said wasn't true, but he possibly wouldn't have been this open with her if he hadn't known how much she was hurting. He looked so satisfied with himself that she couldn't tell him she knew what he'd been up to. No harm in letting him think he pulled something over on her. "*Ya*. I feel a little bit better."

"The job offer still stands, by the way," Adam said. "Wouldn't you rather work for *familye* anyway?"

His words made the whole situation worse because she had thought of Daniel and Barbara as family. She hadn't realized that until now. Barbara was like a sister to her, and even though she and Daniel had only a working relationship, she cared about him like he was a brother. Ugh. The whole thing was a big, depressing mess. "I'll give it some thought," she said, only because she knew she had to say something or Adam would continue to pester her.

But Adam wasn't stupid, and he called her on it. "What's there to think about?"

"Lots of things. Having enough work to earn *mei* pay . . . working for Jalon."

"Ah. Well, I can tell you with confidence he's easy to work with."

"Work with. Not work for."

"You'll be working with him, Leanna."

But she wasn't so sure. "He's been in *mei* business a lot lately."

Adam didn't look surprised at this revelation. "He cares. That's why."

"I don't want that to extend to *mei* work life." That, and for some reason she still wasn't completely convinced his nosiness was only out of brotherly concern. There was something off about this pressure to work for—or with—him. Now Adam was adding to it.

Or maybe not. Maybe she was overthinking everything and the job offer was simply that, a job, and the coincidence with her firing was just that, a coincidence.

Suddenly she felt every ache from her fall, plus a growing headache over trying to puzzle all this out. She also felt like a bit of a baby, knowing what Adam had gone through after his accident. "I've got some cleaning to do," she said, not wanting to let him see how she was hurting.

"You should rest instead," he said. "You don't want to pull on those strips."

"Another voice of experience."

"*Ya.* This mess," he said, gesturing to the clutter surrounding them, "can wait. I have a feeling it's been waiting for a long time anyway."

"You know me so well."

"I do, so listen to me for once." He wheeled himself over to the front door, then turned and looked at her. "Sure you're all right?"

She wasn't all right, but she nodded anyway, and even managed a smile. "You know me. I'll get over it."

He gave her one last look and then left.

Leanna's smile slipped from her face. Losing her job, being blindsided by Daniel's coldness. It would take awhile for her pride to heal, especially after being doubly humiliated in front of Roman.

No, she wouldn't get over this. Not for a long time.

CHAPTER 6

By the time the workday ended, the shop floor was so clean Roman thought he could eat supper off it. So were the work tables. And the outhouse in the back. Roman couldn't believe it when his brother told him to clean *that* before the end of the day.

It wasn't that dirty, since it was only rarely used by customers. Desperate customers, to be specific. Still, he cleaned it thoroughly, and not only because he had something to prove to Daniel. Roman appreciated cleanliness and tidiness. There was a place for everything and everything had a place. His grandmother had taught him the saying, but Roman lived by it. Still, it didn't make the job any more pleasant, and it wasn't what Roman had expected when his brother hired him back. In fact, everything Daniel had him do today was not only unnecessary, but demeaning.

Which was probably the point.

He washed his hands in the water from the cooler at the back of the shop, pulled open the top, saw that it was nearly empty, and then refilled it from the pump near the barn. He was surprised when his brother bought this particular house since it had been owned by an English family. All Daniel did was remove the electricity. He kept the plumbing, and even had a generator to work this pump.

In their district in Draperville they would have been required to remove all plumbing and use only a well for water, which Roman thought was ridiculous. It was one thing not to be plugged into the grid. He understood the reasoning behind that—too much dependence on the world made one less dependent on the community, and in turn on God. He'd experienced that firsthand living with Matt. It was too easy to forget God in the day-to-day things. But making life purposefully more difficult than it had to be—that didn't make any sense. It never had, but his parents and the Amish in Draperville lived that way. Daniel seemed to have left that part of his life behind.

Roman carried the five-gallon, stand-up cooler back to the table and put the lid on it. He stretched and then yawned. It had been a long day, and not without its share of problems. More than one customer had asked why Leanna wasn't there. Apparently she hadn't missed a day of work since she'd been hired. Daniel gave the curt response that she didn't work there anymore, but no further explanation. They had several new orders, and one was a simple chain saw chain replacement, something Roman could easily and quickly do. Daniel had set it to the side and said he'd get to it in a couple of days. The customer seemed fine with that, but Roman wasn't. Instead of cleaning the outhouse he could have had that chain replaced by the end of the day.

To top it all off, Daniel also said very little to him

while he was working. Roman had accepted that. It wasn't as if he had a choice, after all. He couldn't force Daniel to talk to him, and considering their past, he didn't have a right to even try.

Before he went to the house, he glanced at Leanna's empty workstation. Spare parts littered the table—screws, bolts, a couple of nails, a pair of wrenches. It was a little untidy, as if she'd left in the middle of a repair job. He hadn't touched her space, and not only because Daniel hadn't said anything about it. It seemed wrong to clean it right now, despite being tempted to straighten up the table.

He remembered how she tried to ask for her job back. The pleading in her eyes and voice. She'd worn her desperation on her sleeve, and considering he'd done the same thing when he got here this morning, he had a lot of sympathy for her.

He blinked. Why was he even thinking about her? The situation wasn't his business, and Leanna wasn't anything to him, not even a coworker now.

Still, the tears he saw in her brown eyes . . . They had affected him. He didn't know why or how.

Shaking his head, he shoved her out of his mind and headed for the house. When he walked into the kitchen, Barbara was preparing supper. Roman walked over and stood next to her by the counter near the sink. "Can I help?"

"You still know how to make potato salad?"

He nodded. "You bet."

"The potatoes are in the bowl, already cooled. You'll find the other ingredients in the pantry."

He went to the pantry and gathered the seasoning for the potatoes, then the small jar of mayonnaise in the large cooler on the floor nearby. He knew from going to the other homes in Birch Creek during Sunday services that gas-powered refrigerators and freezers were allowed here, but Daniel didn't have one.

As he mixed the potato salad, another short burst of peace came over him, which was odd. Then again, he'd always enjoyed cooking, even though his father and mother hadn't encouraged him to help in the kitchen. But he would sometimes cook with his grandmother, at her insistence. He wasn't the best cook, but he was adequate, and every once in a while he would make supper for him and Matt when they had some extra money and weren't relegated to eating boxed dinners.

After he finished the potato salad, he set the bowl on the table. Daniel came in and, unsurprisingly, didn't acknowledge him. Instead he went straight to Barbara and whispered in her ear. She nodded, and then Daniel took the platter of warm ham steaks from her and set it on the table. He still didn't look at Roman as they all sat down and prayed for the meal.

Roman closed his eyes, but went through the motions. Praying before a meal was such a habit for him that he'd done it even while living in the English world. But he rarely paid attention to what he was doing. He opened his eyes. He saw that Daniel was still praying, so he closed them again. His brother had always been the pious one too.

Finally he heard the sound of dishes being moved and he opened his eyes. Barbara handed Roman the platter of ham. He took a piece and gave the platter to Daniel. Now that he was sitting next to his brother, he could see how troubled he looked. Dark shadows were underneath his dark-blue eyes, and his mouth formed a deep frown.

Roman glanced at Barbara and saw that she, too, looked just as troubled. He shrank a little in the chair. He'd known it would be difficult for him to be here, but he'd focused more on his feelings, a little on Daniel's, and almost none on Barbara's. He wanted to fulfill his promise to his grandmother, but for the first time he thought maybe this wasn't the best way to go about it.

They all ate in silence, with Daniel and Barbara exchanging a couple of looks. Something was definitely going on between them, and if Roman was the source of conflict for them, he didn't want that. He'd already caused enough problems. He set down his fork and said, "I can sleep in the barn tonight."

Daniel and Barbara both looked up from their plates. "Did you just say you'd sleep in the barn?" Daniel said, looking genuinely surprised.

"You will not sleep in the barn," Barbara added.

Roman shook his head. "I know I'm not welcome here."

"That's not true." Barbara looked at Daniel . . . and his brother said nothing.

Defeat rained on him. Daniel didn't want him here, and he probably never would. Then resentment replaced the defeat. He didn't need this. He didn't need Daniel either. Shooting up from the table, he said, "I'll leave. I'll find someplace else to stay. I'll get another job, too—"

"*Nee.*" As if he'd come out of a stupor, Daniel tossed his napkin on the table. "You'll stay here. You'll work here. End of discussion."

"But . . ." He looked from Barbara and back to Daniel, confused. He was giving his brother an out. Why wasn't he taking it?

"Roman." Barbara got up from her chair and went to him. "We want you to stay."

"Maybe *you* do," Roman muttered.

"I've got chores to take care of." Daniel shoved away from the table and left the kitchen.

Barbara sighed, looking in the direction Daniel left.

Roman sank down in his chair, his anger diminishing. "Daniel has a right to be angry with me."

"He's not angry with you." But Barbara's words sounded doubtful.

"I don't want to cause problems between you two."

"You're not, and you won't." She put her hand on his arm. "Give him some time. I know he'll come around."

Roman doubted it, but just like he couldn't turn down his grandmother, he couldn't turn down Barbara either. After a long pause, he nodded.

"*Gut.*" She let out a long breath and leaned against her chair. "I'm glad you changed *yer* mind."

He looked up at her, noticing how tired she looked. The trip to Draperville must have been harder on her than he realized. He popped back up again. "I'll do the dishes," he said.

"*Nee*, I can do them."

"Please. I want to help."

After a long pause she said, "*Danki.* I'd like the help."

As he cleared the table while Barbara put up the left-overs, Roman wondered for the dozenth time if he was doing the right thing by being here.

You are.

The still, small voice spoke to him as if he'd heard the words. He balanced the dishes in his hands as he stared at the doorway. He could leave. He had told Barbara he would stay, but he could easily go upstairs, pack up his things, and leave the same way he'd done it before—without a word and without being beholden to anyone.

Except for that still, small voice. It kept him planted in place, kept him from doing something on impulse that would have ruined the slim chance he had with Daniel.

He would stay. He had to, but not because of his job or a home. There was a greater purpose in him being there. He just wasn't sure what it was.

• • •

"I'm glad you're able to help me can the tomatoes," Phoebe said to Leanna the next morning, wiping her forehead with the back of her hand.

Leanna nodded. *Not like I have anything else to do.* Her palms and knees were skinned over, and her chin was covered with the white strips, while a purplish bruise had grown overnight. But she was okay, and not in as much pain. Malachi had stared at her chin for a few moments at breakfast until Jalon told him to eat his oatmeal. Malachi complied with a scowl, since he didn't like oatmeal, and had left half of it in the bowl before joining his uncles and the younger Yoder children as they walked to the schoolhouse a mile down the road.

Jalon and Adam had left to work on the barn after breakfast, and now it was nearly noon and Leanna was up to her elbows in tomatoes. She was tired of boiling, blanching, and stuffing the tomatoes into jars. Phoebe, on the other hand, even though she had arched her back a few too many times and had to sit down a little more often than usual, seemed to enjoy the process.

"We're blessed to have so many tomatoes," she said. "The garden was plentiful this year." She smiled and pulled a batch of jars out of the electric canner that ran on an inverter.

Leanna nodded and mustered a smile. Yes, they were blessed, and knowing that Phoebe had grown up poor, she understood how much her sister-in-law appreciated the bounty. Leanna knew she should appreciate it, too, but all she could think about was Daniel and her job. Her *former* job. Even though she was still upset, she also knew she still had to apologize to him for reading the letter. She wouldn't get her job back. She knew Daniel was firm in firing her. But it would clear her conscience, and it was the right thing to do.

The kitchen door opened and Phoebe's mother walked in, carrying Phoebe's youngest brother, Elam, and a basket full of green peppers. "Believe it or not, we had too many!" her mother said as she set the basket on the counter and balanced the toddler on her hip. "I thought you might like a few since Jalon enjoys stuffed peppers so much."

"*Ya.* I can make that tonight for supper." Phoebe walked toward her mother, only to stop for a moment.

"Phoebe?" Her mother went to her.

"I'm okay." She put her hand on her abdomen. "Just a strong kick. He likes to move around."

"He?" Her mother lifted an eyebrow. "Are you sure it's a *bu*?"

"Positive. A *maed* wouldn't kick that hard."

"Excuse me," Leanna piped up. "I happen to know I was an extremely active *boppli*, as *Mamm* used to tell me."

"Can't say I'm surprised," Phoebe's mother said.

Phoebe and her mother both laughed as Phoebe started pulling the peppers out of the small wicker basket. Her mother pulled out the toddler seat from the closet and fastened it to one of the kitchen chairs. Phoebe kept the seat handy even before she was pregnant because of her youngest brother. The boy reached for a spoon covered in tomato juice, but Leanna quickly snatched it before he could put his chubby hand on it.

"*Nee,*" she said, moving the spoon. "We have enough of a mess around here."

"I'm surprised you're home, Leanna." Phoebe's mother put two graham crackers in front of Elam. He grabbed one and started gnawing on it.

"I . . . I have some free time." She wasn't ready to explain about her firing, and it wouldn't matter anyway. Most of the community would know by the time they had church this Sunday.

"That's nice you're spending it helping Phoebe." Her mother glanced at her daughter with a look of concern, then said in a low voice, "I know the *boppli*'s not due for another three weeks, but I'm worried she's over-working herself. She seems so tired lately."

Leanna looked at Phoebe, who was arching her back again. Leanna didn't know much about pregnancies and even less about giving birth, but she did know many Amish women didn't slow down their work until right up to having the baby. So for Phoebe's mother to be concerned about her . . . That meant something. Leanna vowed to pay more attention to her sister-in-law until she delivered. She could help out around here more now that she had the time. *More time than I know what to do with.*

The women spent the rest of the day canning tomatoes, stopping only for lunch. Phoebe, however, had also given in to her mother's insistence that she take a nap while her little brother slept. "Leanna and I can finish these tomatoes," she'd said.

"All right." Phoebe left the kitchen with Elam in tow, then returned two hours later. While Elam had a snack, Phoebe worked on making supper and her mother and Leanna cleaned up the kitchen.

When supper was ready, Adam and Jalon came in from the barn. Jalon washed his hands while Leanna got down the glasses for tea and Malachi's plastic milk cup. "See, it wasn't so bad spending the day in the *haus*," Jalon said to her. "You look like you survived it."

She glared at him as he dried his hands. If he was trying to make her feel better, it wasn't working. Her brother could be so dense sometimes.

Supper was delicious, and after cleaning up the kitchen, Leanna felt at loose ends. She went outside and headed for her place, but changed her mind and walked over to the pond near the woods by the main house. The woods were fenced off now that the cows had free rein of the large pasture. She closed the gate and walked through the woods, the trees providing cool shade until she entered the clearing where the pond was. She ice skated here in the winter and fished the rest of the year, but today she didn't feel like fishing. She didn't feel like doing much of anything other than feeling sorry for herself.

She sat down, slipped off her shoes, and dipped her toes into the pond. The water was warm since August had been hotter than usual this year. A couple of dragonflies skittered across the surface of the water, and she looked up at the sky as clouds obscured the setting sun.

She'd never felt aimless before. Even before working for Daniel, she'd spent time tinkering with machines and engines, something her father didn't encourage, but hadn't discouraged either. She'd fixed the washing machine when she was ten and Bishop Yoder's Weed Eater when she was eleven. When she was seventeen, a tractor stalled on her street. The English driver had been taking a shortcut to the dealership so they could repair it, but Leanna repaired it instead. Working on engines came easily for her, and she only had to skim a manual to understand how a machine or engine worked. She was fully capable of working for her brother and Adam, but she couldn't shake the feeling that she would be giving something up by giving in and taking the job. She just wasn't sure what that was.

"What do you want me to do, Lord?" She had a habit

of talking to herself out loud, but this time she wanted God to hear the words from her lips and not just from her heart.

A rustle sounded in the trees nearby, startling her. She twisted around. "Malachi? Sweetie, I'm not in the mood for hide-and-seek today."

"It's not Malachi." Roman Raber stepped out from the trees.

Ugh. He was the last person she wanted to see. She put her back to him, drawing her knees up to her chest again. Hopefully he would get the point and disappear.

"I didn't mean to bother you."

She heard him come up behind her and then sensed him standing next to her. "This is private property, you know," she said, looking straight ahead.

"I know. I just didn't realize it was *yers*."

She glanced up at him, and that's when she noticed he was drenched. His shirt was soaked from the shoulders to the back, and sweat glistened on his neck and face. "Are you sick or something?"

He looked down at her. "*Nee*, why?"

She looked at the pond again. "You're really sweaty."

"I was jogging."

"Jogging?" Now she couldn't resist looking at him again.

"Yeah." He started to sit down, but then stopped. "Do you mind?"

She did mind. This was the man who took her job. The one who hurt her employer—scratch that, her former employer—and left him in a lurch. He wasn't worth her time or attention.

But he was also the same man who had carried her toolbox home for her when he didn't have to, although she didn't want to give him any points for that. She shrugged. "Suit *yourself*. I was about to leave anyway."

"I'll *geh*." He straightened, but didn't move. After a long, stretched-out silence, he said, "This is a great place. I used to come here every once in a while, when I, uh, used to live here."

"I didn't know that." She spent a lot of time at this pond. "Why didn't I run into you here before?"

He shrugged. "I don't know. Every time I came by there was *nee* one here."

She didn't say anything. She shouldn't say anything. She wasn't interested in anything about him. She should keep her mouth shut—

"Why did you come here?" she blurted, curiosity getting the best of her.

"To think. And dream," he said, as if the last two words were an afterthought.

"About what?" Goodness, what was wrong with her? Why was she asking him these questions? She should be leaving, not talking with him. Or rather he should leave and let her have her pity party in peace.

"*Mei* future, mostly. Or rather *mei* lack of one." He crouched down next to her and picked up a rock, then threw it across the pond. It landed with a plop in the middle. "That was supposed to skip," he said.

"You're throwing it wrong." She jumped to her feet, found a smooth stone, and then side-armed it. Even though she had perfect form, the stone landed straight in the pond. Her cheeks heating a little, she bent down and found another stone, then tried to skip it again. It shot straight for the bottom of the pond.

"Impressive," he said, his tone slightly sarcastic.

She glared at him and made another attempt. Then another. Finally, out of frustration she picked up a large rock and tried to throw it as far as she could. Instead it slipped out of her hand and landed on her toe. "Ow!"

"Are you okay?"

She stepped away from him. "Don't patronize me."

"I'm not. I'm genuinely concerned."

"Don't be." Why hadn't she been able to skip the stones? Or even throw one? She never missed, and she could hurl a rock clear to the other side of the pond without effort.

He picked up another stone, this time skipping it smoothly across the pond, adding more insult to a pile of injuries. He glanced at her. "I'm sure you're just having an off day."

"I'm sure I am." She turned her head and looked up at the clouds as if they were the most interesting thing she'd ever seen. "I wasn't trying to skip them, anyway," she said, the blatant lie rolling out of her mouth with ease. "Skipping stones is too easy."

"I remember you made a lot of things look easy."

She'd had no idea he'd even paid attention to her while they both worked in the shop, with the exception of a few times when either one of them needed an extra set of hands to work on a job. Well, there were those moments he stared at her, only to avert his gaze when she caught him. But that didn't mean anything.

"Here." He handed her another stone. "Try it again."

She hesitated, but then took the stone. When she did, she noticed he had nice hands. She glanced at her own. While she kept them clean, there was motor oil and grease embedded in the skin that she couldn't get out. Suddenly she felt self-conscious and dropped the stone and then put her hands behind her back.

"Why did you do that?"

"I don't feel like skipping stones, okay? Besides, I don't want to make you feel bad by outskipping you."

He gave her an odd look, but then grinned. "Whatever you say."

She took a step back. His smile . . . Had she never seen him smile before? Because if she had she would have remembered it being so . . . nice.

The smile disappeared as concern went over his face. "You're looking at me funny."

"*Nee*, I'm not." Without thinking she bent down and picked up a stone and skipped it. This time it not only skipped, it skipped seven times. Her mouth dropped open in shock. "Personal best," she said, grinning, forgetting about her pity party and that she found Roman annoying. Of course, grinning was the wrong thing to do, because it made the strips on her chin stretch. *Uh-oh*. Her smile left as she quickly and gingerly touched the tapes. "Are they still in place?" she asked Roman.

"Let me see." He faced her and looked at her chin. She noticed he had to look up slightly. "You're *gut*. Who taped you up?"

"*Mei* cousin Adam."

"He did a nice job. I was sure you'd have to have

stitches, but that seems to be doing the trick. How are *yer* hands?"

She held them palms up. "Attractive, as you can see."

"They're not bad either. You took a pretty hard spill."

"Don't remind me." She plopped back down on the ground, her brief happiness disappearing.

Without asking for permission, he sat down beside her. Since this was her pond, she wasn't going to be the first to leave, so she tucked her knees against her chest and set her chin on top of them. "Ow," she said, and then sighed as she pulled away.

He didn't say anything, and she gave him a sidelong look. He was staring straight ahead, and any teasing or good-natured-ness from him was also gone. He seemed pensive, the corners of his mouth tugging down. He had a nice mouth, with a full bottom lip and a thinner top one. That reminded her of his smile a minute ago, and the little leap she'd felt in her stomach when he'd turned to her. "Indigestion," she said.

"What?" He gave her a quizzical look.

"Nix." She glanced up at the sky. The clouds were thicker now and grayer. The cloud cover was making it look darker than it was.

"I'm sorry about what happened yesterday . . . even though I have *nee* idea what happened." Roman turned and looked at her. His face was dry now, his shirt still showing the sweat stains, although they were also fading. A soft wind rustled the leaves, cooling down the air. "I just got here early this morning. I asked Daniel for *mei* job back." He stared straight ahead now. "He didn't say anything about you losing *yers*."

"That's pretty convenient, don't you think? I get fired yesterday, and you show up and get *yer* job back after what you did to Daniel?" She scoffed. "You expect me to believe that?"

He gave her a snide look. "I don't care what you believe. Whatever happened between you and Daniel is *yer* problem, not mine."

"That *really* sounds like an apology to me." A heavy drop of rain landed on her forearm, but she didn't move. She glared at him, and he was giving her an angry look too.

"It is. If I thought I had anything to do with you losing *yer* job, I would quit and find something else."

"Why are you here, Roman?"

"I told you. I used to come here to think—"

"*Nee.* Why are you back in Birch Creek?" She turned and faced him, ignoring another drop of rain.

"None of *yer*—" He suddenly clamped his mouth shut and looked down at his lap. "I made a promise," he finally said.

A promise. She thought about Daniel's letter. About how their grandmother wanted Roman and Daniel to reconcile. Then she knew what promise Roman had made. A promise she shouldn't have known about. "Sorry," she said, the raindrops coming faster now. "I shouldn't have pried."

"It's okay. I shouldn't have left the way I did." He ran his hand through his short hair, and she saw that he had a scar behind his earlobe. How did he get that? She shook her head. *I could do with a little less of a curious nature, Lord. It's already cost me* mei *job.*

Raindrops bounced against the pond as Roman got up. "I don't know about you, but I'm not in the mood to get drenched."

"It's just a little rain." As soon as she said the words, a huge thunderclap sounded, making her jump. Then suddenly the skies opened up and it started to pour.

"You were saying?" He grabbed her hand and yanked her off the ground, then dragged her over to the nearby trees, which gave them a little bit of shelter.

"Shouldn't we head back to *mei haus*?" she said.

"It's just a rain burst." He peeked out from under the canopy of leaves. "The clouds are moving fast. It will be done by the time we get there."

Another thunder burst sounded and she jumped again, this time almost bumping into him. "Hey," he said, putting his hands on her shoulders. "The thunder can't hurt you."

"I know that." She pushed him away, and he let his hands drop to his sides. "I'm not afraid of a storm." A flash of lightning sparked near them. It hit a low tree branch, which cracked in half and dropped to the ground. She noticed Roman had moved a little closer to her. "Now who's afraid of the storm?"

"I'm not afraid," he said, a smile playing on his lips. "I'm protecting you." He didn't look frightened at all.

"Excuse me. I don't need protecting."

The rain fell in a sheet behind him. "Are you sure about that?"

His low voice, combined with the seriousness in his eyes, made her belly jump. "Were you always this annoying?"

He put his hand over his heart. "Me? Annoying?" Then he laughed. "Probably. You were too busy with *yer* work to notice."

"And you weren't interested in working."

"You and Daniel seemed to have it all under control."

She didn't miss the bitterness in his voice, nor the quick drop in his mood. To her surprise he reached out and touched her cheek. "Raindrop," he said. "You need to keep *yer* chin dry."

Now she was completely confused. How could she go from being annoyed, to being entertained, to . . . whatever this tingling was on her cheek where his finger had touched her skin? She didn't feel stuff like this around men, and she especially wouldn't feel anything around Roman. But her mental reassurance didn't help, not when they were huddled under the tree like this, the rain pattering against the leaves, the air cooling her damp skin. Now that they were close to each other, she could see another scar, this time under his left eyebrow. It lifted as he stared at her. "What?" she asked, her arms crossing over her chest, inexplicably feeling self-conscious.

"I never noticed how brown *yer* eyes were before."

"Brown as mud," she said. It was what she thought, too, the few times she'd paid attention to her eye color.

"I wouldn't say that." He frowned a little. "I definitely wouldn't say that." He stared at her for another moment and then looked up at the sky. "The rain's letting up." He moved out from under the tree. "Just sprinkling now."

They emerged from under the tree as a few faded sunbeams managed to shine through the cloud cover.

There was no reason for her to stay here now. The rain was gone, it was getting dark, and her pity party, miraculously, was over. Still, she stood there, alternating between glancing at him and staring at her surroundings.

"Guess I'll head back to Daniel's." He stuck his hands back into the pockets of his pants.

Brought to her senses, Leanna started backing away. "*Ya.* I've got lots to do tomorrow." More canning. Yay.

"Uh, I'll see you later then."

"Right. Later." She watched him walk away, wondering what in the world was going on. Butterflies in her stomach, wondering about his scars, feeling a bit of a rush when he gazed into her eyes. Even though they'd had a decent conversation this evening, he was a loner. An odd one at that, since the last time they'd had a conversation, other than the day after she lost her job, he had barely spoken to her. If anything, he had seemed eager to avoid her when they were working.

That hadn't seemed to be the case a few moments ago.

Leanna stopped up short. She'd been too much in her head lately, rethinking and double thinking the simplest encounters. She doubted she'd ever exchange more than a few words with Roman Raber again, which was fine with her.

But as she went back to her house, she couldn't stop thinking about his great smile.

. . .

Barbara slipped out of bed, put on her slippers and a light robe, and went downstairs where she knew she'd find Daniel. She was worried about him. He'd always had a tendency for insomnia, but with her pregnancy, then his grandmother dying, he'd barely gotten any sleep. Copious amounts of coffee were keeping him going, but he couldn't continue that. It was past two in the morning, and she knew he hadn't had any sleep tonight either.

The scent of coffee grew stronger as she went to the kitchen. She found Daniel at the kitchen table, holding his coffee mug, staring straight ahead. "Daniel?"

He turned to her and blinked. "What are you doing awake?" He shot up and went to her side. "You should be in bed, asleep."

"So should you." She put her arm through his. "Come to bed, Daniel. I don't sleep well when you're not next to me."

He put his hand over hers and gave it a squeeze, then moved away. "I'll be there in a minute."

"Which will turn into half an hour, then an hour, and then another all-nighter." She put her hand on his cheek. "You have to get some sleep."

"I'm fine." He sat back down at the table and took a sip of coffee.

She could tell by the lack of steam coming from the mug that he'd been nursing it for a while. She sat down next to him. "Talk to me, Daniel."

"There's *nix* to talk about." He gave her a weary smile.

"Remember the day before yesterday? You could tell something was bothering me. I have that same intuition when it comes to you." She took his hand and this time she wasn't going to let him go. "It's Leanna, isn't it?"

He nodded. "I didn't want to fire her."

"Then hire her back."

"You know I can't do that." He sighed. "I didn't think things through when I hired her in the first place. A single woman, working alone with a married *mann*. I'm surprised we weren't gossiped about a long time ago."

"Maybe you were, and we didn't know about it. What does it matter, anyway? I trust you."

"You had doubt though."

"I have hormones." She managed a small smile. "We can blame the *boppli*. She can't defend herself."

"So you think we're having a *maed*? Can you tell this early?"

The corners of his eyes softened, and she prayed the child she was carrying was a girl. Of course, her husband would love a boy just as much, but she knew he really wanted a daughter. "One who looks like you," he'd said. She'd never carried a baby long enough to find out what the sex was. *This time will be different.* "*Nee*, I can't tell. I just have a feeling."

"Come here." He pulled her into his lap, and she leaned her head against his shoulder. "I don't want you to be troubled by anything. Not gossip . . . and not *mei bruder*."

So it wasn't just Leanna that had Daniel up tonight. She'd known that, of course, but she was surprised he'd mentioned his brother. "Roman has changed," she said. "Can't you tell?"

"He hasn't changed." His tone was unyielding. "He's here because he feels guilty."

"I'm sure that's true. But I don't think guilt is the

only thing that brought him here. I suspect there's something else. Maybe Roman doesn't even realize the reason."

"Oh, he knows exactly why he's here." His mouth flattened into a grim line. "*Mei grossmammi* wrote to him too."

She lifted her head. "She did?"

He nodded. "She wanted us to reconcile." He shook his head. "I figured I'd be the first to extend the olive branch. I'm surprised he is."

"He was close with *yer grossmammi*."

"I am . . . I *was* too."

Barbara nestled against Daniel's chest, her heart aching a bit for the boy he was, the one who had tried so hard to earn his parents' affection but never had. Thankfully his grandmother had been there to give him and Roman what their parents couldn't.

They sat in the dim gaslight of the kitchen for a few moments. Barbara felt her eyelids grow heavy, and then she jolted awake.

"You're going to bed," Daniel said, his voice gentle.

She looked up at him. "Not without you."

He swung her up into his arms, something he hadn't done in a long time, and carried her upstairs to bed. He laid down beside her, tucking her against him, his hand on her middle, his mouth close to her ear. "I love you," he whispered in a sleepy voice.

She placed her hand over his. "I love you too." She resisted sleep until she heard his soft, steady breathing. Once she knew he was finally asleep, she relaxed. *Please, Lord . . . help* mei *husband. And help Roman too. They can't do this without you.* She threaded her fingers with Daniel's, thinking about the baby she carried. *Neither can I.*

. . .

For the rest of the week Leanna spent nearly all her time either in the garden or in Phoebe's kitchen. Her only reprieve was Saturday, when she fulfilled her promise to skate with Malachi and his uncles. She hadn't been on skates since her fall, but she managed to stay upright this time. Her knees were healing nicely, and that evening after her bath she took off the steri strips. The wound looked okay, but she still needed a Band-Aid.

She sat on the edge of her bed, her hair damp and in need of combing. But all she could think about was how to get out of going to church the next morning, and not because she was sporting a stylish Band-Aid on her chin. By now everyone had to know Daniel fired her. She'd managed to avoid people this week by helping Phoebe, but now she would have to face the whole district.

Maybe she'd go to Mesopotamia and visit her parents instead. It was dark, but she could still get a cab to take her. It was only a couple of hours away . . .

"Nee." She stood up. She wasn't a quitter, and she definitely wasn't a coward. So what if she'd been fired? Like Jalon had said, people were fired all the time. And she couldn't tuck tail and run from her problems. This would blow over, just like everything else did. Grabbing her comb off the dresser, she sat back down and

attended to her hair. Tomorrow wouldn't be easy, but she'd get through it. She'd just ask for an extra dose of strength from God during her prayers tonight.

· · ·

The next morning she got ready for church, which was being held at Patience and Timothy Glick's house. Patience was also Phoebe's midwife, having been certified last year after having two children of her own. Leanna drove one buggy with Adam, while Jalon, Phoebe, and Malachi went in another. Adam kept up a steady stream of chatter, which Leanna suspected was for her benefit, and she was grateful.

But by the time they arrived at the Glicks' her palms were damp again. Still, she put on a smile, and after she parked the buggy, the men went into Timothy's barn. Patience was outside, and she immediately went to Phoebe. Leanna watched the women talk to each other, putting off entering the barn until the last possible moment.

"Ready to *geh* inside?" Karen asked, appearing at her side.

Leanna drew in a deep breath and nodded. *I can do this.* As they walked together, she suddenly remembered Karen had wanted to talk to her the day Daniel fired her. "I'm so sorry," she said, turning to her friend. "I completely forgot to come over and visit."

Karen looked puzzled for a moment, but then smiled. "That's all right. I heard what happened, and I know you needed some time for *yourself.* Besides," she said with a smirk, "Adam said you were pretty busy with canning. That must have been fun for you."

"Torture is more like it. I don't ever want to see another tomato."

"At least you're finished. *Mamm*'s already planned out this week's canning schedule. With Ivy gone, I'll have to do double duty. You can come over if you want."

"Sure. Let me know what time."

Karen looked at her in shock. "Are you serious?"

She shrugged. "I don't have anything else to do."

"But I thought Jalon and Adam offered you a job."

"I'm still mulling it over." Which she wasn't, but it was easier to say that than explain why she didn't want the job. Soon she would have to figure out her next step, though. She could try to get some factory work in Barton, although that held as much appeal as working on the farm. Not that many available jobs interested her, although it would probably come to a point where she would have to set aside her interests and make a living. She sighed.

"Are you okay?" Karen asked.

Leanna nodded. "We don't want to be late for church." As they walked, she asked Karen, "What did you want to talk about the other day?"

"*Nix.*" She didn't look at Leanna.

It wasn't like Karen to give one-word answers. Now Leanna felt bad. "Are you sure? We can talk after church."

Karen waved her hand. "I promise, it was *nix*. Don't worry about it."

They entered the Glicks' barn and sat down on one of the benches. Leanna steeled herself for the stares, but no one looked at her. In fact, it was as if it was a regular Sunday service. Which it was, and Leanna realized she was making a big deal out of nothing. That seemed to be her pattern lately.

The service started, and Leanna was determined to focus on worshiping God and not on her problems. That determination went out the window as soon as she saw Roman sitting on the opposite side of the barn. He was seated next to Daniel, but there was a significant space between them. He looked straight ahead, seemingly listening to the sermon too. But then she saw him stifle a yawn behind his hand. "How rude," she said.

"Shh." Karen poked her in the arm. "Not so loud."

"Sorry," she whispered, and focused on the rest of the service and not Roman. Soon she was involved in worship, and before she knew it, church was over.

After the service, Leanna went inside the Glicks' house. "Is there anything I can do?" she asked Patience. Several ladies were gathering dishes to take out to the tables in the backyard.

"You can secure the tablecloths," she said, gesturing to the window. "A few of them have come undone."

Leanna went outside and pinned down the tablecloths. As she did, she spotted Roman standing by the barn. Alone, not surprisingly. She turned from him, ignoring her concern over him standing off by himself. He chose to separate himself. He could easily join the rest of the men, who were standing around in small groups, talking. Instead he wanted to be alone. Fine. Let him be alone. He wasn't her problem. She had enough problems of her own.

The shout of happy children distracted her, and she saw Malachi and the Bontrager boys chasing one another around, along with a few other small children. She was half tempted to join them. Okay, more than half. She mulled it over, though. Was she too old to be playing games, especially since she didn't have any children of her own? Then again, a game of tag right now would do her good. She needed to revel in the freedom having fun always brought her, whether it was through skating or playing volleyball, or even quietly fishing. A game of tag was definitely on the list.

Her decision made, she finished securing the tablecloths, went to a large tree near the tables, and started to slip off one of her shoes. She stopped when she heard female voices behind her.

"I heard she got fired," a woman whispered. She recognized Tabitha Smucker's voice.

The back of Leanna's neck prickled, but she didn't turn around. She had excellent hearing, and she didn't want Tabitha to know she was eavesdropping. She held on to a thin thread of hope that maybe she was talking about someone else.

"About time," her sister, Melva, chimed in. "She should have never gone to work with him in the first place."

"Patience's husband says she's a *gut* mechanic."

Leanna fell back against the tree. So much for hope.

"That's a *mann*'s job," Melva piped up. "Her parents were always too permissive with her."

"Do you still think they were having an affair?" Tabitha asked, barely lowering her voice.

"*Ya*. Definitely."

Leanna froze. An affair? Her cheeks heated as her stomach dropped, but she forced herself not to turn around until the women had gone back into the house. She stared at the children, but she didn't see them. Was this really happening? How could anyone suspect her of having an affair with Daniel?

She walked away from the kids and the tables, heading toward the back of the Glicks' yard. A small flower garden was in the corner. It was a prayer garden Patience made shortly after she and Timothy were married. It was nothing fancy, of course, but there was a two-person wooden swing and, most important for Leanna, it was partially secluded from the rest of the property. Right now she had to get away from everyone. She hurried and sat down in the swing, clasping and unclasping her hands as the swing rocked back and forth.

Leanna was used to being gossiped about. Her height, her impulsive speech and straightforwardness, and her independence had always been topics of conversation since her family moved to Birch Creek when she was a teenager. She'd been able to let a lot of it roll off her back. Words like "skinny Minnie," "big mouth," and "tomboy" had never really bothered her. Even remarks about her choice of career hadn't kept her from pursuing it. Then there was her penchant for playing with kids. She was sure some people didn't approve, and up until recently, she hadn't cared.

But this was different. It didn't matter that Melva and Tabitha were known as the community gossips. What did matter was that they thought she was being immoral. That she was sleeping with a married man right under his wife's nose. Just the thought of it made her sick to her stomach. What had she done to deserve that speculation? Her mind whirred as she tried to figure out what she could have done to make people think she and Daniel were having an affair.

Still deep in her thoughts, she barely heard a man clear his throat. When he did it again, she looked up. Great. Roman was standing in front of her. Just what she needed.

"You okay?" he asked, peering down at her.

She wanted to say yes, to tell him she was fine and taking a small break to smell the flowers. But she couldn't lie. She shook her head and stared at her lap.

"Thought so." Once again without asking permission, he started to sit down next to her, this time on the swing.

She jumped up before he was fully seated. "Wouldn't want anyone to get the wrong idea." She meant to be flip. Instead her voice was thick with hurt and shame. Embarrassed, she turned her back on him.

"Leanna."

Without thinking she closed her eyes, feeling them burn. He'd said her name so gently. With concern and care, something she never would have expected from him. But he'd been doing and saying the unexpected ever since he'd shown up again in Birch Creek.

"What happened back there?" he asked. "I saw you start to take off *yer* shoes, and then you suddenly went white as a sheet."

He was close to her now, which made her move away.

Composing herself, she faced him. "Indigestion," she said, forcing a smile.

"You seem to get that a lot," he replied, and then tilted his head and kept looking at her. He had to lift his head slightly to look her in the eyes, but he either didn't notice or didn't mind. "For some reason, this time I don't believe you."

"I don't care what you believe." She wasn't going to reveal what she'd overheard. Then a thought occurred—what if he'd heard the same gossip? He'd been here for nearly a week now. Maybe these lies had been circulating for a while . . .

She brought her fingers to her lips. "That's why he fired me."

"What?"

"I know why I got fired." She didn't look at Roman as she let the thought sink in. It made perfect sense—more sense than her getting fired for no reason or even over reading Daniel's personal correspondence. Daniel had to have known about the rumors too. And even though she was still upset over the gossip, she was also relieved. Letting her go had been the right thing, even if it was unfair. And now, at least, she had the real answer.

"Why did you get fired?" Roman asked, his calm voice breaking into her whirling thoughts.

Desperate to divert from the question, she crossed her arms over her chest. "Why did you follow me here?"

"Like I said. You looked like you were going to throw up a minute ago." He searched her face. "Although *yer* color looks better now, which is *gut*."

"Why were you paying attention to me in the first place?"

To her surprise, his cheeks reddened. "I wasn't. Not exactly."

"Now's *mei* turn not to believe *you*."

That made him smile a little bit. "You and Daniel and Barbara are the only people I really know here."

"Who's fault is that?"

His half-smile disappeared. "Mine, and *danki* for reminding me."

"*Mei* pleasure." But it really wasn't. "Where's *yer bruder*?"

"Talking to Timothy and Asa. Probably explaining why it's taking so long to get their appliances back to them."

That piqued her interest, despite herself. "What's wrong with them?"

He briefly explained the problem with Timothy's chain saw and Asa's lawn mower. "It's *nix* complicated. But there's so much work to do. We're barely keeping our heads above water."

Leanna was surprised by his honesty, and she thought she detected some frustration on his part. How she wished she could help. But now she knew she couldn't step a single foot on the Rabers' property. Not without fueling more rumors, and she wasn't about to do that. Not just for her sake, but for Daniel's and Barbara's. Another awful emotion flowed over her. Had Barbara heard the gossip? Hopefully not, but Leanna needed to assure her that nothing had ever gone on between Leanna and Daniel, just in case she did hear something. "What a mess," she muttered.

"*Ya.* I'd say so. It would help if Daniel would let me do more than clean tools and take out trash."

She looked at him, surprised. "That's all *yer* doing?"

"Basically." He stuck his hands into his pockets. A bee buzzed around his head, touching lightly on his black hat before flying away. "I thought it might change after I'd been here for a while, but I should have known better."

"Maybe he still doesn't trust you," she said without thinking.

If Roman was insulted by her comment, he didn't show it. "Oh, he definitely doesn't." His face pinched. "I know he doesn't trust that I'm going to stick around. And I get that. But I'm not completely useless when it comes to being a mechanic. Regardless of what you and Daniel think."

"I never thought you were useless." But hadn't she? Hadn't she thought he was lazy and snobby about getting his hands dirty? Had her disdain for him been that apparent?

Without saying anything else, he turned and walked away. She quickly followed him, opening her mouth to say something. But what could she say? If she apologized, he would know she hadn't thought very much of him. And while it was true, for some reason she didn't want him to hear that directly from her. Her attitude had apparently affected him already, and she didn't want to make it worse. She didn't want him to hurt more than she suspected he already did.

She fell back a few steps, and by the time she reached the tables, he had disappeared. She looked around for him, but didn't see him. Had he left? Worse, had she driven him away?

Then Leanna's gaze landed on Tabitha and Melva, who weren't sitting too far from Barbara. Roman suddenly forgotten, she started to panic. What if they started gossiping about her and Daniel again? *Please, Lord, shut their mouths for the rest of lunch . . . or the rest of their lives. I'm not picky.*

She sat down with Phoebe and her mother, but ate very little. And for once, she said almost nothing. Conversation swirled around them as she kept her eyes on both the sisters and Barbara. Finally, after everyone was nearly finished eating, Barbara stood, went to where Daniel was seated with several men, and started to pick up his dishes. She said a few words to him and then went into the house, presumably to help with the light cleanup always needed after a Sunday meal.

Leanna got up and followed her. She had to talk to her before it was too late.

CHAPTER 7

Although Barbara was tired and Daniel had warned her to rest, she wanted to help clear dishes from the tables. "I'm just going to carry them in," she whispered to Daniel when he gave her a disapproving look. "I promise."

"Then after you do, we're leaving," he said, getting up from the table. "I'll find Roman."

"Last time I saw him he was talking to Leanna." She picked up several plates and stacked them, putting silverware on top. She'd been a little surprised to see the two of them walking from Patience's prayer garden, especially when she remembered how they'd barely been civil to each other when Roman lived in Birch Creek before.

She went into the Glick kitchen and put the dishes near the sink and the silverware in a basin on the counter. She'd wanted to clear the table and come into the kitchen for another reason, too—she needed to ask Patience to be her midwife. This was the longest Barbara had carried a baby, and she felt it was time to enlist Patience's services. Right now Patience was emptying glasses into the sink while her friend Sadie helped.

Barbara held back. She'd wait a few minutes for Patience to be free.

"Can I talk to you for a minute?"

Barbara turned around to see Leanna standing there, her hands clasped together, looking like a mix of contriteness and embarrassment. Instantly Barbara understood why. *She knows.* Pain lanced at Barbara's heart for her friend. "Of course," she said. She lowered her voice. "Did you want to talk privately?" At Leanna's meek nod—and there was usually nothing meek about Leanna—she led her into the living room. Fortunately it was empty.

"Should we sit down?" Barbara said, gesturing to a worn but comfortable-looking couch.

"I'd rather stand." Leanna licked her lips. "I'm . . ."

Barbara had never known Leanna to be at a loss for words, or confidence. She moved closer to her friend. "It's only gossip," she said quietly.

"Oh *nee*. You know?"

"*Ya.*" She reached out and gave Leanna's hand a quick squeeze. "But I'm paying it *nee* mind, and you shouldn't either."

"I'm so sorry, Barbara."

"There's nothing to be sorry about. It isn't *yer* fault those women have a wandering imagination and a running mouth."

"I know." She licked her lips again and didn't meet Barbara's gaze. "But I can see why they might come to the conclusion. Daniel and I were working together alone. We shouldn't have done that."

"Leanna, except when Roman was here, you worked

alone with Daniel for over a year before someone started talking about this."

"Are you sure? *Nee* one's said anything about it before?"

Barbara paused. "I don't know. But it doesn't matter. I just wish Daniel had handled it differently."

"He handled it fine. He needed to let me *geh*. If he'd told me about the gossip, it would have upset me." She looked down at Barbara, shame evident again. "I'm upset anyway. I promise, Barbara. *Nix* happened between us."

"It never crossed *mei* mind." Except it did, but she wasn't going to tell Leanna about her own personal faults in letting her imagination run wild when she shouldn't have. "I just wish you hadn't lost *yer* job."

"It's for the best. I know that now." Leanna's face suddenly brightened. "*Danki* for understanding. I couldn't stand it if you were upset with me, or thought I would do something so awful."

"We're friends, right? We trust each other." At Leanna's nod, she put her hand on her forearm. "And I'm glad you and Roman are getting along too. He's going through a difficult time right now." She saw curiosity flash in Leanna's eyes, and she wondered if Roman had confided in her about his troubled relationship with Daniel.

At that moment, Daniel walked into the living room. Leanna's expression tensed, and Barbara moved a little closer to her.

Daniel glanced from one woman to the other and then rubbed his eyebrow. While his face remained impassive, Barbara knew he was on edge. He shouldn't be dealing with this problem. There shouldn't be a problem in the first place, and she was half tempted to confront Melva and Tabitha and tell them exactly what she thought of their gossiping. But it would be better to let the gossip go and hopefully disappear now that Leanna was no longer working with Daniel. She went to him. "Are you ready to leave?"

He looked at Leanna and rubbed his eyebrow again. "*Ya.*"

Her poor husband. He was still struggling with firing Leanna, and Barbara knew he would for a long time. She started guiding him out of the living room. The sooner they got home, the faster he could relax, and, hopefully, rest. But before they had moved more than a few steps, Leanna spoke.

"I owe you an apology, Daniel."

Barbara stopped and looked at Daniel. His frown indicated his surprise, which seemed to equal hers. Leanna had just apologized to her, and even though it was unnecessary, she knew why Leanna had felt the need to do so. But why did she need to apologize to Daniel?

Leanna's gaze darted around the room. "I . . . I found the letter from *yer* grandmother on the floor of the shop and . . . I read it." Her next words came out in a rush. "I'm sorry. I know it was wrong, and I shouldn't have done it. I hope you can forgive me for invading *yer* privacy."

Daniel looked even more confused, but he said, "Okay . . . You're forgiven."

"And I promise I won't ask for *mei* job back anymore. You don't have to worry about that." She glanced at Barbara and then back at Daniel. "I don't want to add any more stress for either of you." She started to hurry out of the room, then skidded to a stop, turned, and said, "I'm so sorry . . . for everything." Then she rushed off.

"Daniel?" Barbara moved closer to him.

"I had *nee* idea she read the letter." His frown deepened. "She thinks I fired her because of that."

Barbara decided to let him continue to believe that. He didn't need to know Leanna was aware of the gossip.

"I'm not happy she read the letter," he added. "It's very personal. But I never would have fired her for it." He looked at Barbara. "You two were in deep conversation when I walked in. Is everything—"

"It's fine." She briefly leaned her cheek against his shoulder. "Everything is *gut* now."

He breathed out a sigh. "I'm glad none of this has come between you two."

She saw the worry and strain in Daniel's eyes and decided to wait to talk to Patience. There was time to discuss the midwife subject. "Let's *geh* home, Daniel. And I want you to promise me something."

"Anything," he said.

"You'll take a nap."

A twinkle appeared in his eyes. "Only if you join me."

She grinned. "You don't have to ask twice."

. . .

Roman spent the rest of Sunday afternoon walking the roads of Birch Creek. Not jogging, since that was more work than a relaxing stroll. Yet he was anything but relaxed. He couldn't get Leanna and their conversation off his mind. He couldn't believe he'd admitted to her that he'd felt useless when they worked together. But there was something about her—the vulnerability he'd seen when she was standing under that tree, looking like someone had knocked the wind out of her—that compelled him to make some kind of connection.

He'd gone over there to . . . Well, he wasn't sure why he'd gone to her. Maybe to cheer her up, although he didn't know what possessed him to think even that. And then when he started talking about the shop, and how Daniel still wasn't letting him do any repair work even though they were overwhelmed with orders . . . It just got to him. Enough that he had to get away from her, from everyone. The urge to flee Birch Creek had hit him again. And now he was walking the roads once more, trying to convince himself to be an adult for once.

He glanced at the sky. It was cloudless and hot, unlike the day he and Leanna had talked at the pond. She'd been a little vulnerable then, too, he realized. She'd also been good company, something he hadn't experienced in a long time. Matt was a friend, but he was more interested in playing video games, something Roman didn't enjoy. He tried a few times, but they seemed like a waste of time to him. While he knew he could depend on Matt if he needed anything, that was more because of the quality person Matt was, not because of any close attachment.

And why was that? Because attachment was something Roman always tried to avoid. Even growing up he hadn't formed any close friendships with kids in his school, mostly because while they'd been interested in playing games, he'd been reading books and dreaming about how he could escape home. He'd been dubbed weird and odd more times than he could count, and he really hadn't cared.

Or had he?

Somehow he found himself in front of the Chupp place. The property had expanded since he'd left Birch Creek. Expanded and improved on. Where there had once been a lone house and barn, now there were two houses side by side, and Roman caught a peek of what was possibly a *dawdi haus* in the back. The barn was to the side, and they seemed to be adding to it. There was also a large fenced-in pasture. A herd of cows grazed lazily, some sitting in the sun, others lounging underneath two large trees.

"Hi."

Roman looked down to see a young boy about five years old with bright-blond hair looking up at him. He'd been so lost in his thoughts he hadn't heard him approach. "Hello," he said.

"You're *mei aenti* Leanna's friend," he said.

"How did you know that?"

"I saw you two talking together. Are you looking for her?" He pulled a green yo-yo out of his pocket and rolled it around in his hand.

"I was just taking a walk. I don't want to bother her."

"Do you know how to yo-yo?"

"*Nee*, I don't." He crouched down. "What's *yer* name?"

"Malachi. You want me to teach you how? I'm really

gut. Jalon gave me lessons, and now I teach *mei onkles*. When *mei boppli bruder* is born, I'll teach him."

"How do you know you're having a *bruder*?"

The boy shrugged and started throwing the yo-yo. "I just do."

Roman chuckled. To be so young and so sure of things. "What kind of tricks can you do?"

"I can walk the dog." He threw the yo-yo down on the edge of the street and dragged it across. "That's an easy trick."

"Show me a harder one."

The boy's blue eyes lit up. "This one's *reallllly* hard." He threw the yo-yo out a few times, then gathered it up into a triangle. The green yo-yo spun in the middle, sunlight glinting off the plastic.

"Impressive."

Malachi snapped the yo-yo back into his small hand. "I've got more tricks."

"You also have a cat to feed."

Roman looked up to see Leanna walking toward them. She was barefoot, and she wasn't wearing her *kapp* right now, but a bright blue kerchief that wrapped her dark-brown hair. She looked fresh, and less strained than he'd seen her since his arrival in Birch Creek. She also looked . . . pretty.

"I'll feed Blue in a minute." Malachi spun the yo-yo in his hand.

"You'll feed him now or I'm taking him back."

"*Nee*," Malachi whined. "He's *mei* cat."

"But he used to be mine."

Roman caught the teasing glint in Leanna's eyes, even

though Malachi didn't. Thinking his aunt was serious, he said, "I'll feed him right now."

"*Gut*. He's sitting by his bowl waiting for you."

Malachi started to dash off, but then turned and waved at Roman. "Bye!" he said, and then ran to the house.

Roman stood. "So that's *yer* nephew. I didn't realize Jalon had a *sohn*."

"Stepson, soon to be adopted. But Malachi doesn't know that. Jalon's going to do it formally after the harvest and after Phoebe has her *boppli*."

"Malachi seems to think it's a *bu*."

"He's probably right. The men outnumber the women around here by a wide margin." She looked at him, and with her standing on the slight incline of the grass, it made her even taller than he was. He probably should mind, but he didn't. Superficial things like that never bothered him.

"What are you doing here?" she asked, and then added, "I seem to be asking you that a lot lately."

What was he doing here? "I wanted to check on you," he blurted.

She tilted her head to the side. "I'm fine. See? You walked all the way over here for nothing."

"Not for nothing. I got to see some cool yo-yo tricks."

Leanna laughed. "I'm sure you did. He's a little obsessed with it, a lot more than Jalon was at that age."

"It's *gut* to find something you have a passion for," Roman said.

"*Ya*. It is."

He stared down at his feet, the conversation grinding

to a halt. Then again, why wouldn't it? It wasn't like they were . . . friends. He wasn't sure how to even be a friend.

"You want to stay for supper?" she asked.

His head popped up to meet her gaze, and before he could think about it, he said, "Sure. I'd like that."

. . .

Daniel opened the door to his shop, stepped inside, and locked it. He'd left Barbara sleeping upstairs, grateful she hadn't woken up when he left the room. She was normally a light sleeper, but she must have been tired. He had no idea where Roman was, which wasn't a surprise. The past week they'd barely spoken to each other, not that Roman hadn't tried. His brother had also tried to do more work in the shop, but Daniel had told him no. He was being unreasonable and he knew it, but he couldn't keep himself from giving Roman jobs he knew his brother would hate. It was petty, and he should ask for forgiveness. But he hadn't been able to bring himself to do that either.

Why had his grandmother done this to them? She put them in an awkward and basically impossible position. Daniel couldn't seem to forgive, even though he should. And Roman . . . Roman would never be responsible. It wasn't in him. How many times had Daniel gone after him when he ran away?

At first his grandmother was the one who sent him out to find Roman, since their parents didn't bother to care. But one time when Daniel was twelve and Roman ten, he'd been gone for two whole days, and their mother and father had said nothing. They acted as though Roman hadn't existed. Daniel had never understood that, and he'd been so afraid for Roman that he spent the entire next morning looking for him without anyone asking him to. When he found his brother hiding in an abandoned tree house in the woods, snacking on peanut butter and crackers he'd taken from home and looking absolutely fine, Daniel was ready to strangle him. The same instinct occurred to him thirteen years later, when Roman disappeared from Birch Creek.

No, he was tired of being his brother's keeper. He had a wife and a child to think about. He didn't have the energy to worry about Roman anymore.

Daniel pushed Roman out of his thoughts and focused on why he was here. He was committing another sin by working in the shop on a Sunday, but he had no choice. He was behind, desperately behind. Firing Leanna and not letting Roman help him had put him in a bind, and he'd lied to Timothy and Asa when he told them their machines would be finished by the end of the day tomorrow. Not lied exactly, but fudged. They would be finished, if he could get started on Timothy's chain saw today.

With a yawn he went to the workstation and got started. He'd drunk several cups of coffee this morning before church, and four during the church dinner, which was why he couldn't fall asleep with Barbara this afternoon. He hadn't been able to sleep hardly at all the past couple of weeks. There was too much to worry and think about. His grandmother's death always loomed in his mind and heart. Barbara would say he wasn't taking time to grieve, but he didn't have the time to take. Then there was Roman, and, as always, there was work.

Then there was Barbara, and their baby. He'd been counting the days and she was further along with this pregnancy than any other. He'd thanked God for that, and all during the morning service he'd tried to give that particular anxiety to the Lord because it was driving him *ab im kopp*. Yet he couldn't let go of it, couldn't stop wondering how his wife was doing when she was out of his sight.

Life felt like a hundred-pound millstone around his neck, and he didn't see any relief in sight.

He was turning a screw in place when his eyelids grew heavy. He snapped them open and finished tightening the screw. All he needed to do now was weld the two materials together, which wouldn't take him long. They didn't do much welding in the shop, and Leanna was actually better at it than he was. But this was only a little more extensive than soldering. He went to get his welding helmet and turn on the generator that powered the blowtorch. It roared to life, and he had to hurry before someone heard it, especially Barbara. He'd get a lecture for sure if she caught him in here, and he would bet plenty of grief for working on a Sunday. His plan was to finish part of the job, then slip back into bed before she discovered he was missing.

Daniel moved the welding material to his workstation. He fired up the torch. Too late he realized he was not only holding the flame too close to his face, but he'd also forgotten to pull down his helmet. The torch fell out of his hand. He cried out and covered his eyes with both palms.

CHAPTER 8

Leanna couldn't stand awkward silences, so that had to be the reason she'd invited Roman to stay for supper. At least that was what she told herself. But any awkwardness on Roman's part had disappeared by the time the meal ended. Adam had eaten supper over at Karen's and Malachi was at his grandparents', so it was just Jalon, Phoebe, her, and Roman. Jalon and Roman had fallen into easy conversation, with Roman asking about the cattle and how Jalon and Adam fed and watered them. They also talked about the expansion plans for the farm. Leanna stayed uncharacteristically quiet as she watched Roman interact with her brother. He was animated when he talked to Jalon. Animated and engaged and completely different from the way he'd been when they had both worked for Daniel.

When they finished eating, Leanna cleaned up while Phoebe retired to the living room to relax and read. Jalon joined her, saying he wanted to catch up on some reading, too, but Leanna knew better. Her brother would be asleep within five minutes.

Since supper had been simple—egg salad sandwiches, pickles, cut vegetables, and a blackberry cobbler for dessert—it hadn't taken her very long to tidy the kitchen. She turned to Roman, who was standing near the back door, staring out the window. She could practically see him turning inward, and anticipating more awkward silence, she said, "Would you like to take a walk outside?"

He turned and nodded and then opened the door for her. When her bare feet hit the soft grass, she heard the wail of a siren in the distance. She stopped, bowed her head, and prayed that whatever emergency the vehicle was headed to, everyone would be safe. When she opened her eyes, she saw Roman staring at her.

"Were you praying?" he asked.

"*Ya*. I always do when I hear a siren."

"Wow. I've never seen anyone do that before."

"It's a small gesture." Leanna waved him off, a little embarrassed by the compliment. "Not a big deal."

"I think it is."

They continued to walk, not saying anything until they were in front of the *dawdi haus*. He studied the house for a moment. "So this is *yer* place."

"*Ya*." That she lived in the *dawdi haus* had come up at the supper table. "It's small, but it's perfect for me."

"Hard to imagine a woman living by herself in her own *haus*." At Leanna's scoff he added, "In *mei* home district, I mean. The rules there can be ridiculous."

"So you don't see a problem with me living alone?"

"Not if you're happy."

"I am." She lifted her chin. "I like *mei* place, and *mei* job . . ." She looked away. "Sorry. I'm used to defending myself to Jalon."

"You shouldn't have to defend *yerself* to anyone."

There it was again. Sincerity. She appreciated his straightforwardness. "*Danki.* I've been trying to convince him of that. *Mei bruder* can be hardheaded sometimes."

"He's a smart *mann*, though. He and Adam have some pretty forward-thinking ideas about farming and animal husbandry. Again, I'm making a comparison to *mei* home district."

They had started walking without her even realizing it, past her house and to the back pasture. "Is it really that strict?"

"*Ya.* But some people thrive under a lot of rules. *Mei* parents, for example. They don't have a problem with anything the bishop tells them they have to do."

"The rules don't come just from the bishop, though. They are ordained by God."

"But bishops are human too. Imperfect just like the rest of us."

"That's true." She thought about Bishop Troyer again, although it still seemed that Roman's district was even more strict than hers had been.

They had reached the thick oak fence, and Roman leaned on it and put his forearms on the top slat of wood. "Anyway, I'm not interested in talking about *mei* old district."

"What are you interested in?" This time she wasn't asking the question on a whim or impulse. For some reason she genuinely wanted to know.

"Engineering. I think."

"Really." Now that was interesting. "What kind?"

"Mechanical, mostly. Although I've dabbled in all

kinds. I've got some electrical designs I've been working on for the past several years."

"But you don't sound sure."

."I am," he said, not looking at her, and sounding about as confident as an elephant walking a tightrope.

A bee buzzed around her head, and she batted it away. When he didn't say anything for a few moments, she asked, "Is that what you were doing when I saw you writing in *yer* journal? Designing things?"

"Mostly. I've got other stuff in there. Private stuff."

She'd learned her lesson about getting too deep into someone else's business, so she wasn't going to pry further.

"I do like to design things." A somber expression covered his face. "At least I used to."

"You don't anymore?"

He shook his head. "I've put that to the side for now." The bee came back, this time landing on Roman's head.

"Hold still," she said, then reached out and batted at the bee. The edge of her hand brushed against his curls. They were soft, and now that she was this near him, she could smell the soap he used. Clean and kind of woodsy. Definitely nice.

"Are you sniffing *mei* hair?"

She jumped back, her face on fire. "*N-nee*. Why would I do that?"

He leaned against the fence and looked at her. "Why would you?"

The flicker of amusement in his eyes annoyed her. She needed to put him in his place, and fast. She also needed to explain that she wasn't sniffing his hair. She was batting away a bee, which could have saved his life, especially if he was allergic to bee stings. He should be grateful to her for being such a quick thinker.

"You have nice eyes," she said instead.

His nice eyes widened with surprise. "Uh, thanks?"

Why had she said that? She wasn't even thinking about his eyes. Well, maybe a little. She jumped back, feeling stupid. Why did she have to blurt everything on her mind? "What I meant was—"

"It's okay. You've got nice eyes too."

For once she was rendered speechless. Then she realized he was either making fun of her or being courteous. In her current confused state, she didn't appreciate either. "You don't have to lie."

He gave her a blank look. "I'm not lying. Were you lying about mine?"

She always made it a policy never to lie, although she had told a little white one lately. Not this time, though, even though she could save a little face if she did. *"Nee."* And because she wasn't sure what to say next, not to mention a little worried that she might blurt something else stupid, she said, "You don't have to give me a compliment because I gave you one."

"I didn't."

His eyebrows were knitted together now, and just as she was starting to think about how *nice* they were, he turned and faced the pasture again. Which wasn't a good thing, because now she was appreciating his profile. "For goodness' sake," she muttered.

"What did you say?"

"Nix," she replied quickly. Desperate for a change of subject, she blurted, "Is that why you left the Amish?"

He turned, one of his nice eyebrows lifting. "What?"

"Did you leave the Amish to do engineering?" This was close to prying territory, but she had to do something or she'd be admiring *all* of him, and she couldn't allow that to happen.

"That's the main reason. I wanted to *geh* to school and get *mei* engineering degree." He looked out at the pasture again. "It didn't turn out the way I expected. Now I'm back here."

She scratched her chin, but then stopped, remembering the scab there. Her wounds from her fall had healed, but they itched periodically. "You sound like you've been sentenced to prison."

"Maybe I have." His frown deepened. "Haven't you ever felt trapped?"

The intensity of his gaze amplified the question. Before losing her job she'd felt free to do what she wanted. Now she was stuck here, too confused and mentally paralyzed to figure out her next step. *"Ya,"* she admitted. "I have."

"It's suffocating."

"I wouldn't *geh* that far." Sure, she had no idea what she was going to do with herself now that she didn't work for Daniel anymore, but she didn't feel smothered. Well, maybe a bit by Jalon, but not by anyone else.

Roman picked at the white paint on one of the fence slats. "'You, my brothers and sisters, were called to be free.'"

Leanna frowned. "What?"

"A scripture verse *mei grossmammi* said to me when I was young. I never fully understood it, though. If we're called to be free, then why do we have to live under all these rules? Where's the freedom in that?"

Leanna was familiar with the verse. "Did she tell you the rest of the scripture? The part where you're not supposed to indulge in the flesh and serve others?" She turned to him and said, "'For the entire law is fulfilled in keeping this one command: Love your neighbor as yourself.'"

He turned away from her. "*Ya.* She said that too."

"But you're only seeing what you want to see."

"I see what's reflected in *mei* life. Whenever I try to do something, whenever I have a plan, it gets thwarted."

"Then maybe you're working too hard to fulfill *yer* plan instead of God's."

Roman heaved a sigh. "I thought they were one and the same."

"Sometimes they are. I thought God's plan was for me to work for Daniel, and that fit right along with what I wanted to do. Now . . . I'm not sure what's next for me. But I do know I'm not trapped. I can leave when I want."

"You want to leave the Amish?"

"Of course not. I mean I can travel. I can leave Birch Creek, and I often do. At least I used to, before things got busy at work." She sighed. "Now I guess I can leave anytime."

"I didn't know you liked to travel."

"Oh, *ya.*" She leaned against the fence. "I love going to new places."

"Me too." He paused and then asked, "Have you ever wanted to *geh* to the mountains?"

"Which ones?"

They talked about a few mountain ranges, and while Leanna had never seriously considered traveling so far from Birch Creek, visiting the Rocky Mountains sounded exciting. "Maybe one day I'll *geh* there. Because the whole point I'm trying to make is that the rules aren't a cage. Did you find more freedom in the English world?"

He paused and then shook his head. "To be honest, I felt even more trapped." He gave her another look. "I'm sure if you want to *geh* see the Rockies, you will. You're the kind of person who can do anything she sets her mind to."

His words felt . . . nice. "*Danki* for saying that."

"I should be the one thanking you." He put his hand on her wrist. "You've given me some things to think about."

She glanced at his hand, expecting him to move it away, because surely he was accidentally touching her. Instead he slid his fingers down to her wrist, his gaze following and then reaching up to meet hers. She could only imagine what he was seeing, because her eyebrows felt like they had shot up into her hairline.

"Sorry," he mumbled, snatching his hand away.

She didn't know what to say. Suddenly everything turned awkward between them again. She should say something. But what? Danki *for touching my wrist? For looking at me in a way that made* mei *stomach flutter?* Because she wasn't upset or annoyed or even confused by what he'd done. She was . . . pleased.

"I should get back." He moved away from the fence. "Barbara is probably wondering where I am."

"I'm sure Daniel is too."

He looked down at the ground and shrugged. "Not so sure about that."

Leanna was about to assure him he was wrong, that Daniel did care, even though he had a hard time showing it. If he hadn't, he wouldn't have been so hurt when Roman left. But before she could speak Roman was already walking away from her, like he'd done that morning at the Glicks'. And once again, she was hurrying to catch up to him.

When they reached the driveway, the tension between them was thick, and she didn't know why. "*Danki* for supper," he said, still not looking at her. In fact, he was looking everywhere but at her.

Had she done something wrong? Said something she shouldn't? Pried too deeply? She was about to apologize—for what, she had no idea—when his head lifted.

Then he looked at her. As usual, he had to tilt his face up slightly to see directly into her eyes. "This is going to sound *seltsam*," he said, his gaze pointed at his feet again. "But . . . um, I wondered . . . Is there a way . . ."

The way he was pulling out his words was painful. "Roman, whatever you have to say, just tell me."

He cracked the knuckle on his finger and then jumped a little, as if he'd surprised himself. Finally, he said, "Could we be friends?"

Her heart nearly melted at his quiet request. Suddenly she was seeing Roman in a new light. He wasn't an aloof, snobby man who thought he was too good to be a mechanic, or someone who was too dissatisfied with rules to be Amish. He set himself apart for a deeper reason, one he'd hinted at earlier, and that was probably ingrained in him more than he even knew. "Of course," she said, surprised at how soft she sounded. Almost delicate, and that wasn't a word anyone used to describe her.

He smiled, and her heart softened even more. "I'll see you later then."

"*Ya,*" she said, unable to pull her gaze from him. "I'll see you later."

Then he turned, put his hands in his pockets, and walked away.

"Me and Roman . . . friends," she said when he disappeared down the road. She turned to go to her house. Then she smiled. "Who would have thought?"

CHAPTER 9

Barbara paced the ER waiting room, fighting her tears and the ache in her stomach. She'd ridden with Daniel in the ambulance two hours ago, but when they arrived at the hospital, she wasn't allowed to go back to the examining rooms with him. All she knew was that the burns on his legs were so severe that the first responders had to sedate him.

"It would have been much worse if you hadn't found him when you did," the paramedic said when she explained what happened. "This whole shop could have caught fire."

The thought made her stop pacing. She hadn't heard Daniel slip out of bed earlier that afternoon, but when she woke up and didn't find him in the house, she had a feeling he was in the shop. After letting Leanna go he'd had to work more hours, even with Roman's help. What she didn't understand was why there was still so much work to do, but she was staying out of that. It was between Daniel and Roman.

When she went to the shop, she heard Daniel crying out. The door was locked, and she quickly got the spare key, opened it, and found Daniel bent over, slapping at his legs with a tarp. The blowtorch was on the floor, the flame still lit. Daniel's trousers were on fire, and somehow Barbara managed to grab the tarp, finish extinguishing the fire, and then turn off the torch's flame. Daniel crumpled to the floor in pain as she ran to the phone shanty to call 911.

She kept asking for updates, but the receptionist had the same answer each time. "As soon as I know something, I will tell you."

Barbara went back to pacing, hugging her arms around her waist. How had the accident occurred? Daniel was always careful. Safety had always been a priority with him. So was honoring the Sunday Sabbath. It didn't make sense.

The emergency room doors opened and Barbara saw Roman hurry in. He went straight to her. "How is he?"

"I don't know." She glanced at the doors again. "They won't tell me anything."

Anger flashed on Roman's face. "They'll tell me something." He stormed over to the receptionist, and Barbara could hear Roman's angry words as the receptionist told him the same thing. "That's not *gut* enough," he said.

"It's the only answer I can give you." The receptionist had spoken in bored tones to Barbara, but now she could see Roman had the woman shaken. Barbara went to him. "This isn't helping," she whispered in *Dietsch*.

Roman gave the woman a disgusted look and then followed Barbara back to the waiting room. It was empty and had been since she and Daniel arrived. "You need to sit down," he said to her.

"I'm fine standing."

"Sit," he said with the same determined tone he'd used with the receptionist.

She complied and then he joined her, sitting on the edge of a chair facing her. "What happened?"

"He was out in the shop using the blowtorch." She shook her head. "I don't know why he was working on Sunday."

Roman's face pinched. "I have an idea," he muttered.

"He had on his welding helmet when I got there, but it wasn't covering his face." She explained how she found him and called 911. "How did you find out?"

"I was walking back from the Chupps' and Charley Ridge stopped me."

"Our English neighbor down the road?"

"*Ya.* He wanted to know if everything was all right since he'd seen the ambulance stop at the *haus.*" A guilty look crossed his face. "I'm sorry I wasn't there."

"This isn't *yer* fault."

He leaned forward and put his hands between his knees, but didn't say anything further.

Twenty minutes later, a nurse came through the double doors that separated the waiting room from the exam rooms. "Mrs. Raber?"

Barbara stood and hurried to her. "How is Daniel?"

"Stable. We had to assess whether he'll need a skin graft on his legs and then bandage the wounds before we could let you come back there." Sympathy colored her features. "Burns are hard to look at," she said. "We were trying to spare you. We have them wrapped up now and you can come back."

"Can I come back too?" Roman asked.

"This is Daniel's brother," Barbara explained.

"Sure." She pushed a silver disc to open the double doors and then led them to a room in the back of the ER. "Before we go in I want to explain the bandages on his eyes. The sedative the paramedics gave him was mild so he was able to tell us what happened. The flame from the torch didn't actually burn his eyes, but the heat did affect them a bit, which is why we have bandages over them. His legs have second-and third-degree burns, but because he had the presence of mind to grab that tarp, mostly second. We don't think he'll need a skin graft, but we'll have to keep an eye on him overnight to be sure."

"So he's going to be admitted?" Roman asked.

"He'll be here for a few days. His wounds need to be cleaned and dressed often, and we have to keep an eye on them for infection. The bandages on his eyes will stay on for twenty-four hours, and then we'll take them off and see how his vision is." She looked at Barbara. "I know this all sounds bad, but it could have been so much worse."

She was tired of hearing that. It didn't matter to her if things could be worse. What mattered was that Daniel was burned and in pain. "I want to see him," she said, her voice thick.

When she walked into his room, she sucked in a breath. He was lying on the hospital bed, white bandages over his eyes, an IV in his arm, and his legs covered with bandages. "Daniel?" she said, going to his side. When he didn't respond, she looked at the nurse.

"He's on some pretty strong pain medication, so he might be asleep."

Barbara looked at his chest as it rose and fell in a steady rhythm. He was wearing a hospital gown. Tears spilled as she let out a cutting laugh. "For once you're actually asleep."

"We'll be transferring him upstairs soon," the nurse said.

"Can I stay with him?"

"Absolutely." The nurse looked at her and smiled before leaving the room.

"Here." Roman moved one of the chairs to Daniel's bedside, and Barbara sat down. She took Daniel's hand and held it, feeling the roughness of his fingers and palms on hers. "Oh, Daniel," she said. She kept holding his hand, not saying anything else and not wanting to wake him up. Roman remained quiet too.

An hour later the nurse came in just as Daniel began to stir. "We're ready to move him now."

"Barbara?"

"I'm here," she said, standing up but not letting go of his hand.

"Hurts," he said. Then he pulled his hand out of hers and touched the bandages on his eyes. "What—"

"Don't touch those, Mr. Raber." The nurse gently took his hand and put it to his side. "We'll explain everything when you're not so sedated. Now we're taking you to your room."

"Room?" He turned to Barbara. "What room?"

"You have to stay in the hospital," Barbara said in *Dietsch*. Maybe he would have better understanding in his own language. "You've burned *yer* legs, and we have to be careful of your eyes for now."

"Oh." He didn't say anything else.

Barbara started to leave with him when Roman said, "I'll *geh* back home and take care of things. I can run the shop tomorrow too."

"*Danki.*"

"Do you need anything else?" he asked.

"I need him to be well. That's all."

Roman left as Barbara got into the elevator with a man who was pushing Daniel's bed. She'd never been in a hospital. Her hands shook. She was scared for Daniel, scared of this place, and scared of the pain she suddenly felt in her abdomen.

A little over an hour later Daniel was settled in his room. The night nurse introduced herself, along with someone who said she would be taking Daniel's vitals every so often during the night, whatever that meant. The nurse put something else in Daniel's IV, and Barbara saw that his chest rose and fell again, signaling he was sleeping. He hadn't said anything from the moment they'd left the ER.

When she knew Daniel was asleep, Barbara went to the bathroom. She stared at her pale complexion in the mirror as another pain overtook her. Tears streamed down her face. She'd felt this pain before, and she knew what it was. She found the faint blood streak on her underwear. "*Nee,*" she whispered. "Please, God . . . *nee.*"

Another pain overcame her, stronger, harder than she'd ever felt. When it passed, she was sobbing. She looked around the bathroom and saw a sign that said

"*Call for help.*" Having no choice, she pulled on the cord. Soon there was a knock on the door. "Mrs. Raber?"

"*Ya,*" she said, choking on her tears.

The door opened and the nurse came inside, closing the door behind her. "What happened?" she asked.

"I lost my baby."

. . .

That night after caring for Daniel's horse, Roman went into the shop. He turned on the gas lamp and saw the remnants of his brother's accident. It had been hard to see Daniel in the hospital bed, and Roman could only imagine how much pain he was in. When he was a kid, he'd burned his hand on a hot stove, and that had only been a small burn. But it ached for hours.

His heart heavy, he picked up the welding equipment and scorched tarp from the floor. He couldn't believe his brother had not only broken the Sabbath by working, but that he'd been so careless with dangerous equipment. That wasn't Daniel. Now that he thought about it, his brother hadn't been himself since Roman arrived. Roman thought it had to do with him, that his brother still resented his leaving last year. And he was sure that was part of it, but this . . . this didn't make any sense.

Roman put the welding equipment away and the tarp outside and then looked at the pile of tickets on his brother's desk. Some orders needed finishing and newer ones hadn't even been started. Daniel had assured Roman he had everything under control each time Roman asked if he could work on a project. Now he could see his brother had been lying about that the whole time.

Which led him to think about Leanna. If Daniel was so inundated with work, why had he fired her? And why had Leanna suddenly accepted it, as if Daniel had done the right thing? He sat down at the desk and tried to make sense of everything, including the time he'd spent earlier with Leanna. He hadn't expected to reveal so much, or for her to question him in such a thoughtful manner. He hadn't felt any judgment from her, and she hadn't given him pat answers. Just more food for thought.

Then there was him touching her wrist. What had possessed him to do that, other than the desire to get closer to her physically? The feelings were different and new to him and not . . . unpleasant. He'd never really felt the need to connect with a woman, although he'd never found women unattractive. They were to be held at arm's length, like everyone else. Leanna . . . She was the last woman he thought he'd have any connection with. But there he was, asking, almost begging, for friendship.

It had to be the loneliness, something he'd felt more acutely since coming back to Birch Creek, more than he had before in his life. It didn't make sense, but there was no other explanation for it.

He couldn't think about Leanna right now. He hadn't wanted to leave Barbara at the hospital, but he would have been in the way and she needed him here. Tomorrow morning he would close the shop and head to the hospital. Hopefully there would be more news about when Daniel could come home. He would try to convince Barbara to come home, too, at least for a little while.

He found some paper and scribbled a message on it. *Closed today.* He taped the paper inside the window on the door, turned off the lamp, locked the door, and went into the house. Every floorboard creaked as he went upstairs. The house had an empty feeling to it. All these years he'd yearned to be alone and never minded being by himself. Now he wanted Daniel and Barbara here.

He was about to go to bed, but then stopped and got on his knees, something he hadn't done in a long time. The thought that he could have lost his brother if the accident had been worse wouldn't let go. Instead of praying for himself, he prayed for Daniel, thinking about his grandmother's words. *You two need each other.* They seemed prophetic now.

As he drifted to sleep, his last weary thought was about how for once in his life, when things were tough, he hadn't fled. He hadn't even been tempted.

. . .

The next morning Leanna woke up later than she had in years. She'd always been an early riser. Even when she was visiting family or on vacation she had woken up before the sun. But now it was dawn, and she was just opening her eyes. "Roman's fault," she said as she sprang out of bed. Not only had she spent the evening thinking about him, but she'd dreamt about him, too—about him touching her wrist . . . and of all things, kissing her.

"Ugh." She pulled her dress over her head and then unbraided her hair and brushed it out. The dream itself wasn't ugh. In fact, it was anything but ugh. Still, kissing Roman? All he did was touch her wrist yesterday, and that had been fleeting. Which reminded her that in her dream he'd also held her hand. It had felt warm, strong, and—"Ow!" The brush was trapped in her hair, and she had to untangle it. Great, she wasn't paying attention to anything today. For once she was glad she wasn't working in the shop. If she was this distracted, it could be dangerous.

She quickly braided her hair and put it up, then fastened on her *kapp*. She slipped on her shoes and got ready to go help Phoebe with more canning. Today it was meat, specifically beef. She wasn't a fan of canned meat, but it was good in soups, chilis, and stews when it was seasoned right.

When she went outside, warm air hit her. The sun wasn't even fully up and it was already hot and sweltering. She was halfway to the house when Blue came up to her. She bent over and picked up the cat. "Being ignored again?" she said, rubbing her cheek against the top of his head. She knew he wasn't ignored at all, since he was so spoiled.

A bird swooped by, which made Blue squirm in her arms. He scrambled to get down. "All right, all right," she said, trying to keep from dropping him while setting him down instead. When she crouched down, his back claws dug into her neck. "Ow!" she cried out and then let him go. She put her palm to the scratches and then pulled it away, half expecting to see blood and was relieved when she didn't. "Crazy cat," she said, going into the house.

When she got to the kitchen, she passed Jalon and Adam, who were sitting at the table with Phoebe, and went to the sink. She rubbed her hands with soap and washed her neck.

"What happened to you?" Adam asked.

"Blue happened." She rinsed off the soap and dried her neck. Then she angled the scratched skin at them. "Is it bad?"

"Just a few marks." Jalon took a swig of his coffee, but he didn't look at her face.

"Sorry I'm late for breakfast." She sat down, but no one said anything. "Where's Malachi?" she asked, reaching for syrup for the waffles on the table.

"Upstairs. He let Blue out a minute ago and saw that you were coming over," Jalon said.

"I know, I know. I shouldn't have overslept." She looked at Phoebe, who was seated in her chair but not eating anything. Actually, none of them was eating, even though the food was on the table. "What's going on?"

"Daniel's in the hospital," Adam said.

Leanna nearly dropped the syrup. "What happened?"

"An accident in the shop. Yesterday. His legs are severely burned."

She frowned. "What was he doing in the shop on Sunday? How was he hurt? Why didn't anyone tell me?" She pushed back from the table. "I have to *geh* see him and Barbara."

"Leanna, wait."

She turned and looked at Jalon. "What?" she said impatiently.

"You can't *geh* see him."

She put her hands on her hips. "What do you mean I can't *geh* see him? He's *mei* friend."

"Leanna, please," Phoebe said, going to her. "Listen to Jalon."

She looked from Phoebe to Jalon, then at Adam. All of them seemed to be of the same mind. "Why don't you want me to *geh*?" she said, a cold dread falling over her.

"Because . . ." Jalon rubbed the back of his neck and didn't say anything else.

When she looked at Adam, his gaze darted away. Then she saw the compassion in Phoebe's eyes. *Oh nee.* "You know." She took a step back, shocked. "Do all of you know?"

"Leanna—"

"Have all of you heard the gossip about me and Daniel?" she said, her voice halfway to a scream. She tried to control herself, but all control was quickly slipping away.

Her brother didn't say anything, only nodded slowly.

"That's why you were pushing for me to quit." She went to Jalon, who got up from the table. "That's why you were talking all that nonsense about marriage and *familye*."

Guilt crossed his features. "I meant it, Leanna. I wasn't bringing it up because I don't believe you can't get married—"

"I don't want to get married! How many times do I have to tell you? And why didn't you tell me the truth? Why did I have to find out by overhearing Tabitha and Melva myself?"

"Leanna." Phoebe's voice faltered. "I'm so sorry."

"We were trying to protect you," Adam said.

"I thought—we thought—that if you quit working for Daniel, the gossip would die down and you would never have to know," Jalon added.

She looked at her family in disbelief. "Did you believe it?" A quick pause.

"*Nee*," Phoebe said.

"Of course not," Jalon added.

"*Nee* one takes Tabitha and Melva seriously," Adam insisted.

But she barely heard their words. All three of them had hesitated before answering, and that told her all she needed to know. "I can't believe it," she mumbled, shocked and hurt and ashamed, and wishing she could sink straight through the floor. "*Mei* own *familye* . . . that you and other people in the community would think I would have an affair." Why didn't they trust her? Why had they immediately thought the worst?

She stormed out of the house and started for her place, but then changed direction. She wanted to see Daniel, to make sure he was all right. But she couldn't do that, because despite her anger with her family, they were right. After the rumors going around the community, she couldn't show up at the hospital. That would just fuel the suspicion.

But she couldn't stay here either. Not after knowing what her family really thought of her.

She continued to walk down the street and found herself in front of Ivy's house. If only her friend were here. She needed to talk to her. She needed someone on her side. But Ivy was in Michigan, and she didn't want to bring this up to Karen. For all she knew, Karen felt the same way her family did.

She started to walk away when she heard Bishop Yoder call her name. Surprised, she turned around and saw him motion to her.

She couldn't ignore him, since he was the bishop. Besides, he was also like a father to her. But if Barbara, Daniel, Jalon, Phoebe, and Adam had all heard the gossip, then Bishop Yoder probably had too. Maybe that was why he was calling her over—to find out if it was true. Could this get any worse? Steeling herself for whatever he had to say to her, she walked over to him.

He put his hands in his pockets. "Haven't seen you around for a while," he said.

"I've been busy."

"*Ya.* I heard things have been busy at the shop."

What else have you heard? "I don't work there anymore."

"I heard about that too." He tilted his head and looked at her.

"Did you hear that Daniel and I are having an affair?" *Might as well get it out in the open.* She expected a shocked look on his face, but he remained impassive. She put her hand over her mouth, wishing she could take back the words. "Sorry. It's not true."

"I know. I never thought it was."

"Not everyone thinks so."

"I can't deny that we've got some folks in our community with loose lips. God will deal with them accordingly. But you can't let that get to you. At least not too much."

The fatherly way he was talking to her brought tears to her eyes. "I can't help it. I didn't do anything wrong. Neither did Daniel. And now he's in the hospital and I can't see him. I lost *mei* job and I don't know what to do with myself." And then there was Roman, but she wasn't going to bring him up with the bishop.

"I heard about Daniel. Mary is getting the women together to make some meals. I was just about to *geh* see him." He paused. "Do you want to *geh* with me? I doubt even our most ardent gossips will have much to say if you're with the bishop."

Relieved, she said, "*Ya*. I'd like to."

"I'll call for a taxi. Why don't you come inside for a bit? I know Karen and Mary would like to visit with you."

Leanna nodded and followed the bishop inside the house. As she visited a little with Mary, saying that while she wouldn't make a meal she'd be glad to do the shopping for them, she relaxed a little. It was nice to know there were some people who believed in her.

* * *

A couple of hours later, Leanna walked with Bishop Yoder toward Daniel's hospital room. She was eager to see Daniel and Barbara and offer her support. But as she neared his room, she held back. It didn't feel right going inside, even with the bishop's assurances that it was okay. "I'll stay out here," she said.

"Are you sure?" He scratched his cheek just above his salt-and-pepper beard.

"*Ya.* I'll get some *kaffee* in the waiting room or something." She'd been in this hospital before, when Adam fell out of the tree. She visited him since he'd had to stay here for a week before he was stable enough to move to the hospital in Geauga County. At the time she'd been thirteen, a year older than him and still dealing with the news that he was paralyzed. She'd hated being in the hospital then too. But even though she couldn't do much for Daniel, she could pray while she was waiting for Bishop Yoder to finish his visit.

The bishop went on. A minute later, she had just turned toward the nurse's station to ask where the coffee machine was when Barbara appeared at her side. Leanna put her arms around her, leaning down to give her a hug. When they pulled apart, she said, "How is he?"

"Still sedated. Still in a lot of pain."

Leanna got a good look at Barbara and was shocked. She looked beyond tired, her eyes holding a haunted look. "Have you gotten any sleep?" she asked. When Barbara shook her head, Leanna led her to the nurse's station. "Is there a place where we can sit and talk?" she asked one of the nurses. He pointed to a small waiting room down the hall.

Barbara didn't protest as Leanna led her down the hall. They sat down, and Leanna said, "Do you want *kaffee*?"

"*Nee.*" The word came out sharp. "*Nee kaffee.*"

"All right." Leanna scooted closer and took Barbara's hand. "It will be all right," she said. "Daniel will pull through this."

Barbara didn't look at her, tears streaming down

her cheeks. "I know. The burns aren't life-threatening. They're saying he can *geh* home in a few days."

"That's *gut* news, then." Leanna smiled, but Barbara still didn't look at her. More tears spilled over her cheeks, and Leanna let go of her hand and got a tissue box from one of the small tables in the room. She handed a couple of tissues to Barbara, who took them but didn't wipe her face. Instead she balled the tissues in her hand.

"I wish there was something I could do to help," Leanna said.

"There's *nix* you can do." She looked at Leanna. "*Nix* anyone can do."

Something else was wrong, not just Daniel's injuries. Barbara looked as though she were mourning a death, not her husband's burns. A sick feeling formed in the pit of Leanna's stomach. "Oh *nee*," she whispered.

Barbara's eyes widened and then filled with sorrow. "I should have known you'd figure it out."

"I never told anyone. I promise."

"I believe you." Barbara pressed her lips together. "I lost the *boppli*."

Leanna didn't know what to say. All she could do was put her arms around Barbara and hug her tight as she sobbed on her shoulder. By the time the other woman pulled away, Leanna's dress was wet.

"Sorry," Barbara said, blowing her nose. "I didn't mean to cry all over you."

She took Barbara's hand and squeezed it. "You can cry on me anytime."

That made Barbara smile and sniff. "How did you know I was pregnant?"

"Phoebe. She has the same glow . . ." Leanna felt out of her depth. She had no idea how to console Barbara. *Lord, give me the words . . . if words are needed.*

"I'm glad Phoebe's pregnancy is going well. And Joanna's, and Abigail's, and Sadie's . . ." Tears flowed down her cheeks. "I thought this time would be ours."

"Does Daniel know?"

Barbara shook her head. "I can't tell him when he's sedated, and I don't know how to tell him anyway. The doctor said his recovery is going to take awhile, so he won't be able to work in the shop. He was already worried about getting all the work done before. I'm sure that's why he was out there yesterday. You know Daniel. He wouldn't normally fail to take safety precautions—or break the Sabbath."

Leanna nodded, and she couldn't help but feel as though this was partly her fault. If people hadn't gossiped about her and Daniel, she would still be working there. The accident wouldn't have happened, and Daniel would be free to focus on being with Barbara. "What about Roman?"

"He said he's going to take care of the shop."

Leanna felt a little bit of relief, but Barbara didn't seem to share the feeling. "Is that a problem?"

"Daniel won't be happy about it." She sighed. "If he had let Roman help him in the first place . . ." She shook her head. "What's done is done."

"Mrs. Raber?" A nurse poked her head through the doorway. "I'm sorry to interrupt, but your husband is asking for you."

Barbara nodded, wiped her eyes and nose with the

tissues, and then stood. She looked at Leanna. "Please don't say anything," she whispered.

"I won't." She watched as Barbara left the room, and then she got up and looked out the window. They were on the fourth floor of the hospital, and she looked out at the trees surrounding the building. She closed her eyes and said a prayer for both Daniel and Barbara. She didn't know how long she'd been praying when she felt a quick tap on her shoulder. "I'm ready to *geh*," she said, turning around, thinking it was the bishop. Instead she found herself face-to-face with Roman. He didn't move away from her, and she was backed up against the window.

"I'm glad to see you," he said after the long silence. He held her gaze, long enough that she had the inexplicable thought that he wanted to hold *her*. Or maybe her own feelings were overcoming her common sense. Because right now she could really, really use a hug.

CHAPTER 10

Roman hadn't expected to see Leanna here at the hospital, but he was passing by the waiting room and glanced casually inside when he saw her standing at the window. Her eyes were closed, and he realized she was praying. He continued to watch, not wanting to disturb her, but also drawn to her. *She's my friend.* He had to remind himself of that. And right now, he needed a friend.

Finally he couldn't resist anymore and he went to her, expecting that his footsteps would startle her. When they didn't, he lightly tapped her shoulder, and when she turned toward him, they were closer than he'd expected.

And he didn't move away.

She looked tired, worried, and once again, vulnerable. Which for some reason made him want to take her into his arms, even though he felt like walking wounded himself. When he got up this morning after fitful sleep, the loss of his grandmother had hit him again. She would have been the one he'd gone to about something like this, about his feelings for Leanna and his conflict with Daniel. But she wasn't here to guide him. He also hurt for his brother. Now that he knew the extent to which Daniel was buried under work, he was feeling the pressure. His brother's livelihood was in his hands, and he didn't want to fail. He couldn't afford to.

All these thoughts flew through his mind as he tried not to concentrate on Leanna's pretty deep-brown eyes or the feminine pout of her lips. In the past, *feminine* wasn't a word he would have used to refer to Leanna, but for all her sharp angles and thin figure, there was a definite softness about her.

She suddenly and quickly moved away. "Bishop Yoder should be here any minute," she said, turning around when she was on the other side of the room. "I came with him. Not by myself, so don't get the wrong idea."

Okay, now she was being weird. "Wrong idea about what?"

"Never mind," she mumbled in that way that made him think she was talking to herself instead of to him. He used to find her habit of talking out loud annoying, but now he found it a bit . . . cute. Except right now. This situation was anything but cute.

"Where's Barbara?" he asked.

"She's with Daniel. So is the bishop. As soon as he's done, we'll be going back to Birch Creek."

"I'll wait to see him then. How's he doing?"

Leanna explained that Daniel should be going home in a few days. "He won't be able to work, though."

"I figured that. But don't worry," he said quickly. Too quickly. "I've got it under control." But he felt less under control than he ever had.

"You don't sound so sure."

I'm not. He could admit that to her, right? That's what

friends were—honest with each other. He had opened his mouth to speak when Bishop Yoder walked into the room.

"Hi, Roman." Roman didn't know the tall, thin man very well—he didn't know anyone very well—but from what he could tell, the bishop was a fair man who cared about his district. "*Yer bruder* has been awake for a while, which is a *gut* sign," he said, giving Roman's hand a shake. When he let go of his hand, he added, "I'm glad you're here. I want to talk to you about a few things."

"I'll step out," Leanna said, moving to the door.

"*Nee* need," Bishop Yoder said. "I was just going to tell him about the meals and how we're all here to help him and Daniel and Barbara."

Roman listened as Bishop Yoder explained that some of the women from the church would be coming over with meals, and that while no one was as good at repairing machines as Daniel—"Or Leanna, for that matter," he added—the community would be glad to help him with whatever else they needed. "Just let us know and someone will be there," he said.

Roman nodded, grateful. Even though they were doing this for Barbara and Daniel, two members of their community, he couldn't help but feel they really were helping him out too.

"Leanna, I need to head back," the bishop said.

She nodded. "Me too."

Roman said good-bye to Bishop Yoder and turned to Leanna. He noticed the scratch marks on her neck, and he was about to ask her what happened when she gave him a small wave and left with the bishop.

Which left him alone and disappointed. He'd wanted to talk to Leanna more. He needed to talk to her. But he'd lost his chance.

Roman left the waiting room and went to see Daniel. Barbara was seated in a chair next to him, her chin touching her chest.

"Shh," Daniel said, his voice raspy and weak. He turned his head toward her and nodded.

Roman gave him a nod back and then sat down in the chair on the opposite side of the bed and pulled it closer. Daniel had a glistening smear of ointment around each eye. They were red and the skin around them was blistered a bit. His legs were still bandaged, and a sheet covered only his torso and hips and kept his bandaged legs exposed.

"How are you?" Roman said in a low voice, feeling stupid about asking the question. But he didn't know what else to say.

"I'm fine." Daniel's voice was a little stronger. "I'll be home tomorrow and back to work the next day."

Roman frowned. That wasn't what Bishop Yoder and Leanna had said. He glanced at the IV hooked into Daniel's arm. Knowing he was probably getting pain meds from it, he chalked Daniel's optimism up to that.

He waved his hand toward his legs and winced. "This is just a little setback."

"This is more than a setback," Roman said. "You're injured. Pretty badly."

"I can get through it," he said, gritting his teeth.

Roman looked at the IV again. If Daniel was feeling pain under IV meds, he wouldn't be able to stand working in the shop while taking an aspirin, which would be about the strongest medicine he could take while working around tools and machinery.

Daniel closed his eyes, and Roman remained silent. He couldn't think of anything to say to his brother. He had no idea how to comfort him or give him confidence that he could trust Roman to handle the shop.

After a long silence, Daniel said, "You don't have to stay."

Roman glanced at Daniel. His brother's eyes were still closed, and there was an underlying finality to his words. A familiar stinging hurt went through him. Even under pain, Daniel didn't want Roman around. "What about Barbara?" he asked. "What can I do for her?"

"*Nix*. She's fine too."

"She's exhausted, Daniel. I thought I'd try to convince her to come back home with me."

Daniel finally looked at him with squinty eyes. Then he let out a breath and his face relaxed as he nodded. "She slept here last night and that's not *gut* for the . . . for her sleep. She needs to *geh* home."

At least they were finally agreeing on something. "I'll make sure she gets some sleep," Roman said. "And I'll open the shop tomorrow, so you don't have to worry about that."

"*Nee*. It will be okay if it's closed for a couple of days."

"Daniel, I can finish up some of the projects, especially the ones that are past due." He paused, an idea coming to him. "I can ask Leanna to help—"

"*Nee!*" The word was said with such force that Barbara woke up.

With bleary eyes, she leaned forward. "What's wrong?" she said, sleep in her voice.

Daniel sucked in a breath, and Roman didn't miss him pushing on the button at his side, which he knew dispensed the pain medication. "Everything is fine."

Barbara looked at Roman, who gave her a tiny shake of his head. She nodded and took Daniel's hand, stroking it until his body relaxed. "*Geh* home with Roman," he said, sounding sleepy.

"*Nee.* I want to stay here with you."

Roman stood and moved to the other side of the bed. He put his hand on Barbara's shoulder. "Do as he says," he said quietly to her. "It's the best for both of you."

Daniel's eyes were already drifting shut, and his hand went limp in Barbara's. "Okay." She withdrew her hand and looked up at Roman with hazy eyes. "But I want to come back later tonight. I don't want him to be alone."

Roman nodded, although whether she was coming back tonight would be up for debate later. "I'll call the taxi and meet you downstairs."

Barbara picked up Daniel's hand again and kissed the back of it.

An unfamiliar feeling wound through him. Not jealousy, because he wasn't jealous of his brother's marriage, but a feeling he couldn't explain. What was it like to have someone love you so much? He'd never felt love, other than from his grandmother. But that wasn't the type of yearning that pulled at him. He felt empty. Hollow. As if something, or someone, was missing.

He used the phone at the nurse's desk to call the taxi and then waited in the hallway for Barbara. She came out a few minutes later, and now he could fully see how tired she was. As they started to leave, a nurse called her over to the desk. She put her hand on Barbara's as she talked to her. Barbara nodded and then joined Roman. As they got into the elevator, Roman saw the sheen of tears in Barbara's eyes.

"Are you okay?"

She nodded and looked away.

"Is there something you're not telling me about Daniel? Is his condition worse?"

She shook her head. "You know everything I do about it."

He was about to press her further, but decided not to. She looked defeated, almost as if she was in mourning. He chalked it up to her fear and stress about what could have happened if she hadn't found Daniel in time.

On their ride home, Barbara fell asleep and the taxi driver wasn't very talkative, leaving Roman with his own thoughts. Normally he liked drivers who kept to themselves, but right now all he felt was isolation. And rejection.

He shouldn't have been surprised that Daniel didn't want him to run the shop. His brother didn't trust him with little, and he wasn't about to trust him with much. But Roman was determined to prove himself in a way he'd never done before. This determination was different from what he felt when he was trying to get into college. Because he knew Daniel's and Barbara's livelihoods weren't the only ones at stake. In many ways, so was his. He closed his eyes and prayed he was up to the task.

. . .

The day after she went to the hospital with the bishop, Leanna helped Mary and Karen wrap up small packages of banana bread. Since Joanna was pregnant with her second child, she had stopped making baked goods to sell in the Schrocks' store, and she had asked Karen if she would like to take over. Karen had agreed, and this was the first batch of baked goods she was planning to sell.

For once Leanna didn't mind such a mindless task, wrapping the banana bread in tight Saran Wrap and placing a sticky label on the top. She was thinking about Daniel. And Barbara. Roman too. She'd prayed for all three of them last night, especially focusing on Daniel's healing and Barbara's grief. She also prayed for Roman, knowing he would have to shoulder the burden of the shop by himself. She'd done the same thing. It wasn't an easy job, and she knew what she was doing. Roman was basically going in blind.

More than ever she wanted to go over to Daniel's. Not to get her job back. She meant her promise not to ask for it back. But Barbara shouldn't be going through her grief over losing the baby alone. And Roman would probably need some help. But she couldn't reach out at all. Her hands were tied, and it frustrated her.

"Leanna, that label is upside down."

"Oh. Sorry." She tried to rip off the label, but it wouldn't come off the plastic wrap.

"Just start over," Karen said, handing her the roll of wrap.

Leanna took off the wrapper and rewrapped the bread. "How many of these loaves did you make?"

"Thirty. Joanna said hers were *gut* sellers at the store." A nervous look passed her face. "But I'm not as *gut* a baker as Joanna."

"You're an excellent baker," Mary said, putting a sticker on another loaf and doing it correctly. "I taught you everything you know."

Karen laughed, and even Leanna chuckled a little bit. Mary was known more for her cooking than her baking.

"I'm sure they'll sell fine."

"I hope so."

Mary stood up and arched her back and then went to the cabinet and started taking down cups. "I'm going to take the *buwe* something to drink," she said. "They've been working out there in the hot sun all morning."

"Do you want some help?"

Mary shook her head. "*Nee*, I've got it. You two finish up in here."

"You're quiet," Karen said after Mary left. "Worried about Daniel?"

"*Ya*. I wish there was something I could do to help."

"Maybe now that he's going to be out of commission for a while you'll be able to get *yer* job back."

She shook her head. "That won't happen."

"You never know."

But she did know. And now she also knew that Karen had no idea why Leanna had been fired, which she found comforting. At least the gossip hadn't reached everyone's ears. Ready for a change of subject, she said, "How are you and Adam doing?"

By the flush on Karen's face, Leanna knew they were doing quite well, but she waited for Karen's answer anyway. "Fine."

"More than fine, I'd say."

Karen's hand went to her cheek. "*Ya,*" she said shyly. "We're more than fine."

"I'm glad you two found each other. Adam deserves to be happy."

"Is he?" Karen asked, suddenly looking doubtful.

"Is he what?"

"Happy." She bit her bottom lip. "I'm assuming he is, but I . . . I want to be sure."

Leanna frowned a bit. She was surprised Karen had doubts about anything when it came to Adam. "Trust me, he's happy. Happier than I've ever seen him."

"Oh. *Gut,* then." Karen busied herself with wrapping another loaf of banana bread.

Her reaction was unexpected. "Are you happy?"

Her head shot up. "*Ya. Ya,* of course. Adam is a wonderful *mann.*"

"Do you love him?"

"Absolutely."

Leanna leaned forward. "Then what's wrong?"

"Wrong? I didn't say anything was wrong." She slapped a label on the bread. "Everything is right. Just perfectly right."

This was one of many reasons Leanna was glad she wasn't in a relationship. They were too complicated. Karen, who was normally an open book and never hid anything, was so flustered she couldn't tell Leanna the truth. "I don't believe you," she said. No need to be gentle. "Has Adam done something? I know he's *mei* cousin, but sometimes he does stupid things, just like Jalon does. Must be a guy thing—"

"*Nee.* He hasn't done anything."

Leanna peered at her when Karen didn't elaborate. "That's the problem, *ya*?"

After a pause, Karen nodded. "I thought we'd be engaged by now. It's been over a year."

"Adam doesn't like to rush into things." Leanna frowned. The words were true, but hadn't Adam promised he was going to propose to Karen? Frankly, Leanna was surprised he hadn't by now. "Do you want me to talk to him? I can knock some sense into him for you if you want."

Karen chuckled, but it sounded flat. "There's *nix* wrong with Adam," she said. "But there might be something wrong with me."

"That's ridiculous," Leanna said. "It's also not true."

"Then why hasn't he proposed? He's been pulling away lately too."

Leanna frowned. That was also unexpected. She looked at Karen. "I don't know what's going on with him, and since you don't want me to get involved, I will show great restraint and honor *yer* wish. But maybe you shouldn't wait around for him."

Karen's eyes widened and her mouth dropped open. "You want me to break up with him?"

"What? *Nee*. Heavens *nee*. You're the best thing that's happened to him, and dare I say vice versa. What I mean is you shouldn't wait for him to propose. What's wrong with you proposing to him? You do want to get married, right?"

She nodded. "*Ya*."

"Then you should make it happen."

Karen fiddled with the edge of the plastic wrap. "What if he says *nee*?" Karen said softly.

"He won't."

Karen looked at her. "But what if he does? I wouldn't be able to take it if he did."

"Maybe that's what's holding Adam back," Leanna said. "He might be afraid you'll say *nee*. In fact, I'm sure that's the exact reason."

"But I wouldn't say *nee*."

"Exactly." She sat back and tried not to show her frustration. The irony that the two of them had the exact same fear but had yet to talk about it to each other made her want to lock them both in a room until they worked it out. Instead she said, "He won't say *nee* either. For goodness' sake, I don't get this. If I was in love with someone and wanted to marry him, I wouldn't wait around for a proposal."

Karen's eyes widened with shock.

Leanna looked at her, frowning. "What?"

"You said love and marry."

"So?"

"You said them in the same sentence while you were talking about *yourself*."

Karen scooted close to her. "Who are you seeing?"

Leanna was dumbfounded. "I'm not seeing anyone."

"Now who isn't telling the truth?" Karen laughed. "Ivy is going to be so mad I found out you were dating someone before she did."

How did this conversation not only turn on her, but get so out of control? "I'm not dating anyone." But Roman's image suddenly came to mind. She shook her head to clear it. "I'm not seeing anyone."

"Then why are you talking about marriage?"

"Because I'm talking about you and Adam. Not—and I repeat *not*—about me."

"Are you sure? It would be so like you to keep this hidden and then surprise all of us with *yer* wedding announcement."

Karen had lost her mind. "I'm not getting married. And even if I was—which I'm not—I wouldn't be the only person in Birch Creek to keep a relationship secret. It's not like you and Adam were openly dating in the beginning."

"True." She studied Leanna for a minute. "You're not seeing anyone," she said. It wasn't a question but a statement. A disappointing-sounding statement.

"Finally you understand. Now, can we get back to the topic at hand—which is you proposing to Adam?" She clasped her hands together. "The pond would be the perfect place, don't you think? It's secluded and so pretty after harvesttime, with the leaves turning all kinds of beautiful colors."

Karen smirked. "I didn't take you for such a romantic."

"I'm not." But Leanna felt her cheeks heat a little. She was actually getting excited about Karen asking Adam to marry her. She cleared her throat. "I'm just making a suggestion."

"The pond is out. For one thing, there are too many mosquitoes."

"I never noticed that."

"That's because you're too enamored with it. That's a place special to you, not to Adam and me."

"Then what place is special to you?"

Karen gave her a shy smile. "That's a secret."

"Oh," Leanna said, pretending to be hurt. "I see how you're going to be." Then she laughed. "So you're going to ask him, then?"

"I'll think about it."

"*Gut* grief." She slapped her forehead. "You two will be old and gray by the time you get around to marriage." She grinned.

"Who knows, you might get married before we do."

"I can guarantee that won't happen."

"I think you protest too much."

"I'm not protesting. I'm speaking the truth."

Mary came back that moment, and Leanna and Karen dropped the conversation. They finished packaging the bread, and once they put it up, the other two women started making lunch. Leanna offered to help, but after Mary and Karen exchanged a dubious glance, she took back the offer. "You don't happen to have a broken washing machine, do you?" Leanna asked, drumming her fingers against the back of one of the kitchen chairs. The conversation about Karen and Adam had taken her mind off the Rabers, but now that she didn't have anything to do she was starting to worry again.

"What?" Mary said with surprise as she peeled a cucumber.

"Our washing machine is fine," Karen added.

"Oh. Anything else broken?"

Karen handed her a bag of carrots and a peeler. "Here, this will keep you busy."

Leanna sighed as she sat down and started peeling. Another mindless task. If only there was something she could do to be of use to Daniel, Barbara, and Roman. *Lord, please show me how I can help.* She continued that prayer for the rest of the day, but God never gave her an answer.

• • •

The next two days were a blur for Roman. After Barbara slept most of Monday afternoon, she insisted on going back to the hospital to be with Daniel. Roman knew better than to argue with her and had called the taxi himself. She packed a bag, along with a few things for Daniel, and then left. She still didn't look rested even though she'd slept for a long time. Roman was used to worrying only about himself. Now he had Barbara and Daniel, not to mention the shop, heaped on his unsturdy plate.

Several visitors had come to the house on both Monday and Tuesday, mostly women bringing casseroles and other food for the family. A couple of Daniel's customers stopped by to tell him there was no hurry about their engines—to take his time getting them back to them. He appreciated that.

But when he opened up on Wednesday morning, things were different. A couple of the Amish men who had heard about Daniel's accident came and picked up their machines. "It's *nix* personal," they'd said. "We just need them back as soon as possible."

But Roman couldn't help but take it a little personally. He'd also had to field a few phone calls from English customers checking on the progress of their machines, and when he told them they would be late due to unforeseen circumstances, a couple of them were upset and threatened to write bad reviews online about their business. Apparently Daniel had been promising them for a while that their engines would be finished.

After he hung up the phone on the third angry customer of the day, he heard the bell above the door ring. It was Asa Bontrager, who owned the engine Daniel had been working on the day he'd been burned. Roman walked to the counter, wondering if Asa was angry.

"I heard about Daniel," Asa said. "Abigail sent these." He put a plate of brownies on the table.

They looked delicious, but Roman didn't have an appetite. He hadn't had much of one since he returned to Birch Creek. *"Danki,"* he said.

"They're pretty *gut*. Her *schwester* Joanna's been teaching her how to bake." He put his hand on his flat belly. "I've been her guinea pig. Not that I'm complaining, because it's all *gut*. But I might have to start working for Andrew's farrier business to burn the extra calories."

Roman wasn't normally interested in small talk,

especially when he wasn't sure who Andrew was. In fact, he usually avoided it. But right now he needed the break from trying to reassure disappointed customers. "Daniel likes chocolate, so I'm sure he'll appreciate it."

Asa looked around the shop. "Looks like you've got a lot of work here. Do you need any help?"

"Only if you know how to repair machines," Roman said, half serious.

"If I did, I wouldn't have brought you mine."

Roman nodded, slumping a little against the counter. "I'm sorry, but we're still working on *yers*. It won't be done for a few days."

Asa nodded. "It's fine. *Nee* worries. I told Daniel on Sunday that I could wait on it until he got caught up on work. But he insisted he would have it done."

"He likes to keep his word."

"*Ya. Yer bruder* has a reputation for his integrity. And as his accountant, I can say he's got *gut* business sense. It's just a shame about the accident." He glanced around the shop again. "Where's Leanna?"

Roman paused. Asa wasn't the first person who asked about Leanna, although most of the customers who inquired were English. It seemed all the Amish in Birch Creek except Asa knew Daniel had let Leanna go. "She . . . doesn't work here anymore."

"Really?" Asa looked shocked. "I was in Shipshe last week visiting *familye*, so I didn't realize she'd left."

Roman waited for him to ask not only why Leanna wasn't there, but also why Daniel had worked on a Sunday. Instead all Asa said, "I hope she's happy at her new job."

"Uh, me too," was all Roman could manage.

He and Roman chatted for a little bit longer, and by the end of the conversation Roman could see Asa was a good guy. Roman appreciated his discretion and his grace when it came to his machine repair taking longer than promised. Now that he had to interact with his brother's customers, he was discovering that most of the people in Birch Creek were like Asa—friendly, welcoming, and understanding. He was starting to realize why Daniel had decided to stay here permanently.

After Asa left, Roman went to his workstation. He glanced at Leanna's empty station, something he'd done off and on all day. She should be here. It wasn't right that she wasn't.

He turned his focus to Asa's machine and went to work. He was slow because he was out of practice. He also wasn't close to being as skilled as Daniel and Leanna were. By the end of the day he hadn't made much progress, and dealing with the customers who came in and interrupted his work hadn't helped.

When he closed up shop, his stomach was growling and he was trying not to panic. He couldn't do all these jobs himself, not at his slow work rate and not with so many jobs behind. More and more people would get frustrated and ask for their machines back, and he wouldn't blame them.

He plopped down at the kitchen table. He was going to fail before he even started. Unless . . . No. Leanna was staying away for a reason, and he was sure it was a good one. Otherwise she would have offered to come back. She was that type of person.

But what reason could be more important than helping Daniel and Barbara?

Roman popped up from the chair and left the house. He hurried to the barn and hitched up the buggy. It was a long shot, but he had to try. He couldn't take care of Daniel's shop alone. He needed Leanna.

· · ·

After an exciting day of wrapping bread and peeling carrots, Leanna ate supper with her family as usual. Things were still strained between them, even though Jalon and Phoebe and Adam had all apologized to her separately, explaining that they truly hadn't believed she and Daniel were having an affair. "The rumor just caught us off guard," Phoebe had said. "It still does. I don't understand how anyone could spread that kind of gossip around and still sleep at night."

Leanna couldn't understand it either, but right now her mind was on the Rabers, not on Melva's and Tabitha's big mouths. When Phoebe offered raspberry crumble for dessert, Leanna shook her head. "I'm turning in early," she said, getting up from the table. "Unless you need help with the dishes?"

"We've got it," Phoebe said. She ruffled Malachi's head. "Right, *sohn*?"

"I don't wanna do the—"

"Malachi," Jalon warned.

"Right." Malachi looked up at Leanna. "Me and *Mamm* are doing the dishes."

Leanna gave him a small smile before heading for her

house. When she stepped inside, she frowned. Clutter was everywhere, and she was annoyed with herself that she'd let it go for this long. Since she ate her meals over at Jalon's, her sink wasn't full of dishes, but some cups and a couple of plates needed washing. "Might as well start on that first," she said, acknowledging that cleaning her house was preferable to stewing about her inability to help Daniel and Barbara. *And Roman. Don't forget Roman.* How could she when he wouldn't leave her thoughts? Or her dreams. Or her—

"Enough." She turned on the tap. She had just filled the sink with hot soapy water when she heard a knock on her door. Hopefully it wasn't Jalon coming over to check on her again. Or Adam. She didn't even want to see Phoebe right now. All she wanted was to be alone.

Reluctantly she opened the door. To her surprise, Roman was standing there. Her stomach filled with dread. There could be only one reason he was there. "What's wrong? Has something happened to Daniel?"

Roman shook his head. "*Nee.* Not that I've heard. I think they're still planning to let him come home on Friday." He paused. "Can I talk to you?"

She nodded and started to open the door wider, then caught herself. No one was around, but she wanted her behavior to be above reproach. She stepped outside and shut the door behind her. "It's pretty messy in there right now," she said, glad that for once her bad housekeeping came in handy.

"I can't imagine that. *Yer* workstation is tidy."

"*Ya*, but that's because it's work. And it's never been that tidy." She frowned. "I left it a mess."

"*Nee*, you didn't. And even if you did, it wouldn't matter." He looked down at the ground before glancing up at her again. "I have a favor to ask. A huge one."

"Name it. I'll do anything to help Daniel and Barbara."

"I was hoping you would say that." He paused again, and Leanna could see that whatever he had to ask her, it wasn't easy for him. "You probably know Daniel was still behind on a few projects when he had his accident. Okay, more than a few. It was why he was working on Sunday."

Leanna nodded and let Roman continue.

"You also know that *mei* mechanic skills aren't that great."

She didn't like seeing him this way. He looked exhausted and unsure of himself. Even a little desperate. Obviously, he was feeling out of his depth, and she didn't blame him. Daniel was the backbone of that shop, regardless of who was working with him. "How can I help?" she asked softly.

His expression brightened a bit. "Come back to work. You can have *yer* old job back, or even work part-time. I'll take anything you're willing to give."

She stilled at his request. She wanted to say yes, and not only for the business's sake. Roman wasn't asking this lightly. But the situation was still the same—she would be working alone with a man. A single man this time, which would get the gossips' tongues flying even faster than a flock of angry birds.

"Please, Leanna. I wouldn't ask you this if I didn't need you."

"I-I can't help you."

He paused, looking confused. "Why not?"

"I can't tell you." Oh, this was hard. She could see him deflating in front of her.

Then his gaze turned sharp. "Can't . . . or won't?"

She hated the accusation in his eyes. But she couldn't lie to him either. Her mouth turned to dry cotton as she admitted, "Can't."

"Is this *yer* way of getting back at me?"

"Back at you? I don't understand."

"You still think I took *yer* job."

That thought hadn't occurred to her since she first accused him of it. "*Nee*. I don't think that. Not anymore. Roman, you have to believe me. I want to help, but I can't."

He shook his head and backed away. "This isn't like you. You don't back down from a challenge."

The personal way he was speaking about her struck home. "How do you know that?"

"Remember when you worked on an engine for three days straight? You worked late in the evening, even though Daniel kept telling you to *geh* home. You said you were going to figure out what was wrong *nee* matter how long it took."

"And I did," she said, stunned that he remembered not only that incident, but in quite a bit of detail. It turned out to be such a small, simple problem that she was annoyed she hadn't figured it out right away. But when she finished with that engine, it was the most satisfying job she'd ever done. *And he had noticed.*

But she had to stick to her course. "This isn't a challenge, Roman."

"Then what is it? Because I'm on a sinking ship in that shop, and I don't know how to swim."

She closed her eyes. He was being so brutally honest, and she couldn't cast him a lifeline. Wasn't there some way she could help? Some way she could lift the burden from him, even a little, without bringing more hardship on everyone else? She opened her eyes, defeated. "I'm sorry, Roman. I can't."

He took off his hat and shoved his hands through his hair. "I thought we were friends, Leanna."

"We are."

"Friends don't treat each other this way. They don't leave them in a lurch."

"Roman, I—"

"Never mind. I shouldn't have come here." He spun around and stormed off.

She looked at his retreating back. She couldn't leave it like this. There had to be something she could do to help. *You don't back down from a challenge.* That was true. So why was she backing down now? *What can I do, Lord?*

As Roman walked away, she turned and saw the old shed in the back of the property, the one Jalon kept threatening to break up and use as firewood. It was by the garden and right now housed gardening tools. She rarely paid attention to it. It was just a rickety, old shed that had served its purpose.

But maybe it could have a new purpose.

"Roman!" She ran after him, stopping him as he got into his buggy.

"What?" he snapped, but she didn't take offense. She knew he was in a pressure cooker right now.

She tugged on his arm. "I need to show you something."

"Leanna, I don't have time—"

"I think I can help you."

For a moment she thought he was going to ignore her and leave. Then he put down the reins and jumped out of the buggy.

Without thinking she grabbed his hand and led him to the backyard. It was growing dark, and the sky behind the garden shed was filled with glowing, streaky clouds. "Here's *mei* solution. At least I think it is. I haven't thought it completely through—"

"An old shed?" he asked.

"That's what it is now. But maybe it could be a new workshop." She turned to him and smiled. "I can't work *at* Daniel's, but I can still work *for* him. And for you, too, if I pick up some of the smaller projects and bring them here."

"So you have the hydraulics set up? You have a generator for electricity?"

"Nee." Her frown deepened with disappointment. "I didn't think that far ahead. This was a dumb idea," she muttered.

But Roman wasn't listening to her. He rubbed his chin with his finger. "This might work." He was mumbling, but she could hear the growing excitement in his voice as he was looking the building up and down. "It won't be that hard to get this shed in shape for a workshop. It won't be pretty on the outside—"

"Who cares?" She was starting to catch his enthusiasm.

He continued to examine the building. "It doesn't look structurally stable, though."

"Let me worry about that. I have plenty of *mann*— and *bu*—power around. It should take a day to get rid of the rotting boards and put in new ones."

"I can bring over some of the power tools from Daniel's shop. I saw that he had a few extra ones."

"He picked them up at an auction a few months ago. He always said it's a *gut* idea to have backup."

"That's Daniel, always practical." Roman nodded again, as if he was rolling the plan through his mind. "Should take me a few hours tops to equip it for you. If you had it ready by day after tomorrow—"

"Tomorrow," she interjected.

"Day after tomorrow, Friday," he said firmly, "I could come by after work that night. If I don't finish, I'll stop by early Saturday morning and complete the job. It would be bare bones, though."

"I can deal with that." She started to bring her palms together in excitement when she realized she was still holding Roman's hand. Not only holding it, but at some point they had entwined their fingers.

He looked down at their clasped hands, and she expected him to let go. Instead he hung on to her hand and looked back at the shed. "This could work," he said. "This could actually work."

She moved closer to him as she squeezed his hand. "This *will* work, Roman. We'll make it work, for Daniel's sake." She squeezed his fingers one more time and let go. "I need to talk to *mei familye*, and you should get back home. I'll stop by—" She caught herself again. "I'll send one of Phoebe's *bruders* over to let you know about the progress."

"You can't come over *yerself*? I don't bite, you know." He started to grin, but it faded when she didn't laugh. "All right. I'll expect Phoebe's *bruder*."

Leanna was glad that not only did Roman understand, but he didn't pry. "And Daniel should be home by then, right?"

"I hope so. Barbara has insisted on staying there every night."

Leanna wasn't surprised Barbara would want to be by her husband's side, but it worried her. It couldn't be good for her to try to sleep there, especially after losing the baby. "How is she?"

"Tired. Worried." He sighed. "We both are."

Leanna searched Roman's face to see if he was keeping anything from her and determined he wasn't. Which made sense. Barbara wouldn't have told him about the miscarriage. She wondered if Daniel even knew.

"Okay, we have a plan," he said. "A *gut* one." He yawned, looking at the shed again.

The sun was already dipping beyond the horizon. "You should *geh* home and get some sleep," Leanna said.

"I think I will, now that I know there's hope." He turned to her, the strain that had been on his face disappearing. "You're really something," he said.

She chuckled. "*Ya.* I've heard that before."

"I mean something special." His voice lowered, taking on a husky tone she'd never heard before. One that reached clear to her toes.

Leanna waited until he was gone to breathe. She turned around and took in the fading sunlight. Roman thought she was special. She'd heard that before. From her parents, of course, and Ivy. Her brother also used it as an insult every so often when they were growing up. But because Roman had said it—not to mention the way he'd said it—she believed it. The hand he'd been holding earlier tingled, along with something in her heart. For once she wasn't thinking about work or her future or Daniel and Barbara. She was thinking only about Roman.

CHAPTER 11

Three days later, Barbara sat next to Daniel in the backseat of a taxi as they made their way home. He'd had to spend an extra day in the hospital, which had made him crabby. At least he could see clearly now. The skin around his eyes still looked tender and red from the burns, but he hadn't lost any of his eyesight, thank God. His legs were still bandaged and a nurse would be by to change the dressings as often as necessary, something Daniel had balked at but Barbara had insisted would happen.

Now her husband was looking out the window as they drove into Birch Creek. It had taken nearly the whole day to discharge him from the hospital, a process that was ridiculously long, in her opinion, so by the time the taxi reached the house it was after five o'clock. As soon as their driver, Tyler, put the car into park, he turned and looked at Daniel. "*Nee* charge," he said.

Daniel pulled out his wallet, which he'd insisted Barbara bring to the hospital. "I'll pay you what I owe," he said, his voice a little raspy from disuse. He'd been quiet in the hospital. Overly quiet.

"But this is on me."

Daniel ignored him, pulled out money, and held it out. "Take it."

Tyler looked a little insulted, but took the money anyway. He glanced at Barbara. "If you need anything, let me know."

"I will." Barbara nodded her thanks. Tyler was a nice guy who lived on the outskirts of Birch Creek and, other than Max, was one of their main taxi drivers. He'd driven Barbara and Daniel to places before.

She gathered her small bag from the seat and got out of the car. She met Daniel on the other side, and he tried to take her bag. But she wouldn't let him. "I've got it," she said.

"You don't need to be carrying that. Think about the *boppli*."

She pressed her lips together. Other than Daniel's injuries, it was all she thought about. She hadn't been able to tell him about the miscarriage. The cramping had subsided, and the bleeding was next to nothing. It was as if she'd never been pregnant. Except there was a deep hole in her heart that grew with every baby she lost.

The nurse who tended to her when she first miscarried had been compassionate. She'd also been empathetic. "I'm so sorry. I lost my first baby," she said when she brought Barbara the things she needed. Fortunately, her dress had stayed clean, and Daniel had slept through the whole thing anyway. "I have three children now." The nurse placed a comforting hand on Barbara's shoulder. "It will be okay. You'll get through this."

Barbara nodded and tried to smile, tried to be happy for this woman as she tried to be happy for other expectant mothers. But it was getting harder to do. And she couldn't share any of this with Daniel, not while he was trying to recuperate in the hospital. She'd have to wait for the right time.

The door to the shop opened and Roman stepped outside. He turned and went to Daniel. "They finally let you *geh*," Roman said, grinning.

"What were you doing in *mei* shop?" Daniel said.

Barbara turned and saw the two men, standing across from each other. Dread pooled in her belly as she saw Roman's expression become defensive.

"Working," Roman said.

"I told you I don't need *yer* help."

"And I heard you. But you're wrong. You need *mei* help. Mine and Leanna's."

Daniel's face drained of color. "You hired her back?"

"*Nee*." Barbara listened as Roman explained that Leanna was working on projects at her house. "Her *familye* rehabbed an old shed, and I set everything up for her to do the smaller jobs."

"So she's not working *here*?"

Roman shook his head. "I asked her to come back, but she wouldn't. It was her idea to work from her *haus*. Which is fine, but it was more trouble than just coming back here. I guess whatever happened between the two of you was more than she could overlook."

A muscle jerked in Daniel's jaw, and Barbara went to him. "It's not what you think," she said to Roman. Obviously, Leanna hadn't said anything to him about the real reason she was let go, and Barbara knew Daniel wouldn't. "Leanna didn't do anything—"

"*Geh* in the *haus*, Barbara." Daniel didn't look at her as he faced off with Roman.

"But—"

"*Geh!*"

Barbara's bottom lip trembled, and she looked at Roman, who seemed bewildered, since Daniel wasn't prone to outbursts. If anything, he kept his feelings locked tight inside. Too tight, Barbara thought. Not wanting to upset him, she turned and went inside, fighting the tears that threatened to fall. He'd hurt her just now, but she couldn't be angry with him. He was hurting inside too. And she could only imagine the pain he'd experience when he found out about her latest miscarriage.

• • •

"That was harsh," Roman said as Daniel continued to glare at him. His brother looked better than he had the last time Roman saw him, although he could tell Daniel was in pain. That had to explain his outburst at Barbara. He was swaying a little on his legs, and although he was wearing loose hospital pants, Roman had seen the bandages underneath. He softened his tone. "You should *geh* inside and rest."

"Not until we have an understanding. Which I thought we did at the hospital." A fine sheen of perspiration formed on Daniel's forehead. He wasn't wearing his hat, either. "I want you to stay away from the shop."

"Too late for that." Roman lifted his chin. "Why are you being so stubborn? At least before you would let me sweep and clean up. Now you don't want me to even *geh* inside?"

"I have *mei* reasons." Daniel's face looked pale, his lips a little white.

"What reasons are those?"

"I don't need you to fix *mei* mess."

"I'm not fixing it. I'm helping you."

"And I don't need the help." He swayed to the side, and Roman was there to catch him before he hit the ground.

"And you said I was stubborn." Roman helped him inside and to the first-floor guest bedroom Barbara planned to use for a while. Barbara was there, standing by the window. She spun around, and Roman saw her wipe her cheeks before coming toward them. "What happened?"

"*Nix*," Daniel said weakly.

"He nearly fainted." Roman helped him to the bed. Daniel tried to shove him off, but instead collapsed on the mattress.

Barbara crouched down next to him by the side of the bed. "Daniel?"

"I'm . . . okay."

"You're not okay. You're staying in bed for the rest of the night, understand? And I don't want you to do anything that isn't following the doctor's orders." Her voice turned thick as Daniel's eyes closed. "I can't lose you too," she whispered, brushing his damp hair from his forehead.

Roman hung back in the doorway, wondering what Barbara was talking about. Daniel wasn't going to die, unless being stubborn was a fatal disease. If that were true, Roman would have perished a long time ago. Maybe she was talking about *Grossmammi*. Roman didn't know if his grandmother and Barbara had become close after Barbara and Daniel married, but he wouldn't have been surprised. A lump formed in his throat as he thought about her, and now seeing Daniel asleep on the bed, the thought that he could have lost his brother hit him square in the chest again. He went to Barbara and helped her up. "He's safe while he's asleep," Roman said. "You don't have to watch him."

Nodding, she went to the kitchen and sat down at the table. Her head dropped into her hands.

Roman wasn't sure what to do. When she started to cry, he was at a loss. He was never good with tears, learning from an early age to hide his own. He'd never seen his parents cry, only his grandmother, who had always assured him crying wasn't a bad thing. "You have to let the emotions out," she said one time after she'd read him a sad story. He had wanted to cry, too, and she had said he could. But he couldn't bring himself to do it.

He stood next to Barbara, reached out tentatively, and touched her on the shoulder. He patted it a few times and then said, "What can I do to help?"

She looked up at him, her face haunted. That made him pull out a chair and sit down next to her. "He's going to be okay," he reassured her. "His stubbornness will see to that."

"I know." She sniffed, and he reached for a napkin from the holder in the center of the table and gave it to her. "I'm glad you're here."

He paused, a warm feeling spreading to his chest. "I'm glad I'm here too." He never thought he'd say that before. Over the past few days while Daniel was in the hospital, and when Roman wasn't focusing on work, he thought about how his reasons for being in Birch Creek had changed. He'd come here solely to fulfill a promise and get a job so he could make enough money to leave. And now, only a couple of weeks later, he was starting to feel different. Although things with him and Daniel were probably worse than ever, he still felt as though he should be here. He was needed, and it was a good, if unfamiliar, feeling.

Barbara wiped her nose with the napkin and put her hands in her lap. "It's going to be a challenge to keep him from working."

"Once he sees that Leanna and I have it under control, he'll feel better. He's tired and he needs the rest."

"I was wondering in the hospital . . ." She glanced at her lap. "I don't believe God causes harm or that Daniel deserved to be hurt."

"Of course not."

"But I wondered if God allowed it to happen because he knew Daniel needed to rest. He's been having so many sleepless nights lately, and he's been working so hard. Losing Leanna was difficult too."

Roman glanced at his lap. He knew it wasn't his business, but he had to ask. "Why did Daniel let her *geh*?"

"I can't tell you." Barbara sniffed. "I can only say that

it wasn't fair to any of us. But I'm glad she's willing to help out. I'm also not surprised she is." She put her hand on Roman's arm. "Have you had supper?"

"*Ya*," he lied. He wasn't about to let her make him a meal. "Can I get you anything?"

"I'm not hungry."

"Are you sure?"

She nodded. "I'll probably fall asleep soon, anyway."

Sleep sounded good to him right now, even though it was early. He still had to take care of the evening chores, though. "You're sure I can't get you anything?" he asked.

"*Nee*." She stood from the table. "*Gute nacht*, Roman. I'll see you in the morning."

"*Gute nacht*."

After Roman did the chores, he caught a second wind. There was plenty of daylight left and he decided to take a walk. Leanna had made good on her word that her family would get the shed together in record time, and the next day she'd sent word that she was ready for him to outfit it for a mechanics shop. He'd spent the night before scrounging through Daniel's tools and items that could help him provide power to the shop. He also took Leanna's tool belt to her, which she'd left behind when she gathered her tools. He smiled as he remembered handing it to her. She accepted it as if it were a precious item. She even clutched it to her chest, her grin making her face light up. He wanted to see her smile like that again.

He found himself at the pond and heard children's voices. He peeked through the trees. Leanna was there with Malachi and two other boys. They were fishing, and Leanna was baiting one of the boy's hooks.

"You need to learn how to do this *yourself*, Perry," she said, handing him the pole.

"Worms are gross."

"Don't be such a *maed*," another boy teased.

"I'm not a *maed*." Perry lifted his chin defiantly. "I just don't like worms. At least I'm not afraid of the dark like you are, Nelson."

"*Buwe*, you're scaring away the fish." Leanna put her fingertips to her temples. "Not to mention giving me a headache."

The boys sat down on the bank of the pond while Leanna moved a couple of feet away from them and cast out her line. Then she sat down and pulled her knees to her chin.

A fly came out and Roman brushed it away. It flitted around him some more and he realized it wasn't just a fly, but a horsefly. It bit him, and he jumped from the sting, lost his balance, and came tumbling out of the woods.

Leanna jerked her head, looked at him, and then laughed. "What were you hiding there for?" She got up to her feet and went to him.

"Were you spying on us?" Malachi said, holding tight to his bamboo pole.

"*Nee*. Not spying." Roman could feel his cheeks heat.

"Then what would you call it?" Leanna crossed her arms over her chest, and he saw the twitch of her bottom lip.

"Observing." He crossed his arms over his chest too. "You baited his hook wrong, by the way."

"I did not." She went over to Perry's pole and pulled it out of the water.

"Hey!" Perry said, scrambling to his feet. "What did you do that for?"

Leanna looked at the hook, which was empty. "Did you feel a tug on *yer* pole?"

When the boy shook his head, Roman said, "That's because you baited his hook wrong."

"How could you see that from all the way into the woods?"

"I have superior vision." He had average vision, and he had no idea if she'd baited the hook wrong or not. Knowing her, she'd probably baited it perfectly and it happened to get snatched off the hook. But teasing her was fun, and he needed a little fun in his life right now.

Leanna took the pole, marched over to the tub of worms, and picked up a fat one. "Come here and *observe* as I put the worm on perfectly."

Roman went to her and watched as she secured the worm on the hook with such quick expertise he was impressed. She was handing the pole to Perry when Malachi said, "*Aenti* Leanna, I think you got a bite."

Leanna and Roman both looked at her pole, which was lying on the freshly mowed grass. The pole was moving toward the pond, and then, before Leanna could get to it, with one swift pull it was tugged underwater.

"*Nee!*" Leanna ran to the pond, and before Roman

could do anything she jumped in. "You're not getting *mei* favorite pole," she said, reaching out in front of her. Then she disappeared under the water.

"*Yer aenti* can swim, can't she?" Roman asked Malachi. The three boys were standing at his side, watching the pond expectantly.

"*Ya,*" he said, a tone of awe in his voice. "She can do anything."

Roman was inclined to believe that. He already knew she could repair any kind of machine. She could also skate well, with the exception of the day she was fired, and he didn't blame her for losing her balance then. She skipped stones like a pro—even though she had her off days—and she didn't hold grudges, as evidenced by how she went out of her way to help Daniel even though he'd let her go from her job. Clearly she knew how to fish, and now he knew she had a favorite pole, although she was going to a lot of trouble to get it back.

She was also underwater for a long time.

"Where did she *geh*?" Nelson asked.

Roman glanced at the boy, who seemed a bit older than Malachi and Perry. He didn't sound worried, but Roman saw the hint of concern in his eyes. Roman looked back at the pond. "She'll come up any second," Roman said.

"What if she doesn't?" Perry asked.

"What if she's drowning?" Malachi said, which made all the boys, including Nelson, suck in their breath. Malachi yanked on Roman's pants. "Don't let her drown!"

"She's not drowning." But she also wasn't coming up. He yanked off his boots and plowed into the water where she had gone under. He opened his eyes and immediately regretted it. The water was murky and he couldn't see anything. He reached out and tried to find her by touch. All this for a stupid fishing pole . . .

When he couldn't hold his breath anymore, he shot up to the surface. The sound of laughter reached his ears, and he saw Leanna treading water in front of him, laughing. He heard the boys giggling too.

"What's so funny?"

"Hold still." She swam toward him and pulled something off his head. Then she held it out to him.

He jerked back from the bullfrog she was holding. "Wait . . . What? How did that get on *mei* head?"

"This pond is full of them." She patted the frog's head before letting it back into the water.

He glared at her. "Just tell me you got *yer* dumb pole."

"I did." She held it up. "And it's not dumb."

"It wasn't worth getting all wet for."

Her expression sobered. "*Ya*. It was." She swam past him, her white *kapp* soaked and drooping a little, several strands of watery grass on her shoulders. She got out of the water and wrung the skirt of her dress. Water dripped everywhere. She turned to Malachi. "*Geh* get us some towels," she said. "And take *yer* poles back. We're done fishing for now."

"Aw," Perry said. "But I didn't catch any fish."

"None of us caught any," she said, rubbing the top of his head. "And there's always another day. Now do what I said."

The boys gathered their poles and bait and left the pond. Leanna's back was turned as Roman came out of the water. His trousers were heavy and his shirt clung to his chest. He'd stepped onto the bank when she started to speak.

"I love that fishing pole." She turned to face him. "*Mei grossdaadi* gave it to me—"

She stopped speaking, and just stared at him. Actually, she was focused on his chest in particular, and he couldn't stop watching as her eyes grew wide and then turned a smoky-brown color as she swallowed. Hard. He knew what she was looking at. He was in shape, mainly because of the running he'd done while he was living in the English world. Before that he'd worked hard for his father, since his parents didn't believe in doing anything the easy way. It would be false modesty for him to say he didn't have a decent physique, even though he was on the thin side since he'd left the Amish—and all the good cooking. Up until now, he hadn't thought about how he looked. Not until he saw Leanna looking at him the way she was looking at him now.

She suddenly whirled around, wrapping her arms around her thin frame. "Where are those *buwe* with the towels?" she muttered.

"They just left. Not enough time to get them yet."

He realized she was uncomfortable, and he didn't want her to feel that way, especially around him. "I'll leave," he said.

"You can't *geh* walking around in wet clothes."

"I'm tougher than I look."

She gave him a quick glance over her shoulder, and he thought he saw her smile. "Turn around," she said.

"What?"

"Turn around and sit down."

He shrugged, wondering what she was up to, but he did what she asked. Then he heard her moving toward him. A few more shuffles and he felt her wet back against his.

"Okay, I give," he said, looking over his shoulder. "What's going on?"

"This way we don't see each other. Until the *buwe* come back."

"You don't trust me not to look?" he asked, unable to keep the amusement out of his voice.

"I don't trust myself."

He smirked at her mumbled words, knowing she hadn't meant for him to hear them, and he wasn't going to embarrass her by pointing out he had. The spot where she was leaning against him was becoming warm, and he suddenly hoped the boys would dawdle a bit getting back to them with the towels. He clasped his hands around his knees. "*Yer grossdaadi* gave you that pole?"

"*Ya.* I should have been more careful with it. Normally I stick it in the ground, but you surprised me coming out of the woods like that."

"I didn't mean to startle you."

"I said surprised, not startle. There's a difference."

"I know. And you looked startled to me."

"Humph."

He chuckled to himself and looked at the pond. It had settled down since they jumped in, and now the sun was just above the horizon. The bullfrogs, probably including the one that had jumped on his head, were starting to croak, and the cicadas were playing their evening songs. He reached out and caught a firefly and then let it go. "Were you close to *yer grossdaadi*?" he asked.

"He died when I was six," she said, sighing a little. "We were close, but not for long. He liked to take me fishing. I thought it was kind of boring, though." He felt her move forward a little, but their backs were still touching. "It wasn't until I was older that I realized why he liked it so much."

"Why?"

"Fishing requires you to be quiet. It forces you to be a part of nature, which I believe God intended for us. Our lives can get so hectic sometimes."

"Try living in the English world," he said suddenly.

"*Nee* thanks."

"So you never even thought about it?" He turned his head toward her, even though all he could see was the shell of her ear below the edge of her damp *kapp*. He also saw the freckle on her earlobe. Cute.

"Not for a minute. I'm sure this is where I'm supposed to be. Amish, living in Birch Creek, being a mechanic . . ." She paused. "Although I wish things were different."

She didn't have to explain the reason. Although he was discovering that working on machines wasn't as tedious and unrewarding as he thought, he didn't like the circumstances under which he'd made that discovery.

"But I'll help out Daniel as long as he needs me," she added.

"You're very loyal to him."

"And Barbara." She batted away a fly. "*Mei* loyalty is to both of them."

"Of course." That went without saying . . . but why had she felt the need to say it?

She batted away another horsefly. "How is Daniel? Did he come home today?"

"*Ya.* And he wanted me out of the shop, of course."

This time he felt her shift. "Why?"

Roman let out a long breath. "He still doesn't trust me. I don't know if he ever will."

"I know he was upset when you left the way you did." She paused. "We both were."

"You were?"

"*Ya.* You left without telling anyone. That wasn't right. I know we didn't get along, but you could have at least told *yer bruder.*"

"True." He stripped off one sock and dug his bare heel in the ground. "I'm pretty much a coward that way."

"I wouldn't call you a coward."

"I would." *And I do.* "That wasn't the first time I ran away. I used to take off all the time when I was little." A horsefly landed on his knee and he shoved at it. He wasn't about to get bit again. Off came the other sock.

"Why?"

"To get away from *mei familye.*"

"But I thought you were close to them."

"Only to *mei grossmammi.* She lived with us. *Mei* parents . . . That's a different story."

"Oh." She paused, and then said, "Daniel never talked about his *familye.* I only knew he had a *bruder* when you showed up."

"I'm not surprised." Now that he'd brought up the subject he felt he had to clarify. "*Mei* parents aren't bad people. They made sure we had clothes to wear and food to eat. But they weren't really parents to us. More like caretakers. *Mei grossmammi* was different. She was the one who showed us love." A lump formed in his throat. "She never explained why *mei* parents are the way they are. I only know *mei* mother and father got together through letters."

"Like *mei bruder* and his wife."

"They were pen pals?"

"*Ya.* When I first found out he was writing to Phoebe, I used to tease him about it. I never thought it would turn into something serious, because *mei bruder* wasn't interested in marriage at the time. But once I could see he loved her, and then I met her, I knew they were meant to be together."

"It wasn't that way with *mei* parents. I think theirs was a marriage of convenience. *Mei* father is fifteen years older than her, and she had problems with her *familye* . . ." He looked down at his bare feet. "Daniel and I didn't have any contact with *mei* mother's *familye* at all."

"Aren't you curious about them?"

"I used to be." He shrugged. "Then I realized if they were interested in meeting me, they would have made an effort."

"Maybe they did and you didn't know about it."

"Maybe." He shrugged. "I don't really care anymore."

"How can you not care about *yer familye*?" Leanna twisted a little bit, and now he could see the puzzled look on her face.

"I've had a lot of practice. Where are the *kinner* with those towels?"

"I guess we're dry enough to walk back."

He paused. Was that a forlorn tone in her voice? "Do you want to *geh* back to the *haus*?"

Silence, but he felt her back stiffen against his. "*Nee*," she said in a low voice.

This time he knew she wasn't just talking to herself. She meant for him to hear her. In reply, he moved closer to her back, so that they were almost completely touching from the center of their backs to their waists. They could easily do that, since their torsos were almost the same length. Even though their clothes were still damp, he felt the warmth of her through to his skin. He glanced at his lap and smiled.

"The improvements you made on *mei* shop are really *gut*," she said, her voice steady, as if talking about business while they were sitting this close to each other was normal.

"Glad to hear it. I hope it's made things easier on you. At least easier considering you're working in a new place."

"It is. I'm pretty adaptable, though. I do like the idea that I have *mei* own shop. And I guess the news is getting around because Jedediah King brought by a clock that hadn't worked in thirty years."

"Have you figured out what's wrong with it?"

"*Nee*." He felt her shrug. "But as you know, I like a challenge."

That made him grin. "Why haven't you thought of opening *yer* own shop before?"

"In case you haven't noticed, I'm a *maed*."

"In case you haven't noticed, you're a woman." The

words escaped his mouth, but he wasn't sorry he said them, because they were true. She was an appealing woman he was feeling more drawn to than he thought possible.

"Uh . . . okay. A woman." She cleared her throat and he could feel her shoulders straightening. "*Mei* point still stands. I wouldn't have a lot of business coming *mei* way. Not very many men trust a female mechanic."

"They trust you now."

"That's because Daniel gave me a chance."

"So the thought never crossed *yer* mind about opening *yer* own business after he let you *geh*?"

"*Nee.* I wouldn't want to take away any of his business. He worked hard to establish his shop and his reputation."

"With *yer* help." He plucked a stem of grass out of the ground. "You forgave him pretty easily for firing you."

"You're assuming he needed to be forgiven."

"Usually that's the case when someone wrongs you."

"*Ya* . . . but Daniel didn't wrong me. I deserved to be fired."

CHAPTER 12

Leanna hugged her arms around her shoulders. She was being foolish sitting here discussing her firing with Roman, their backs pressed up against each other. There was no reason they couldn't go back to the house. Knowing those boys, she figured they'd been distracted by something and forgotten about the towels. They probably should go back to the house, since she and Roman were venturing into territory she didn't want to go into.

She knew Roman was curious about why she was fired, but he was being discreet about asking, something she appreciated. But she couldn't tell him. She didn't want him to know about the gossip about her and Daniel. She didn't want Roman to even consider that it might be true, or that she would do something like that to his brother and Barbara.

She popped up from the ground, already missing the warmth of his back against hers. "I'm sure the *buwe* forgot about us." Even though the air was warm, she shivered, and she still didn't look at him. Catching a glimpse of his chest through his wet shirt was enough to stir her confused emotions, along with something else inside her.

"You *geh* ahead."

Leanna turned and looked at him. He hadn't gotten up off the ground. Instead he was picking at the grass, plucking up the blades and tossing them to the side as he stared at the pond in front of him. She wondered if he even realized what he was doing. She moved to stand next to him, but he continued what he was doing, still staring straight ahead. Crouching down next to him, she said, "I'm sorry."

He turned and looked at her, and she could see the light-blond whiskers on his chin. She also noticed his blond curls and suddenly wanted to run her fingers through them. She balled her hands into fists instead.

"Sorry for what?" he asked, looking genuinely confused.

"That I can't tell you why Daniel fired me."

Roman turned toward her a little bit, enough that they were almost face-to-face. "Don't apologize. I should apologize for asking you about it. It's not *mei* business."

"But you're upset."

He shook his head, but the muscle in his cheek jerked again. "*Nee*, I'm not."

Without thinking she touched the place that pulsed. "*Ya*. You are."

He covered her hand with his own and then moved both away from his face. She expected him to drop her hand, but he didn't. Instead he looked down at their hands and then back at her. "We seem to be doing this lately."

"Holding hands?"

"That. And. . ." He inched toward her. "Getting closer."

She swallowed. "Does. . . does that bother you?"

"I'm not sure." His words stung a little. She started to pull her hand away, but he held on to it. "I'm not sure because I'm not used to friendship."

Leanna was pretty sure holding hands with a man meant something more than friendship, but she kept her mouth shut.

"I've never been close to anyone, other than *mei gross-mammi*." He looked at her. "You were right. I was upset a minute ago."

She sat down next to him, still holding his hand. For once she stayed quiet and listened.

"I was thinking about what you said about *mei fam-ilye*. I used to want to know about them. I guess I still do. But not enough to get—" He turned away and let go of her hand. "Rejected."

"But what if they want to see you? What if they've had the same fear and it's kept them from reaching out? *Mei bruder* and *mei* cousin had the same problem last year. They missed out on a lot of years together because Jalon was feeling guilty about Adam's accident, and Adam gave up trying to reach out to him."

"What got them to change their minds?"

She grinned. "Me, of course."

He laughed. "Of course."

"I'm joking. It wasn't me. I just brought them to-gether. God's the one who worked on their hearts." She tapped his chest. "Let God work on *yers*. You might find something you've been missing all along."

"And what about *yer* heart?" he asked.

"*Mei* heart is just fine." But was it? Right now it was

beating triple time being this close to him. All she would have to do is lean forward a little bit and she could kiss him. What she didn't understand was why she wanted to. What was it about Roman Raber that woke up something inside her she didn't even know she had?

"Leanna!"

She turned at the sound of Zeb, one of Phoebe's older younger brothers calling her name. "Over here," she said, getting to her feet.

The boy burst into the clearing, gasping for breath. "Phoebe . . ."

Leanna's blood turned cold. "What about Phoebe?"

He gulped for air. "She's having her *boppli*."

. . .

Karen had spent a lot of time thinking about her conversation with Leanna the other day, and she realized her friend was right. There was no reason she couldn't ask Adam to marry her. So what if it wasn't traditional? Their relationship hadn't exactly been traditional from the start. Her decision made, she had gone to the Chupp house after work to see Adam and propose to him.

Instead she found herself helping Phoebe as she went into labor.

Jalon, Adam, and Phoebe's father were still out getting more materials from the lumberyard for the barn expansion. The older of Phoebe's brothers—Devon, Zeb, Zeke, and Owen—were with Karen's brother Seth at one of his friends' houses. Leanna was at the pond with Malachi, Perry, and Nelson, and Phoebe's mother, along with the youngest Bontrager boys, were at Naomi Beiler's.

"*Mamm* said something about getting together with Naomi and Rhoda today to work on a quilt. Irene offered to watch the *buwe*," Phoebe had said shortly after Karen arrived.

Karen smiled. Naomi Beiler and Rhoda Troyer had both experienced their own share of heartache. Irene was Naomi's daughter and Rhoda's daughter-in-law, and Karen wasn't surprised she offered to watched Phoebe's youngest brothers so the three women could quilt together.

"It's nice *Mamm* has made friends so easily here," Phoebe added.

"Is everyone in *yer familye* still happy here?" Karen had asked, masking her disappointment that Adam wasn't home. She would wait for him, of course. If she went home now, she'd probably lose her courage.

"*Ya*. Very. They don't talk about Fredericktown at all. Not even *mei* younger *bruders*. This is their home now."

Karen had made some tea for her and Phoebe, who seemed especially tired. The baby wasn't due for a couple of weeks, but Phoebe looked like she was in some pain. "Labor pains?" Karen asked, a bit anxious as she handed her the tea.

"Only the false ones. They've been plaguing me for over a month." She put her finger to her lips. "Don't tell Jalon. He'll start to worry."

"I won't."

"*Danki*—" She put her hand to her abdomen and grimaced. "Okay, that was a strong one."

They were in the living room, and Karen moved the footstool over in front of Phoebe, who was sitting on the couch. "Here. Put *yer* feet up." When Phoebe did as she was told, Karen said, "I'll get more tea."

"Okay."

Then Phoebe let out a scream that curdled Karen's blood. "Phoebe!" Karen flew from the kitchen to see Phoebe bent over in pain. She went to her side. "Is it the *boppli*?"

"*Ya.*" Phoebe's face was red, contorted. She gasped for air. "The pain . . . It's coming so fast."

"*Mamm!*" Malachi ran into the house, along with Perry and Nelson. "*Aenti* jumped into the water to get her fishing pole and then Roman jumped after her and now they're wet and they need towels—"

Phoebe let out another cry and Malachi turned white. "*Mamm?*"

Karen jumped up from the couch and went to the boys. "*Yer mamm*'s okay," she said, crouching down and putting her hand on Malachi's shoulder. Then she looked at Perry. "Why don't you *geh* to *mei haus* and tell *mei mamm* to come over? I think Phoebe could use the company."

"Why is she hurting?" Malachi pressed his teeth down on his lip.

How was she supposed to explain this to a five-year-old without worrying him? Too late, he was already worrying. "Sometimes when you're carrying a *boppli* it can hurt. But *yer mamm* is okay. I'm with her. Now *geh* do what I asked you to do."

They nodded, and Malachi gave his mother one

last worried look and ran out the door. Karen blew out a long breath and went back to Phoebe, who was hunched over on the couch. "Do you want to lie down?" she asked.

Phoebe shook her head. "*Nee*. I have to *geh* to the bathroom."

"I'll help you." She assisted Phoebe to her feet and was glad that her friend didn't resist.

They'd walked a few steps toward the bathroom when Phoebe stopped, fear in her eyes. "*Mei* water broke."

Panic threaded through Karen, but she said a prayer for calm. Her mother would be here soon and she would know what to do.

Phoebe clutched at her, but straightened her shoulders. "I need to breathe," she said to herself. "Breathe." She took deep breaths and let go of Karen. "Get some towels," she said.

"I don't want to leave you—"

"I'm fine." Phoebe's face was calm, and she was breathing a little normally now. "Just get the towels and put them on *mei* bed—" Another contraction overtook her and she folded in half. "Hurry."

Karen ran and got the towels, knowing exactly where everything was. She had not only practically grown up here, but had lived in this house when Phoebe and Malachi first came to Birch Creek and Jalon took them in. She gathered as many towels as she could carry and dashed back to the living room. Phoebe was grasping the rocker with one hand and cradling her swollen abdomen with the other. Karen quickly spread the towels on the couch and led Phoebe to it.

"I can't have the *boppli* on the couch!" Phoebe said, her voice turning shrill.

"I don't think you have a choice. You can't even walk."

Phoebe grimaced in pain again and sat down on the couch. "It wasn't this fast with Malachi," she said.

"Was he born at home?"

"*Ya*, with a midwife." She looked at Karen. "Someone needs to get Patience."

"I will once *Mamm* gets here."

"I wish Jalon was here," she said through gritted teeth.

Karen took Phoebe's hand. "Sorry. I'm a poor substitute."

Despite her pain, Phoebe smiled. "*Nee*. If Jalon can't be here, I'm glad you are."

For the next minute or so, Phoebe rode out another strong contraction. "They're getting closer," she said.

Where is Mamm? As soon as Karen had the thought, her mother rushed in. "Looks like we're going to have a *boppli*." She sat on the edge of the couch. "Don't worry, Phoebe. Everything will be fine."

Karen moved away and watched as her mother calmed Phoebe down and helped her as she had another contraction. When it subsided, she calmly looked at Karen. "We'll need hot water," she said. "And a blanket for the *boppli*. *Yer* father went to fetch Patience."

Karen immediately calmed, went to the kitchen, and turned on the tap, letting the water get hot. Or should she boil it? She didn't want to burn Phoebe. Normally she felt capable of anything, but this was completely different.

The back door opened and Leanna burst in, Roman in

tow. They looked wet, and Karen remembered Malachi's ramblings about how they had jumped into the pond. Knowing Leanna, she could only imagine why, but right now she was focused on Phoebe and the baby.

"What can I do?" Leanna asked, going to her.

"I'm not sure." What if Patience didn't get here on time? What if something happened to the baby? What if she hadn't done the right thing in helping Phoebe? *Please, Lord. Let everything be all right.*

CHAPTER 13

Karen kept repeating the prayer as Leanna told Roman to take the boys next door to the Bontrager house and then turned off the faucet. Hot water was spilling over the top of the pitcher. Leanna put one hand on Karen's arm and took the pitcher from her. "It will be all right," she said, setting it aside.

Karen turned to see Patience come into the kitchen. Relieved, she sank against the sink as Patience took charge. "The water needs to be boiled," she said.

Nodding, Karen picked up the tea kettle and began filling it. As Patience left the kitchen, Leanna left, too, saying she was going to check on Roman and the boys. After the water boiled, she turned off the burner, poured the water into a large ceramic pitcher, and took it to the living room. Patience nodded for her to set it on the coffee table and then turned her attention back to Phoebe.

Karen watched as Patience stayed at the end of the couch, coaching Phoebe on how to breathe, her voice calm and soothing. She was the perfect reflection of her name. Phoebe listened, and within a few minutes she was settling down.

"Should we try to move her to the bed?" Karen asked

while Phoebe leaned against the pillow, her eyes closed as she rested from one of the contractions.

"She's okay here," Patience said.

Karen lowered her voice. "She said she didn't want to have the *boppli* on the couch."

"I don't care anymore," Phoebe said, her face scrunching in pain.

Karen hurried to kneel beside Phoebe, holding her hand. Phoebe gripped Karen so tightly she thought her bones would crack. Just as she thought the contraction was over, Phoebe let out another bloodcurdling scream.

"You're doing great, Phoebe!" Patience said.

"*Ya.* You're doing great." Karen wasn't sure what else she should say. She'd never coached anyone during childbirth. She kept holding Phoebe's hand as she drifted down from the painful contraction.

"Phoebe!" Jalon burst into the living room.

"She's okay, Jalon," Patience said. "The contractions are getting closer, though."

Karen looked up at Jalon, who was hovering over his wife. "Here," she said, getting up from Phoebe's side. "She needs you."

Jalon hesitated, looking more unsure than Karen had felt. Then he knelt beside Phoebe and took her hand. "I'm here," he said in a low voice. He brushed his work-roughened fingers over his wife's forehead. "I'm here."

Stepping back, Karen was near the staircase when she saw Phoebe grimace again. "*Boppli*," Phoebe gasped. "I have to push—"

"*Nee*," Patience said. "Not yet."

Knowing she wasn't needed anymore, Karen turned

and headed for the kitchen. She wasn't sure what else she should do. Make tea and coffee? She jumped as she heard another scream. She'd make that tea and coffee. She had to do something until Phoebe's baby was born.

She nibbled on her thumbnail as she walked into the kitchen and then said aloud, "Please, Lord, let everything be all right."

"It will be."

Karen was surprised to see Adam by the kitchen table. "I didn't realize you were here."

"We were pulling into the driveway when Jalon heard Phoebe," Adam said, folding his hands in his lap. "Thomas took care of the horse and buggy and then went to his house to wait for Phoebe's mother to come home. I came in here. Didn't want to be in the way."

"Me either."

"What happened?"

Karen filled Adam in on Phoebe going into labor, sparing him the personal details. She went to the table and sat down. "I'm glad Patience got here so quickly. I was worried I'd do something wrong. Or worse, I would have to deliver the *boppli* myself."

Adam wheeled closer to her and put his arm around her shoulders. "I'm sure if you had, everything would be fine."

"Then why am I still worried?"

"It's only natural you would be."

His deep, steady voice soothed her. That was one thing she loved about Adam. He was strong, like a rock wall in the face of a storm.

"Phoebe's like a *schwester* to you," he continued. "Of

course you want everything to be okay. Just like I do."
He slipped off his glove and took her hand. "Let's pray
that it will."

She closed her eyes, holding on to the man she loved
as they prayed for the family she wanted to be a part
of. Yes, she did think of Phoebe as a sister now. They
had grown close over the weeks she had stayed here in
Jalon's house while Phoebe and Malachi were also living here, before the couple married. She'd been sent as
their chaperone and had left with a good friend.

After they finished praying, she opened her eyes, and
turned to Adam. He was staring at her with his deep,
wise eyes. Eyes she could stare at all day. "Feeling better?" he asked.

"*Ya*. Now that you're here."

He grinned. "See? Everything is all right."

She smiled back, but it faded quickly. "Is it?"

He frowned. "What do you mean?"

"Is it all right . . .?" She couldn't believe she was bringing this up now. But she couldn't wait any longer. She
had to know the truth. "Is everything all right between
us?" His frown deepened, and that wasn't the answer
she was hoping for.

"Of course it is," he finally said, not looking at her
directly.

She pulled away from him. She knew it. She'd felt that
something had been off for a while now. They spent
time together, but he seemed distant. Right now he
seemed miles away, and she didn't know how to reach
him. And Leanna said she should propose. Karen nearly
scoffed out loud. How could she propose to a man who

was having second thoughts about their relationship? She started to rise. "I'm sorry I brought this up."

"Karen—"

"I should *geh* check on Phoebe. She might need something—"

He took her hand and gave it a firm tug. "Patience is taking care of her, and Jalon is right there." He looked up at her. "Tell me what's wrong."

After a pause she knelt in front of him. "Why haven't you asked me to marry you?" Nothing like being straight-forward. Leanna would be impressed.

He swallowed, hard enough that she could see it. "I'm . . . I'm not ready."

"Why not?"

"Do you really have to ask that?" His eyes grew stormy as his voice turned sharp. "Look at us, Karen. You have to kneel in front of me for us to talk face-to-face."

"That's not the only way." She moved to sit in his lap, but he held her from him.

When he didn't speak, she reached out and touched his face, angling it toward her. "Don't shut me out, Adam. Not now."

"I didn't realize I was shutting you out." Then he sighed. "That's not true. I have been shutting you out. Because that's easier than facing reality."

"Reality? I don't understand."

"Reality is this chair." He hit one wheel with a fist. "Reality is the fact that when I'm in a crowd, I can barely see above people's belt lines. Reality is being stared at by everyone, no matter who they are or how discreet they think they are."

Her heart wrenched. He'd never been this candid about his disability. It wasn't the elephant in the room, but he had such confidence and inner strength that she didn't think about it most of the time. He owned his own business, and as far as she knew, he accepted his paralysis. He was an amazing man, one she loved from the bottom of her heart. "I'm glad you're telling me this," she said. "I want us to share everything. Not just the fun times we've had together, or the good fortune God has blessed us with. I want you to talk to me about what's in *yer* heart." She placed her hand over his chest. "I want to know what you're afraid of."

"You're not afraid of marriage at all?"

She paused. "I would be lying if I said I wasn't." She stood and moved to his chair. If he could admit his fear, she could admit hers. "I'm afraid I won't be the wife you want."

"Karen . . ." He took her hand, a look of true pain on his face. "You're everything I've ever wanted. If anything, I'm the one who isn't . . ."

"Isn't what?"

"Isn't what you deserve."

A tear slipped down her cheek. How could he think that? He was the perfect man for her. "So we have the same fear."

"*Yer* fear is unfounded," he said. "Mine isn't. What if you decided you were tired of taking care of a *mann* in a wheelchair?" The words spilled out of him in a bitter cascade.

"Adam, that's what I want." She touched his face again. She loved to touch him, to be near him. "I want to take care of you . . . and to have you take care of me. A partnership. That's what marriage is supposed to be."

He looked away, her hand still on his cheek. "It would be uneven in our case."

She withdrew her hand. "What if the situation were reversed? Or what if I became sick, or hurt? Would you walk away from me?"

He quickly faced her. "*Nee* . . . never. I'd be there right by *yer* side. Where I belong."

"*Ya,*" she said softly. "Where you belong."

"I love you," he said, his voice turning thick. "*Nee* matter what happened, I would love you."

"Then why would you doubt *mei* love for you?" She leaned forward until her mouth was near his. "Why would you believe that what I feel for you is less than what you feel for me?"

He brushed the tears that streamed down her cheeks. "I'm sorry," he whispered. "That wasn't what I meant." He pulled her into his chair and buried his face in her neck. "I'm so sorry."

She hugged him, filled with love, and relief that they had talked this out.

"I love you," he said against her skin. Then he moved his face and kissed her softly on the mouth. "I love you so much."

"I know." She smiled, running her hand over his chin, imagining what it would look like with a marriage beard. "Now that we have all that behind us, can I ask you one more question?"

He nodded. "Anything."

"Will you marry me?"

His eyebrows shot up. "You're proposing?"

"Absolutely. Is there any reason I shouldn't?"

Adam shook his head. "I can't think of a single one." His arm tightened around her waist as he kissed her again, more deeply this time. "And *mei* answer," he said when he pulled away, "is *ya*."

. . .

Roman watched as Leanna played a rousing game of tag with the boys in the backyard. They were at the far end of the yard, far enough from the house that they couldn't hear Phoebe. The game was working as a good distraction, and Roman surmised from the worried glances Leanna cast at the house in between chasing and being chased that it was a good distraction for her too. Her father was taking care of the animals so Jalon and Adam could be inside. Roman had offered to help, but he said he had it under control. One of the Bontrager boys—Perry, Roman thought his name was—had gone inside for a few flashlights, considering it was now dark outside.

He noticed that Malachi was sitting on the sidelines in the shadows. He went over and sat next to him. "Don't you want to play?" he asked the boy.

Malachi turned his flashlight on and off. He shook his head and looked at the house.

"She's going to be okay," Roman said. "Women have *boppli* all the time."

"She looked like she was hurt."

"Well, having a *boppli* hurts." There was no use in

lying to the child. "But after the *boppli*'s born it's okay. She was fine after having you."

Malachi nodded, but Roman's words didn't seem to alleviate his worry. Roman wasn't sure what to say next, since he had no idea how to deal with kids. He'd never been around them, other than the kids in their district. And he'd never interacted with them. Never noticed them, really. Kids and marriage and family had never been on his radar—just his designs, dreams, and future plans.

"Get back here, Jesse." Leanna chased after the boy, who was squealing with laughter. "The tickle monster is coming after you!"

"Nee!" The younger boys ran around in circles while the older ones, who looked to be between about nine and twelve, had stopped playing tag. They'd found a volleyball and were throwing it back and forth with headlights strapped on so they could see while keeping their hands free. They still missed a lot more than they caught, yet none of them seemed eager to go inside their own house. They seemed to know they were all out here to keep Malachi distracted.

Roman leaned over to Malachi. "Do you want to play catch?"

Malachi shook his head, but Roman wasn't going to take no for an answer. He took the boy's hand. "Come on. I'll show you another game."

Malachi followed him, his hand limply in Roman's as Roman approached the boys. He took the flashlight from Malachi and pointed it at the volleyball. It would have to do in a pinch. "Do you know how to play soccer?" he asked.

"A little," one said.

"We don't play it much," another one said.

"The rules are too complicated," the third one said.

"That's because you don't know them," Perry said.

Heading the argument off before it started, Roman held up his hand. "We'll play a modified game." He took the ball and divided the boys into two teams. By the time he was done, Leanna and the younger boys had joined them. "Can we play?" one of them asked.

"Sure," Leanna answered before Roman could say anything. Then she looked at him, the light from her headlamp shining a bit in his face before she lifted her head. "What are we playing?"

Fifteen minutes later, the boys, plus Roman and Leanna, were chasing the ball around the yard—and having a ball doing it. The younger ones were uncoordinated, and it was nice to see how the older ones helped them or even let them score when it was clear they could steal the ball away from them. Even in the dark they managed to have a fairly decent game. Then Leanna got the ball, and she was off.

"*Geh* get her, Roman!" Malachi called out.

Roman turned to see one of the boys offering his headlamp. He slipped it on, and ignoring the fact it was tight since it was adjusted for a child's head, he took off after Leanna. Wow, she was fast. So fast that he had to run at his top speed to reach her as she sped across the Chupps' yard and into the Bontragers' yard. She kept looking over her shoulder and laughing at him, which spurred him on even more. Once she'd rounded the corner and disappeared on the side of the house, he stopped, reversed gears, and circled to the other side of the house, running at full speed.

Suddenly he slammed right into her, and they both fell to the ground. Roman lay on his back, gasping for breath, and he could have sworn he saw stars.

In the distance he heard the boys running, and he managed to get himself up on his elbows. But Leanna was on her side, not moving. He scrambled up and went to her. He slipped off her headlamp and shined it on her. A goose egg was already forming on the side of her forehead, and her eyes were still closed. Why would she have a bump on her head? He glanced around and saw they were near the flower bed, which was bordered by large stones. His stomach dropped to his knees. "Wow, that was a crash," Judah said as he reached them.

"I think she hit her head on one of those rocks," another one of them said.

"Get back." Roman waved the boys off as he gathered Leanna into his arms. Was she unconscious? Another bad sign. "Leanna," he said, but she didn't move.

"I'll *geh* get *Daed*." One of the Bontrager boys took off for the house.

Roman looked up and saw Malachi, the worried expression on his face. This was the last thing the boy needed to see. "Can you *geh* in *yer grossmammi*'s *haus* and get *yer aenti* a glass of water?" he asked.

"*Ya*."

"The rest of you *buwe*, *geh* with him." Seeming to be able to grasp the situation, they followed Malachi.

Roman brought Leanna closer to him. "Come on," he said, whispering in her ear. "Wake up."

A second later her eyes fluttered opened. "What . . . happened?"

He was so relieved he pulled her to his chest. "Thank God. I was worried you weren't going to wake up."

"Romanff?" she said, her face pressed against his chest, her voice muffled in his shirt. "I can't breaffe."

He pulled her away. "I'm sorry." The bump on her head was alarming. "How many fingers am I holding up?"

"I have *nee* idea because it's dark." She brought her hand to her forehead and gingerly touched the bump there. "Ugh. That's going to give me a headache." She started to move out of his arms but he wouldn't let her go. Not yet. Not until he was sure she was okay.

"I got the water!"

Roman jerked up his head and saw several flashlights bobbing toward him. As they neared, he saw that Malachi was rushing toward them, water sloshing out of a cup. The other boys were right behind him.

Leanna moved out of his arms and to a seated position. She winced, but then smiled as Malachi gave her the cup. She took a sip. "That hit the spot."

"You've got a big bump on *yer* head," Malachi said, shining a flashlight in her eyes.

She squeezed her eyes shut. "I know. Impressive, isn't it? You can put the flashlight down now, Malachi." Before he did, Roman caught her grin—and the pain in her eyes. "But more important—did Roman get the ball?"

"Nope," the boys said in unison.

"Then we won!" She put her hand up for a few high fives, then let it weakly fall.

Two more flashlights headed toward them. It was Phoebe's father and Judah. Malachi and his uncles quickly and confusingly filled Thomas in on what had happened. Once he heard the fractured story, he said, "Get some ice on that, Leanna. I've got some in the *haus*." He turned to Roman. "Can you take her inside and get it for her?" Then he grinned. "I've got a grandbaby to meet."

"Phoebe had her *boppli*?" Leanna asked.

"*Ya*. Karen came over and told me right as Judah showed up." He shook his head. "Been an exciting day around here. *Buwe*, you come with me." He looked at Leanna. "Mary Yoder said she'd take them to her *haus* while Malachi and I spend some time with his new *schwester*. And my wife should be back any moment."

"Phoebe had a *maed*?" Leanna said, a dreamy look in her eyes.

"*Ya*." Phoebe's father's lower lip quivered. "We've got another *maed* in the *familye*."

The boys and Phoebe's father left. Roman got to his feet and offered to help Leanna to hers. He could see the shadow of her waving him off, but when she wavered a little bit, he put his arm around her slim waist and helped her to Thomas's house.

"I'm fine," she said as he guided her to the kitchen.

"I know. You still need to get the swelling down." He found the gas lamp and turned it on, then spied a large gas-powered refrigerator in the kitchen. Again he was reminded how such an appliance would never be allowed in his former district. Apparently that wasn't a rule here. He opened the left door and saw a bin of ice, with several ice trays stacked next to it.

"I think the kitchen towels are in that drawer," Leanna said, pointing to one of the cabinet drawers.

He nodded, closed the fridge, and got a towel. He should have thought about a towel first. Then he put the ice in the towel and took it to her. She took it from him and pressed it against her head, wincing. "What happened, exactly?"

"I thought I'd surprise you and catch you on the other side," he said, sitting down beside her. "Guess we surprised each other."

She pulled the ice away, wincing again, looking tired.

"Here." He scooted closer to her and took the ice pack from her. Then he pressed it against the bump. "Does that hurt?"

"*Nee.* Other than the headache, that is."

"I'll find you some aspirin in a minute." He held the pack against her head, and there was nowhere to look but directly in her face. It was thin, angular, and sharp, at least at first glance. But now he was also familiar with its softness. He smoothed one of her eyebrows with the tip of his finger. What was it about this woman that he couldn't keep his hands off her?

"Something wrong with *mei* eyebrow?" she asked.

"*Nee,*" he said, dropping all pretense. "It's perfect." He heard her breath catch, which made him smile. Then he saw her face turn pink. "Sorry. I didn't mean to embarrass you."

"I'm not embarrassed." Her eyes flitted to the side. "I'm just not . . ."

"Not what?" He moved the ice pack, looked at the bump, and then returned the pack.

"Not used to compliments."

He scoffed. "You get complimented all the time. I've heard people rave about *yer* work, including Daniel."

"Not those kind of compliments." Her skin went from pink to crimson, flushing from her neck all the way to her cheeks. Then she met his eyes. "I don't have people exactly raving about *mei* looks."

He nodded. "They don't rave about mine, either."

"I find that hard to believe."

Now it was his turn to become flushed, not because of her words, but the way she was looking at him, as if drinking in his face. "How did you get this scar?" she said, pointing to the one underneath his earlobe.

"Doing something stupid. Although in *mei* defense, I was three years old. I don't even remember it. I somehow got ahold of one of *mei daed*'s pocket knives. Daniel tried to take it away from me, and I wouldn't let him have it. When I pulled back, the blade nicked *mei* ear." He sobered. "Daniel got into a lot of trouble for that."

"It wasn't his fault." Leanna frowned. "*Yer* father shouldn't have left his tools out."

"True. But even at five, Daniel was supposed to be watching me." He looked beyond Leanna. "He was always looking out for me when we were little. At that time it was the two of us against . . ." He shook his head and checked the bump again. "I think the ice is helping."

"The two of you against *yer* parents?" Leanna said.

"It only seemed that way. Then *mei grossmammi* moved in and things were better for a while." He started to move away from her. "I'll get fresh ice."

But she took the ice pack from him and set it on the table. "I'm sorry," she said, her voice the softest he'd ever heard it.

"For what?"

"For what you had to *geh* through as a *kind*."

He scoffed. "Other kids had it a lot worse. Like I said, *mei grossmammi* loved us."

"But *yer* parents didn't."

"*Mei* parents did the best they could."

"I don't think it was enough."

He swallowed the lump in his throat. "It had to be. They couldn't . . . They can't give any more." He tried to smile. "We have our differences, but Daniel is a *gut mann*. I think I took that for granted growing up . . . and even recently. Mostly because I was too focused on myself. I'm always too focused on myself." He mumbled that last part, and he was glad Leanna didn't seem to hear him. "Anyway, I'm glad Daniel found Barbara. And I know when they have kids, he'll be a *gut* and loving father."

Leanna's eyes clouded and a frown covered her face, which alarmed him. "Are you okay? You're not dizzy or anything."

"*Nee*. I'm fine." The look cleared and she gave him a half-smile. "You keep surprising me, Roman Raber. Here I thought you were a coldhearted guy. Who knew you had marshmallow insides?"

"More like stone."

"I don't believe that," she said. "I think God is already working on *yer* heart." She opened her mouth as if to say something else, but then closed it.

"Speechless again? This must be a record for you—"

She put her hand on the back of his head, brought his mouth to hers, and kissed him.

CHAPTER 14

Leanna had no idea what possessed her to kiss Roman, but now that she was, she couldn't stop. She didn't know anything about technique or if she was even doing it right, but the fluttery feeling in her stomach reached all the way down to her toes. Also, he wasn't pulling away. In fact, he was drawing her closer to him, his other hand on her waist. She rubbed her fingers against his short hair in the back, feeling the beginnings of curls there as it was already growing out from his Yankee cut.

So this was why her friends had giggled about meeting with boys behind the school building, or why levelheaded people would do strange things to get the attention of those they were interested in. This was what excitement truly was. This was . . .

Love?

She pulled away, her mouth still open, her eyes feeling as though they were going to jump off her face. Then she put her fingertips to her lips. "I . . . I . . ." She couldn't think of what to say, not with him looking at her like . . . like he never wanted to stop.

Then she came to her senses. She had just kissed

Roman in her sister-in-law's parents' kitchen. She put her hand to her mouth. "This is wrong."

The dazed look in his eyes cleared. "Wrong?"

"I don't *geh* around kissing men," she said, still trying to grasp the fact that she was the one who instigated the kiss and that she wanted to kiss him some more, enough that her heart was telling her mouth to shut up and pucker up. Good grief, she was hopeless.

"I could tell," he said.

That brought her up short. "Are you saying I'm a bad kisser?"

His look grew sly, which up until now wasn't a word she would have used to describe Roman, but it was the only one that fit him at the moment. "Would I have kept kissing you if you were?"

That made her smile. So even with zero experience she was good. That was gratifying to know. Then she shook her head. She didn't need those kinds of thoughts clouding the issue. "What I'm trying to say is that I'm not that kind of *maed*."

"I know." His expression grew serious. "And I'm not that kind of guy. What I'm saying is that for a first kiss, it was *gut*."

"How do you know?"

"Because I enjoyed it." The sly look slipped from his face. "And if you want to know if it's *mei* first kiss, it is. Hope that satisfied *yer* curiosity."

It did.

His arms quickly slipped from her waist and he sat back in his chair. They stared at each other for a long moment. When he looked away, the awkwardness that hadn't been between them for a long time returned. Did he regret kissing her? Was he upset that she was his first kiss? Was he wishing they had never locked lips?

"It's okay," she said, jumping up. She laughed, trying to sound cool and collected, but it came out more like a shrieking cat. She grabbed the towel. "I got hit in the head, after all. I lost *mei* senses. I might even have a concussion." The room started to spin a little. Oh *nee*. "I'm not responsible for *mei* actions . . ."

He was right there to catch her, his strong arm around her waist, his eyes holding hers. Now that they were standing, if she kissed him again she'd have to bend her face down a bit because of their height difference. She didn't mind that at all. What she did mind was the frown on his face. Maybe he didn't want to be this close to her anymore.

But he didn't let her go. "Feeling dizzy?" he asked, his brow furrowed with concern.

"A little. I got up too fast."

He took the ice pack from her and set it on the table. "I'm walking you back home." When she started to protest, he took her hand and shook his head, his look so intense that she nodded and followed him, pushing aside the doubts bouncing off each other in her mind.

"I'm usually not this clumsy," she said. "I don't fall when I skate, I never miss when I skip stones . . ." She touched the scratches on her neck. "Blue's never done this before." She started to frown. "And I've never slammed into someone while playing soccer."

"Seems this is an evening of firsts, then." He smiled. "You don't have to explain *yerself* to me. You've had a bad day—"

"More than one lately," she said, on a sigh.

"Come on. Let me walk you home."

When they got to her house, her head was really throbbing. Before they reached the front door, she glanced at Jalon's house. The lights were on in almost every room, and she suddenly noticed the noise and laughter coming through the screened-in windows. "I can't believe I forgot about *mei* new niece!" She let go of Roman's hand and started for Jalon's.

"Leanna, slow down—"

But she ignored him as she walked through the back door and straight to the living room, ignoring the pain in her head. She'd lie down later. Right now she wanted to meet her niece.

Phoebe was sitting on the couch, Jalon seated on the floor by her side, holding the baby. He couldn't take his eyes off his daughter, and a lump formed in Leanna's throat.

Karen came up beside her. "They're getting ready to *geh* to the bedroom," she said. "Patience wanted to give Phoebe some time to recover before she got up. Everything went well. The *boppli* is perfect."

"She definitely is." She walked toward Jalon and knelt beside him. "What's her name?"

"Hannah," he said. Then he looked at her and frowned. "What happened to you?"

"*Nix.*" She looked at Hannah, and she was indeed perfect.

"Okay, parents and *boppli* to the bedroom," Patience said. "Let's give them some time together. There will be plenty of time to spend with Hannah later."

Leanna stood, and in the corner she saw Karen and Adam holding hands. They both looked different, and when Karen looked down at Adam, and Leanna saw his smile, she knew they were finally engaged. The thought made her turn and look for Roman. She found him, hidden in the shadows. She went to him and saw there were tears in his eyes. "What's wrong?" she said.

"Hannah." He swallowed. "That was *mei grossmammi's* name."

. . .

Barbara brought a bowl of chicken noodle soup to Daniel's bedside. "I thought you would be hungry since you didn't eat supper."

He took the bowl from her and took a sip, but then set the bowl aside. "The pain meds," he said. "I don't have much appetite when I'm on them."

"Hopefully you'll be off of them soon." She smiled, even though it was a strain. She was trying to keep up good spirits, but it was getting harder. Not only was it difficult to see Daniel like this, but keeping the secret about their baby was tearing her apart.

"And then I can get back to work." He patted the empty space beside him. "You look tired. Why don't you get some sleep?"

"I don't want to bump *yer* legs or disturb *yer* bandages."

"You won't."

"I'll sleep on the couch." She put her hand on her abdomen. There was nothing there, and nothing would be brought forth from there. The nurse in the hospital suggested she see a doctor about the miscarriages, but Barbara knew she wouldn't. She couldn't bear to hear the news that she would never have a child, even though she was beginning to believe that in her heart. The story of Sarah in the Bible had always given her hope. But she wasn't Sarah. She was an ordinary woman who was barren.

"Barbara?"

She turned to Daniel and hid her turmoil. "Can I get you anything else?"

"Lie next to me."

She couldn't bring herself to move. "Tomorrow night," she said, getting up from the side of the bed. "I will tomorrow night." She ignored the sorrowful look on his face and left the bedroom.

She cleaned the kitchen and was almost finished when Roman walked in. "Sorry I've been gone so long," he said.

She hadn't seen him all evening, but that wasn't unexpected. When he lived with them before, he would disappear and return without apologizing. Daniel thought it was rude, and he was angry whenever it happened. Yet Barbara tried to see Roman's side. More than once Daniel was going to say something to him, to demand Roman show her respect. But Roman did, in his own way. He often helped with the dishes, and sometimes he even helped cook. Now he was outwardly showing her respect, and she was glad to see the change.

"It's okay," she told him. "You don't have to apologize."

"*Ya*, I do," he said seriously. Then he added, "Phoebe Chupp had her *boppli* tonight."

Pain stabbed at her anew. "That's … that's wonderful."

"*Ya*." Roman smiled. "A little *maed*. One who will be completely spoiled, considering she's surrounded by her *bruder* and so many male *onkles*."

"I'm happy for her." She pulled deep within her and smiled, facing Roman. "She's doing well, then?"

"*Ya*."

"What's the *boppli*'s name?"

"Hannah."

This time Barbara's smile was genuine. "That's a lovely coincidence."

"I thought so. A reminder of the circle of life." He paused. "How's Daniel?"

"Better. He's resting right now."

Roman nodded. "I'll get upstairs, then. *Gute nacht*, Barbara."

"*Gute nacht*." Then she remembered something. "A letter came for you today. I put it on *yer* dresser upstairs."

He looked surprised and nodded again. "*Danki*. I'll see you in the morning."

After Roman disappeared upstairs, Barbara sat down at the kitchen table. All around her were reminders of what she'd lost, and what she'd never have. Everything collapsed inside her, and she held her head in her hands and sobbed.

. . .

Roman picked up the envelope and glanced at the return address. It was from Matt, which surprised him a little. He hadn't expected to hear from him. Then again, now that he understood the concept of friendship, maybe he shouldn't be surprised. Matt had given him a home when he needed one, had hung out with him when he was alone, and had offered to help him when his grandmother died. Roman hadn't appreciated him enough. As he ripped open the envelope, he went and sat down on his bed. His eyes widened when he saw another envelope inside, along with a yellow sticky note in Matt's handwriting.

Got this today. Thought you might want to look at it. Matt.

He hadn't given Matt his brother's address, so Matt had to have taken the extra step to find it. He understood why when he saw where the letter was from. Dupree State University. Figuring they wanted to know why he hadn't registered for classes this semester, he haphazardly opened the envelope and scanned the letter.

Dear Mr. Raber,

I'm sorry you're receiving this letter on such late notice, but your application just came across my desk. My secretary insisted I look at it. Normally we don't receive letters from students requesting entry into our program. Everything is done online these days, and I see you have already been accepted. But after reviewing your application and the ideas and designs you submitted, in addition to your ACT and SAT scores, I'm pleased to tell you that you've been awarded a

grant for full tuition for this academic school year.
This is a new grant program that seeks to help bright,
innovative students achieve success in the field of
engineering.

I see that you haven't registered for the fall semester. My hope is that this grant will encourage you to do
so. We want you to be a part of our program, Mr. Raber.
Congratulations, and feel free to contact me personally
if you have any questions.

Sincerely,
Richard B. Hawkins
Dean, College of Engineering
and Applied Science

Roman's mouth dropped open. Dupree State was
offering him a grant? A full-tuition grant? It wouldn't
cover all his expenses, and he'd still have to get a job
and find a place to live. But now going to college was
doable, more doable than it had been two weeks ago.

He set the letter aside, his foot tapping on the floor.
He'd thought this door had been mostly shut, although
there had always been the chance that he'd receive government financial aid. But now he wouldn't have to
apply for that. He could go to college. He could get his
degree, and he would fulfill his dream. He wouldn't
even have to worry about leaving Daniel in that much
of a bind, since Leanna was now working for him again.

His foot stilled. Daniel. Was there really any chance
for reconciliation, especially now? Even when he physically couldn't do his job, Daniel still wouldn't accept
Roman's help. What hope was there that his brother

would ever truly forgive him? And even if he did, could they possibly have a normal relationship? Roman wasn't sure.

He stood from the bed and walked to the window, looking out into the black night. He should be thinking about his future, now that this opportunity had opened up. A random one that never would have happened if he hadn't taken the unorthodox step of sending Dean Hawkins an actual letter, along with a few sketches. And if he hadn't done that, the secretary wouldn't have passed along his letter to the dean. And if the department hadn't had a new grant program in place, Roman wouldn't have been offered tuition money. So many coincidences . . .

Or was it God's plan?

Yes, he should have been thinking about all of that. Instead Daniel was on his mind. And Barbara, and Leanna, and Malachi and the Bontrager boys . . . even baby Hannah. For the first time he felt as though he was a part of something, not standing on the outside trying not to look in. He was experiencing friendship, and in Leanna's case, something more. He remembered her kiss, the softness of her lips, the shock and then pleasure he felt holding her in his arms as they both experienced something so important, and so wonderful, for the first time. Could he walk away from that? From everything?

Roman turned and glanced at the bed. The letter lay open, the gateway to a future he'd been chasing for nearly a year. All he had to do was make a phone call to the dean and he was set. Once again a choice lay in front of him. But it wasn't as difficult as the one he'd faced when his grandmother died. In fact, this decision was an easy one.

He picked up the letter again and put it in his pocket. Tomorrow he would be stepping into his future, and this time he wasn't turning back.

. . .

Dear Ivy,

I really, really, really wish you were here right now. I have so much to tell you, and I don't want to have to do it in a letter. But I'm about to burst if I don't tell someone, and you're the only one I trust. Plus, I know you're the only one who will understand.

First things first—I have a niece. She's so cute, just a tiny thing. But, boy, can she cry! Malachi's already complaining about her wailing, although he's a doting older brother. Jalon, of course, can't get enough of her. It's only been two days, but Phoebe's already talking about getting on her feet and making breakfast in the morning, but I won't let her. In fact, I'm closing my shop tomorrow so I can help out there, giving some of the other women who've been helping a break. Don't worry, I'm not cooking. The men will have cereal in the morning, and they will like it.

Speaking of my shop, I didn't tell you—I have a shop. I didn't dare call it that at first, but it really is becoming a place where I'm feeling comfortable. I miss working with Daniel, but I like having my own shop. I know it will end once Daniel gets back on his feet, which knowing Daniel will be sooner than later. I know Roman and Barbara want him to wait until he's fully recovered, but he's stubborn. I'm staying out of it, except to make sure I do as much work as I can. Except for tomorrow, of course. I'm needed here at home, and surprisingly, I'm looking forward to doing some domestic stuff. It's really not that horrible—at least not that much.

You know what else isn't horrible? Kissing. How do I know? Because I actually kissed Roman Raber. You remember him? He's Daniel's brother, and I used to complain about him when he worked with us last year. He came back to Birch Creek two weeks ago, and I wasn't happy about that. He's cold and aloof and lazy. At least I thought he was. He's changed. I'm learning some things about his past that I didn't know, which makes me feel bad for jumping to conclusions about him. He really is here to help out Daniel, and he works just as hard as Daniel does, sometimes harder since he's not naturally gifted at working with machines. He's the one who fixed up the shed so I can work there. He really is brilliant, and I had no idea.

I also don't have any idea how I feel about him. I always said I couldn't imagine liking a man enough to kiss him. But I hit my head and . . . Well, that's a long story and I'll tell you about that when you get back, but I think I had a concussion because why else would I kiss him? Even more confusing was that I liked it, and he liked it too. Ugh, I feel like I'm acting like a twelve-year-old about this. This is why relationships are such a bother. I don't like feeling like this, but I have to admit that when we kissed it felt . . . good. More than good. See why I'm confused?

Don't worry, I'm not going to marry him or anything. We haven't even gone on a date. We're just friends. Friends who shared a kiss. That happens, right?

Leanna balled up the letter and threw it into the trash. She felt stupid even writing this stuff down. Leanna trusted Ivy with everything. But this seemed too personal . . . and too embarrassing, mostly because she sounded like a preteen talking about her first crush. How many times had the two of them secretly laughed at their friends' foolish behavior when they were talking about the boys they had crushes on? Or how friendships went by the wayside once they were so involved in their relationships? Leanna and Ivy had each other, and they both had always been fine with that.

So what did that mean for her and Roman? What was going on with her and Roman, anyway? She couldn't believe she actually kissed him two days ago—and liked it. That wasn't in her plan, ever. Especially with him.

She flopped onto her bed and stared at the ceiling. Ivy wasn't due to come back home for another month, and any plans Leanna had to go visit her in Michigan had been scratched because of the work she was doing for Daniel. She really needed her best friend's wisdom right now. She closed her eyes. *Lord, help me out here. What am I supposed to do about Roman?*

Her eyes flew open. She felt silly for even asking God for help for something like this. But she really was confused, and she couldn't forget the way he looked at her with such concern when she bumped her head. Or how she felt the bristles of his five o'clock shadow when she kissed him. Or the way he said he liked the kiss. Or—

She heard a knock on the front door and sat up, shoving aside her thoughts. She bounced up and went to answer the door. "Barbara?"

Barbara stood there, wringing her hands. She looked tired. Exhausted, actually. "Daniel doesn't know I'm here," she said. "I don't want him to know."

"I won't tell him." Leanna opened the door and let her in. She turned to Barbara, her surprise changing to shock when she noticed the dark circles beneath her eyes. "Do you want anything?" she said. "I don't have much. Just, um, two boiled eggs. Maybe some orange juice, but that might be from last month. I really should clean out *mei* fridge. But I could make *kaffee*, or tea."

Barbara shook her head. *"Nee."* She was still wringing her hands. "Can I just sit down for a little while?"

"Of course." Leanna led her to the couch in the living room. Barbara didn't so much sit but sink into it. Leanna perched on the edge and waited for her friend to say something.

After a long moment, Barbara said, "I finally stopped bleeding from the miscarriage."

Leanna nodded, her heart breaking for her friend. She thought about Phoebe and baby Hannah, and how special the miracle of birth was. She hadn't been there to see the actual delivery, but holding Hannah in her arms when she was only hours old had turned her insides to mush. It wasn't fair that Barbara was robbed of the chance to experience motherhood, not once, but twice.

Barbara stared at the wall in front of her. "I want to be happy for Phoebe. I'm trying to be. But I've had six miscarriages in three years. I'm so tired of losing babies." Tears streamed down her face. "How can I tell Daniel? He doesn't even know I lost this one. And what if I can never have a child?"

"We'll just have to pray and believe something different. God can do anything."

"I know. But what if he chooses not to?" Her voice was small. "What if he says *nee*?"

Leanna opened her mouth, only to close it. What could she say? A few scriptures came to mind, along with some prayers, but it didn't seem enough right now. She moved closer to Barbara and took her hand again. "Whatever the answer is, God will give you the strength to accept it."

"I wish I could believe that. I want to believe it."

"You can. And whenever you doubt, remember that you're not alone. Daniel will be by *yer* side. You will face this together. And, of course, I'll be here." She managed a smile. "I'm not going anywhere."

Barbara nodded, but Leanna could see that her words hadn't sunk in. "You always see the positive side of things," she said. "I hope you never lose *yer* optimism."

"You can borrow some of it," Leanna said. "I have plenty to *geh* around."

That made Barbara smile slightly. "You're a *gut* friend," she said on a yawn. "And a wise one." She leaned against the back of the couch and closed her eyes. "I'm so tired," she said.

"Then rest." Leanna went to her bedroom and got a pillow and a quilt from her bed. She put the pillow at the end of the couch. "Lie down. Take a nap, and then you can *geh* home. How did you get here, anyway?"

"I walked."

"You're not walking back home, that's for sure."

Barbara lay down and shut her eyes. She gave Leanna a brief nod, and Leanna put the quilt over her shoulders. By the time she straightened, Barbara was asleep.

Leanna went outside and sat down on the steps of her small front stoop. She looked up at the sky, prayed for Barbara and Daniel, and then closed her eyes and felt tears squeezing from them. Her heart was breaking for her friends. "Ugh," she said, her fists clenching, thinking about Tabitha and Melva. "People can be so stupid sometimes." She needed to forgive them, but it was hard, especially when she saw her friends suffering. There was nothing else she could do to help them. She could only pray.

. . .

Daniel eased himself out of bed, grimacing as he put his feet on the floor. The pain wasn't as bad as it was at first. That had been excruciating. The doctor kept telling him how lucky he was that his burns weren't "that bad" and that he would heal fairly quickly. Daniel hoped so. It had been a week, and he had to regain control of his shop—and his life. He'd been in bed too long.

His fists clenched at his sides. The last thing he'd wanted was to put Barbara through any stress. The second last thing was for Roman to work on jobs. It was Daniel's responsibility to fulfill those repairs. Not Roman's. He hadn't wanted his brother to see how far behind he was on the orders. Now Roman probably knew everything. He knew how much Daniel had let people down, and now he'd let down his wife. His brother was witnessing Daniel's failure, and it was tearing him up inside.

The fact that he should be grateful wasn't lost on him. Roman was saving his business, or at least making sure it wasn't going under any further. But just the sight of his younger brother made him angry and resentful, even more than he'd been when Roman first arrived. In fact, he was filled with anger almost all the time now. In the hospital he'd been inundated with pain, not just physical but emotional. Through the haze of medication the past came back, haunting him, reminding him that no matter what he did, how responsible he was, how much he tried to look out after Roman, his parents didn't care. Worse, they didn't seem to notice. The only time his father had come close to being upset was when Roman cut himself with a knife when he was three. Daniel had gotten a talking to, but that was it. He'd been relieved, actually, to see that his father could express some kind of emotion. But that had happened once. Even at his grandmother's funeral, he hadn't seen his father or mother shed a tear.

He carefully stood and pulled on a robe. His legs were still swollen from the burns, but the swelling had subsided enough that he'd been able to walk more the past couple of days. After a trip to the bathroom he headed for the living room. He needed to convince Barbara to sleep in their bed. She'd slept in an uncomfortable chair the entire time he was in the hospital, and he couldn't stand the thought of her sleeping on the couch again the way she had the past two nights. More important, he needed her by his side. He'd missed her soft breathing beside him as she slept, her warm body against his, the way she reached for his hand in her sleep. He didn't believe her excuse that she didn't want to disturb him. She was angry with him. He could tell, even though she was doing everything she could to hide it.

Could he blame her, though? He'd made a huge mistake—more than one lately—and she was paying for it too.

When he didn't see her in the living room, he assumed she was in the kitchen since the light was on. As he entered, he saw Roman at the table, his journal open. He was reading a letter, and Daniel didn't have to guess who it was from. A stack of them were beside the journal, wrapped in a rubber band. Daniel had his own stack tucked away in his dresser drawer. This wasn't the first time he'd seen Roman rereading their grandmother's letters over the years. As for Daniel, he'd only read his own letters once and then put them away. His grandmother was caring and had been the only source of love and affection he'd had growing up, but he didn't need her letters as a crutch.

When he saw Roman's small smile as he continued to read, however, Daniel felt a tug in his heart. Had she written something different to his brother? Something more special? A familiar thread of envy wound through him. Roman always thought he was the outsider in the family. He seemed to have no idea their grandmother favored him.

Daniel was about to leave when Roman looked up.

He tucked the letter back into the pile and gathered them up along with his journal. "I'll *geh*," he said, moving to stand up.

"Stay. I'll *geh* back to *mei* room."

"Is Barbara back?"

Daniel paused. "Did she leave?"

"*Ya.* A couple of hours ago." Roman frowned. "She said she needed to take a walk."

"And you didn't *geh* with her?"

"Why would I do that? She wanted some time to think." He set down the journal. "Surely she's back somewhere on the property by now."

Panic stabbed at Daniel. Unlike Roman, Barbara didn't take walks at night. "I've got to find her." He started for the back door but Roman stepped in his path. "Move!" Daniel said.

But Roman stayed in place. "Daniel, you're not even dressed. I'll look outside. It's dark, but—"

"And that's why we have to find her!" Daniel's gaze went hazy with panic. "What if she's missing?"

Roman put his hands on Daniel's shoulders. "She's not missing. She probably stopped off somewhere to visit. Where does she usually *geh* when she takes walks?"

"That's just it. She never takes long walks. She always likes to stick around home, and it's already dark." Or was it that he never let her take a long walk, at least without him. He shook his head. "She's in trouble. I know it."

"Daniel, calm down. We'll find her. I'll *geh* outside and search for her."

"And what am I supposed to do? Wait here and do nothing?"

"*Ya.* Let me help you for once. You don't want to make things worse."

Daniel lifted his hand, ready to push Roman out of the way and throw on some clothes and boots.

Roman stopped him. "You can trust me," he said.

Daniel shook his head. "*Nee,* I can't. I've never been able to rely on you. You don't follow through on *yer* word. You never have."

"I will tonight. I know how important Barbara is to you. She's also important to me." To Daniel's surprise, Roman's eyes filled with tears. "Besides you, she's the only *familye* I have."

Daniel took a step back, Roman's words soaking in. Roman was right. Now that their grandmother was gone, they had only each other, and Barbara. Yes, their parents were alive, but they were never truly parents, just the people who gave birth to them and made sure they didn't starve or live on the streets.

"Please, Daniel. I was so scared when you had the accident. I know we don't get along, and I'm not sure we ever will." He paused, his bottom lip trembling. "But I love you, *bruder.* And despite everything, we have to stick together. So let me help you. I'll find Barbara and bring her back."

Daniel's legs felt weak and he reached for the chair behind him. Roman grabbed it and pulled it out for him. Daniel looked up at him. He'd never seen his brother so filled with emotion. Raw emotion that neither one of them would have dared to show growing up. "Hurry," he said, his throat constricting with worry.

"I will." Roman went to the back door and opened it,

but then turned around. "I'll take a quick look outside, but . . . are you sure you have *nee* idea where she might have gone?"

He shook his head and then paused. "Leanna's. They've grown close since Leanna started working here. Try there first."

A flash of something went across Roman's face, and then he nodded and dashed out the door.

Daniel put his head in his hands, tears streaming down his face. *Please, God. Let* mei *wife be okay. She's everything to me.*

CHAPTER 15

Roman had never run so fast in his entire life. Even when he got frustrated in the English world and ran to let off steam, he'd never moved at this pace. He wasn't wearing running shoes, either, but he had made it to Leanna's in record time. He ran past the main house, where all the lights were off. When he saw her sitting on her front stoop, he skidded to a halt.

Leanna jumped up. "What's wrong?"

"Barbara . . . here?" he said, gasping.

"*Ya*. She's inside sleeping."

Relieved, Roman leaned over, putting his hands on his knees and gulping air. Suddenly he felt Leanna at his side, the light touch of her hand on his back, only to disappear when she moved away.

"Is Daniel all right?" she asked.

Catching the note of panic in her voice, he lifted his head and nodded. "He's worried . . . didn't know she left . . ."

The moonlight cast a shadow on Leanna's face. "I'll wake her up." She moved to go inside, but then stopped. "Did you run over here?"

He was finally able to stand up straight and look at her. He nodded.

"Why didn't you bring Daniel's buggy?"

He paused. He'd been so consumed with finding Barbara that he wasn't thinking clearly. Now she'd have to walk home with him. "I'll . . . I'll *geh* back and get it."

"Well, that would be silly. And a waste of time. You can borrow Jalon's horse and buggy to take her home. She's tired enough as it is."

"*Danki.*"

Roman waited outside while Leanna woke up Barbara. She didn't invite him in, and he wondered about that. As he thought about their kiss again, this time doubts set in. She had kissed him first, but maybe she thought she'd made a mistake. He thought about how quickly she had tried to pass it off as the result of bumping her head. Was that even possible, to kiss someone after being knocked out? But she'd seemed lucid. He ran his hands through his hair. When had all this gotten so complicated?

Leanna and Barbara came out of the house. In the illuminating moonlight Roman could see the fatigue in Barbara's face. He went to her and put his arm around her shoulders. "Daniel's worried about you."

She sighed. "I know. I'm sorry. I should have told him I was leaving. I didn't think I'd be gone that long, and he was sleeping so I didn't want to wake him up." She looked up at him with worry in her eyes. "Is he all right?"

"*Ya.* Although I had to make him stay home and wait. He wasn't too happy about that." He smiled, but his smile faded when she didn't even crack one in return.

"I'm sure he wasn't." She moved away from him and looked down at the ground.

This wasn't the first time he sensed something was off about Barbara, something beyond being tired and worried from Daniel's accident. But he wouldn't pry. He was just glad he found her quickly, and that she'd been able to go to Leanna and find a little bit of rest.

Leanna drove the buggy to the driveway and jumped out when Roman and Barbara reached her. "I'll have Jalon come get it in the morning," she said.

"You can come with us." Barbara went to her. "It's okay."

Leanna hesitated and then shook her head. "It's better that I don't. Jalon won't mind coming to get the buggy."

"I'll bring it back," Roman said.

"*Nee*, you've got too much work to do tomorrow."

"Then I'll come back tonight." He had no idea why Leanna wouldn't make the drive to Daniel's house, or why she insisted Jalon come get the buggy. Or why she was being so frustrating.

"All right." Barbara nodded and then gave Leanna a hug, the top of her head barely reaching Leanna's shoulder. "*Danki*," she said, her voice so soft Roman almost didn't hear her.

Roman drove the buggy back to Daniel's. His brother was dressed and waiting outside, and as soon as he saw the buggy, he hurried to it, wincing in pain as he did. He helped Barbara down and pressed her against him. "Why did you leave?"

She looked up at him, still trapped in his arms. "I needed some time alone." Her voice broke, and Daniel pressed her against him again.

Without a word Roman got back in the buggy and

left his brother and Barbara together. He hoped they would work out whatever was wrong. So much was happening he didn't understand—problems between Daniel and Barbara, Leanna's firing and her refusal to go anywhere near his brother's house, and, of course, the kiss. By the time he reached Leanna's, his stomach was in knots. He hated this feeling, one that was fully familiar to him as he grew up. This was why he didn't get involved. Didn't let people inside. That made him feel . . . and he didn't want to feel. Not this confusion and dread and worry. When it was just him, he could keep his focus narrow. Keep himself busy so he wouldn't be affected. But now . . . He was deeply affected. And he didn't know what to do about it.

· · ·

After Roman and Barbara left, Leanna turned to go back inside the house. It was late, and her head started to throb again. So much had happened in the past several hours she could barely comprehend it. All she wanted to do was fall into bed and sleep until morning. Hopefully Roman would come to his senses and not return Jalon's buggy tonight. He needed sleep too.

She was about to step inside when her bare foot touched something on the stoop. She leaned down and picked up a folded envelope. "Where did this come from?" She opened the door to let in some of the light from inside and saw it was addressed to Roman. He must have dropped it while he was here. She hadn't seen him holding anything, but maybe it fell out of his pocket. He had run all the way from Daniel's, so it would have been easy for the envelope to work its way out of his pants pocket.

She started to fold the envelope, but then noticed the return address. Dupree State. Had Roman applied there? She thought back to their talk at the pond. He had mentioned going to college to pursue his dream to be an engineer, but was this an acceptance? Something jolted inside her. It could just as easily be a rejection. Either way, it was a reminder that up until two weeks ago, Roman had been in the *bann*. He had left the Amish willingly, and apparently had plans to go to college. That wouldn't change after such a short period of time.

Leanna sat down on the stoop and held the envelope. If he'd been accepted, would he leave right away? Would he go like he did the last time, without a word, not even good-bye? The thought made her eyes burn. "Ugh," she said. Who would have thought she'd ever be teary about Roman Raber?

She lifted her chin. If he left, it wouldn't be a big deal. He'd done it before, and she and Daniel had managed. Now that she had her own shop, she didn't have to worry about gossip, and she could keep taking on jobs for Daniel. They didn't need Roman before.

But she needed him now. Not because there was enough work for the three of them to do. Or because she would miss his company. Or even because he had become a closer friend than she'd ever imagined. She needed him. She'd seen his loyalty to Daniel, his care for Malachi when the young boy was worried about his mother. Roman didn't know that even while she was playing tag, she had been watching him distract Malachi.

Then there was the enthusiasm he showed playing with the boys. The kindness he expressed with Barbara. His worry over Leanna being hurt. He was a good man, even if he didn't think so. But she knew. And God knew too.

How was she supposed to let that go? How could she forget him when he left?

She heard the sound of a buggy approaching and shook her head, letting out a curt laugh. She should have known he would bring the horse and buggy back right away. She looked at the envelope in her hand. She had to give it back to him. But as he pulled into the driveway, she tucked the letter underneath the back of her *kapp*. It was uncomfortable, but she didn't care. She wasn't ready to find out the truth just yet. She would delay as long as she could.

. . .

When Roman pulled into the driveway, he saw Leanna sitting on her stoop again. He drove the buggy to the barn and started to unhitch the horse. She got up and walked toward him. When she started to take the reins from him, he said, "I've got it."

"I can do it."

"I said I've got it!" He yanked the reins away from her, which wasn't easy since she could easily reach around him with her long arms and take them from him. But she took a step back instead.

"All right," she said quietly, wrapping those long arms around her waist.

But for some reason, her easily agreeing made him

even more irritated. "You don't trust me to take care of *yer* horse, do you?"

"Technically it's Jalon's horse."

"That's not the point and you know it." He led the horse to the barn, having enough sense about him not to yank on the poor animal. But as he put the horse up, even giving him extra feed for disturbing his sleep so late at night, he had to fight to maintain his composure. She didn't trust him, just like Daniel didn't. He was reaping what he sowed. In the past he would have shrugged it off. But he couldn't do that now. The shame of how he treated his brother and Leanna when he left last year dug deep inside him. His selfish actions had consequences, something he'd never thought of. He was reaping those too.

He turned off the lantern in the barn and went outside, intending to head straight home. He passed right by Leanna's house, not bothering to look back.

"I trust you."

Her words, softly spoken, made him halt. He turned toward her. She was still standing on the stoop, the door of her house open behind her, the glow of the light outlining her tall, thin frame.

"I couldn't have said that after you left. Or even when you first came back." She threaded her fingers together. "But I feel like I know you now. The real you. Not the one you always show to the world."

He couldn't move, could barely breathe. She trusted him? He couldn't believe it, but then he realized this was coming from Leanna. She didn't lie. She didn't play games. She wasn't going to compliment him to make him feel good. She would tell him the truth. Recognizing that propelled him to her. "*Danki* for believing in me. Only one other person ever has."

She nodded. She had said the right words, but there was still distance between them. "How is Barbara?"

"Tired. She and Daniel were talking when I left."

"*Gut.* I hope they work things out."

The last words were muttered, and he knew she hadn't meant to say them out loud. "I hope so too." After another long silence he asked, "Why didn't you come back to the *haus* with Barbara and me?"

She looked away from him and shrugged. "I'm tired."

"I'm sure you are. But you're the type of person who wouldn't let being tired get in the way of supporting a friend."

She faced him and crossed her arms over her chest. "You sound like you know me."

"I do." He closed the gap between them. "I do know you, Leanna."

• • •

Leanna had never felt so out of her depth in her life. She couldn't think straight, or feel straight, when she was around Roman. How could he know her, when right now she didn't even know herself—or even what she wanted?

He took one tentative step toward her and held out his hands. "What's going on here between us?"

She looked at his hands and had the sudden urge to

slip one of hers into his. She sighed. "I don't know. I'm so . . . confused."

"If it makes you feel any better, so am I. This is all new territory."

She met his gaze and asked him the one question that had been on her mind for the past several hours. "Are you mad that I kissed you?"

He tilted his head as he looked at her, his eyes lifting up so they could meet hers. Then he gave her a small smile. "*Nee*. Definitely not."

She almost leaned against the doorjamb with relief.

"But I think that's part of why I'm confused. I hadn't expected any of this when I returned to Birch Creek. Honestly, I thought I'd be here for only a little while. Just enough time to make things right with Daniel. As you can see, that didn't *geh* according to plan."

As he spoke, she thought about the envelope in her *kapp*. That was his real plan. College. A life in the English world. Her chest squeezed.

"When I decided to come back, I thought I could isolate myself. I did it before. I didn't get involved with anything or anyone when I was here last time."

This time she stepped toward him. "Why did you keep to *yerself* when you didn't have to?"

A flash of pain crossed his features. "You don't get involved—you don't get hurt."

She moved closer to him, her heart constricting. "That's *nee* way to live, Roman."

"It's the only way I know how."

She couldn't stop herself from holding out her hand. Without hesitation he took it, and they sat down together on the stoop. In the light from the house she could see his chest rising and falling, the tension that gripped his jaw. She couldn't imagine growing up with the parents Roman had. Her father had been distant at times, and he and Jalon didn't get along, but her mother had always been loving and supportive. Her father had also given her an important gift—the freedom to be her own person. He didn't try to make her conform to the typical Amish woman standard. He allowed her interest in machinery, even if he didn't share it or fully understand it. That gift had shown how much he loved her, and she had always been 100 percent sure of that.

"I figured I'd always be alone," he suddenly said, his voice barely a whisper.

Leanna held his hand tightly. "You've never been alone."

"I know. I had *mei bruder*, and of course *mei gross-mammi*. And it wasn't like our parents abandoned us, at least not physically."

"That's not what I'm talking about. God was there with you."

He moved away from her, scoffing. "Didn't seem like it," he muttered.

"Why did you join the church then, if you don't believe?"

Roman let go of her hand, a flash of anger in his eyes. "I never said I didn't believe. I do believe. That's what made it so hard. Why couldn't *mei* parents love me? Why couldn't God change them . . ." He choked. "Why couldn't he change me?"

"I don't know why he didn't change them. And you don't need changing."

"Daniel would disagree with you."

"Daniel is hurting too. "

Roman's eyes narrowed. "What are you, some kind of Amish psychologist?"

She almost laughed at that. "Hardly."

"You could have fooled me. You seem to have me pegged."

Leanna folded her hands over her knees. She grew very quiet, and very still. Two things she rarely was.

"Leanna?" He moved closer to her. "Did I upset you? If I did, it wasn't intentional. Like I said, I'm new to all this."

"I'm not upset." She leaned forward. "I just don't get how I can understand you, yet I don't have a clue about myself."

"Okay, now I'm completely confused." He scooted over a bit more, until their shoulders were almost touching. "You're the most self-assured person I've ever met."

"Except I'm not." He had laid himself bare to her emotionally, and she could do the same—even if she hadn't realized she needed to until this moment. "I'm a confirmed bachelor. You know that, right?"

His lips twitched. "Okay. An odd change of topic—not to mention wrong word usage—but I'm listening."

"Fine. I'm a confirmed bachelorette, although that word sounds too frilly to me." She drew in a breath. "I always told myself it's because I'm fine without dating or getting married."

"You don't need a *mann*," he said.

"Right. And technically I don't."

"Technically." His lips twitched again.

"Are you mocking me?"

"Absolutely not. Continue."

"I have *mei* own *haus*, I have *mei* own job . . . well, had—"

"Still have."

"Thanks to you." She smiled a little and then went back to the point. "But more importantly, from what I've noticed, dating and marriage are hard. People act silly when they're in love, and they do dumb things. They also get hurt. I didn't have any interest in that."

His eyes darkened. "Didn't?"

"I didn't want to get hurt, okay? You're not the only one protecting *yerself.*"

"So what changed?"

What had changed? The fluttery feelings in her stomach she'd been feeling around Roman and even when she kissed him weren't enough to make a huge shift in her heart. But while she had been reassuring him that he wasn't alone, she'd been reassuring herself. She had been lonely, even when she was surrounded by her family and friends. Not constantly lonely, but there were times when she was in her little house, sitting alone with only a few *Popular Mechanics* magazines to keep her company, when she felt separated. Jalon was married and had a family. Adam and Karen were together. She was surrounded by couples and families and . . . love.

What *had* changed? She turned to Roman, tears in her eyes, and for once she wasn't embarrassed that he was seeing them. "You," she said, her voice tight. "You changed. And I think . . . I think you changed me."

He sat there staring at her for so long, she thought she had said the wrong thing. Or had said too much. Then he pushed one string of her *kapp* over her shoulder, his eyes searching her face. "*Mei grossmammi* wanted me to come back to Birch Creek and reconcile with Daniel. She said we needed each other. But I also need something else." He took her hand in his. "I need you."

CHAPTER 16

Barbara sat on the edge of the bed, still wearing her dress and *kapp*, wrinkling the skirt of her dress in her hands. She hadn't said anything to Daniel as they walked back into the house, and she had kept quiet as he climbed into bed. His eyes had been questioning, searching, but she couldn't bring herself to speak. She couldn't even bring herself to lie next to him, even for a moment.

"Barbara."

She tensed at the gentle way he said her name. He didn't deserve her shutting him out like this. But she didn't know what else to do. Tears slipped down her cheeks, and she let them fall, surprised there were any left.

Behind her Daniel got out of bed and moved to sit next to her. He didn't say anything for a long time. Didn't reach for her hand. They sat a few inches apart, but the gulf between them was cavernous.

Finally, he said, "I'm sorry."

She closed her eyes against the brokenness in his voice. He didn't have to explain what he was sorry for. He'd already apologized, numerous times.

"What can I do to make it up to you?"

After a long pause, she said. "You don't have to make up for anything."

"I do. You haven't forgiven me, so I need to do something."

Something in her snapped and she turned to him. "You don't need to do *anything*. Don't you understand? You're always working too hard, drinking too much *kaffee*, staying awake at all hours. You're always worrying and hovering and . . . You're always doing, Daniel. You never just . . . stop."

His eyes widened with surprise. "I don't understand."

She blew out a breath. "Never mind." She didn't understand it either, only that they couldn't keep going on like this. She also knew she couldn't keep her secret anymore. "I lost the *boppli*," she said dully, staring in front of her.

She felt him stiffen beside her. "When?" he asked, his voice tight.

"The day of the accident. While you were in the hospital." She glanced at him and saw his head fall into his hands. Then she heard him sob, and everything hard and brittle inside her broke into pieces. She took him in her arms. "It's not *yer* fault, Daniel."

"It is." He looked at her, tears spilling. "The accident was *mei* fault. I wanted to take care of you and the *boppli*. I made it worse and—"

"Shh." She pulled him even closer and he pressed his face against her shoulder. Strangely, comforting him was also comforting her. "I'm afraid, Daniel. I'm afraid I'll never have a *boppli*."

He looked up from her shoulder and then took her in his arms. "It's okay. God will make a way."

"You sound like Leanna."

"She knows?"

"I had to talk to someone."

He stiffened again. "You should have come to me."

She looked up at him. "I couldn't bear to tell you I lost another *boppli*. I couldn't stand disappointing you."

"Listen to me." He cradled her face in his hands. "You haven't disappointed me. Am I disappointed about losing the *boppli*? *Ya. Mei* heart—" He took in a deep breath. "*Mei* heart is breaking over it. But I'll heal. We will heal. And we can try again."

She pulled away from him. "I can't . . . I can't *geh* through this again."

He stared at her and then wiped the tears from her cheeks. "Then we won't."

She shook her head. "I can't spend the rest of *mei* life not being with you either."

"That's not what I meant. We've both been focused on having a *boppli*, so much that it's taken over our lives. There's so much pressure, pressure I've put on you and myself." He waved his hand. "I'm stopping that now. If we're meant to have a *boppli*, God will bless us with one."

"And if I get pregnant again?"

"Then we'll see a doctor right away. I won't hover over you or put any stress on you. And if we lose another *boppli* . . . we'll get through it together, with God."

She'd always known her husband had a deep, abiding faith in God, but she'd never seen him so intense about it before. "Are you sure?"

"*Ya.*" He tucked her into the curve of his arm. "I love you, Barbara. Nothing will ever change that." He pressed a kiss to her temple. "And if you want to *geh* back and work at Schrock Grocery, you have *mei* blessing."

She looked up at him with surprise. His statement was so out of the blue. "Why are you bringing that up?"

"I had a lot of time to think in the hospital. I realized how unfair I've been to you. And it stops now."

She almost told him yes, that she would like to work for the Schrocks again. She had enjoyed her job at the small grocery store. But she also liked being home, knowing that her husband was close by. Not hovering, but working hard to support his family. Showing her how much he loved her the best way he knew how. "I don't think so," she said.

He held her away from him, puzzled. "Why not?"

"Who would bring you *yer* lunch every day?"

"I can get *mei* own lunch," he said.

"I know." She leaned against him. "But I want to be the one bringing it to you."

He pulled her close against him, and she felt his lips against the top of her *kapp*. She leaned into him, the despair she'd been carrying lifted. Not completely. She still needed to mourn, and she knew Daniel did too. But for right now she had hope, and she had her husband. That was enough.

. . .

As Leanna walked into Aden Troyer's barn on Sunday morning, Roman's college letter burned a hole in her *kapp* where she'd put it before she left the house. She hadn't seen Roman since he left her house nearly a week ago, kissing her lightly on the back of her hand and telling her good-bye. Even after they admitted they needed each other, she wondered if the good-bye would be permanent someday. If he was missing the envelope, he hadn't come back to find it. And she knew he had to be busy working, because she was too. A few more customers had heard about her workshop and had brought their machines straight to her. She made sure to tell them she was helping out Daniel while he was still recovering. She didn't want anyone to think she was in business for herself.

And each night after supper she had gone back out to her workshop to work on the clock Jedediah King dropped off. She still had no idea what was wrong with it. She'd taken almost the entire thing apart and still couldn't find the problem. But she wasn't giving up. She would never give up.

Leanna found her seat at the end of one of the benches. She searched around for Roman. She had to give him the letter. The guilt had nearly overwhelmed her this morning. She shouldn't have held on to it for so long. She saw Daniel as he entered the barn. He looked filled with trepidation, which she wasn't surprised to see. He had broken the Sabbath, and he would be required to confess and ask for forgiveness sometime during the service. She expected to see Roman right behind him, but he wasn't. Panic hit her. Had he left? Had he decided reconciling with Daniel wasn't worth sticking around? That she wasn't worth him staying?

"Can I sit here?"

Leanna looked up to see Barbara smiling at her. She calmed her nerves and scooted over on the bench, setting her thoughts about Roman on the back burner for a moment. When Barbara sat down, she leaned over and whispered, "You look better."

"I'm feeling better. Thanks for taking me in the other night." She gave Leanna's hand a squeeze. "Thanks for being such a *gut* friend."

The service started, and Leanna searched for Roman again. The congregation sung hymns, and she joined a couple, even though some of her notes were off-key. When they were finished singing, she looked for Roman once more. He wasn't there.

She was about to ask Barbara about him when Bishop Yoder got up and looked out over the congregation. He brought his fist up to his mouth and coughed, which made Leanna sit straighter in her seat. *Uh-oh.* Since she'd known Freemont for a long time, even before he became bishop, she could tell he had something important and not so pleasant to say.

"It's come to *mei* attention that there has been a problem with gossip in our congregation." His eyes scanned the crowd, but he avoided looking at Leanna. "I've preached about this before, but it seems that it's a message we need to hear again."

Leanna felt her cheeks heat. Surely he wasn't going to bring up what people were saying about her and Daniel? She looked at Barbara, who was staring straight ahead, but her hands were clenched in her lap.

"'Speak not evil one of another, brethren.'" That's

from the book of James. Some folks among you, some sitting right in these benches, have been speaking evil, and I am speaking to those folks now. You have been spreading lies, talking behind backs, and making judgments that aren't true and are based on absolutely nothing. What might seem like idle talk and conjecture has ended up causing pain and hurt. You know who you are, and you know the consequences *yer* gossip has caused."

He cleared his throat and then coughed again. "I'm not going to name names. Not because I'm protecting you. God knows what you've done and will deal with you accordingly. I'm protecting the ones who have been damaged by *yer* words and who are innocent." His gaze went to Leanna, and she thought she saw him barely nod. "'Let no corrupt communication proceed out of your mouth, but that which is good to the use of edifying, that it may administer grace to the hearers.' This is from the book of Ephesians, and we need to heed these wise words. We are to build each other up, not tear each other down."

The bishop continued to preach on the topic of good speech and encouragement, but Leanna barely heard him. She glanced at Melva and Tabitha, who were sitting one bench away and within her view. They both remained impassive, and Leanna wondered if they even realized the bishop was talking about them. It didn't matter. The message was important, and she agreed with Bishop Yoder that it was a message the whole congregation needed to hear.

And after Daniel made his confession and asked for forgiveness, everything felt right again. *Almost everything.*

After the service, Leanna and Barbara walked outside. Barbara went to Daniel and whispered something in his ear. He nodded, and they both came over to her. Daniel looked a little sheepish as he spoke. "Hi, Leanna. Interesting sermon today."

She smiled a little. "*Ya*, it was."

"Coincidental too. I was going to come see you tomorrow. Barbara and I talked about it, and it wasn't fair for me to fire you." He raised his hand when she started to speak. "Before you say anything, I want to ask you to come back to work for me."

She was so shocked her mouth dropped open.

"I'd understand if you didn't. I should have talked to you about what happened instead of just letting you *geh*. And if you say *nee*, I'll accept that. Just know that there's always a job for you at my shop."

"*Danki*," she said, still trying to process what he was saying.

"I promised Sadie I'd help with lunch," Barbara said.

"And I see Asa," Daniel added. "I need to talk to him." He and Barbara excused themselves, leaving her to watch them walk away.

She wasn't focused on getting her job back—although the offer was nice and unexpected. She was more struck with how Barbara and Daniel were more relaxed, more comfortable with each other. More at peace. She smiled. It was what she had prayed for.

"Leanna."

At the sound of Roman's voice she spun around. "You're still here!" she blurted.

"Of course I am. Where else would I be?"

"I, uh . . ." She thought about the envelope in her *kapp*, and she raised her hand to retrieve it.

"Can I talk to you for a minute?"

Leanna dropped her hand. Unlike Daniel, Roman didn't seem at peace at all. There was only one reason for that. *At least he's going to say good-bye this time.* Her stomach dipped. "Sure."

He led her over to the parked buggies, finding a spot secluded from everyone else. Then he faced her, looking straight into her eyes. "Was the bishop talking about you this morning? About someone gossiping about you?" he asked without preamble.

Wait, he was there after all. And this was what he wanted to talk about? After a quick moment of relief, she felt stressed again. *"Ya."*

"You and *mei bruder*?"

Again, she nodded, growing more nervous. How did he know? "Did someone say something to you?"

"Not directly to me," he said. "I was running late this morning, which was why I didn't come with Barbara and Daniel. As I came inside, I passed by a couple of the ladies. They were looking at you and Barbara sitting next to each other."

Dread formed in the pit of her stomach. "And they said something?"

Roman nodded. "They said Barbara should beware of a wolf in sheep's clothing."

Leanna felt like she'd been punched. What had she done to make those two women dislike her enough that they would say something so cruel?

"And when the bishop started talking, Daniel started

shifting in his seat. Then I glanced over and looked at you and Barbara . . ." His mouth formed a grim line. "Is that why Daniel fired you? Because someone suspected you two of having an affair?"

Leanna couldn't move. She couldn't read Roman's facial expression, either. It reminded her of when he first worked for his brother. Suspicious. Aloof. Even cold. "*Ya*," she whispered. "That's why he fired me." She waited for him to continue, but he didn't say anything, just stared at her with the guarded expression she disliked so much. Then she took a step back. "You believe them, don't you?" Before he could say anything, she exploded. "How could you believe that about me? About *yer bruder*?"

"I don't." He moved closer to her, putting his hands on her shoulders. "Leanna, I don't believe a word of it. But why didn't you tell me? Why did you keep this to *yerself*?"

She looked away. Didn't he know how much shame she felt?

"Leanna." He tilted her chin toward him. "You can tell me anything, even something as stupid and unbelievable as that. And the bishop's right—God will deal with them."

"Listen to you," she said, managing a smile as his hand left her face. "Having some faith in God, I see."

"I'm trying. He's been showing me a lot lately. Mainly about *mei* future."

"Speaking of." With regret she reached up to her *kapp* and pulled out the envelope. "You dropped this the other night."

He took the tightly folded envelope from her. "You kept it in *yer kapp*?"

"I don't have any pockets, okay?" She moved away from him. "And I'm sorry I didn't get it to you sooner. But I also didn't see you the rest of this week."

"I've been swamped at work." He put the envelope in the pocket of his pants. "I think I'm starting to get caught up. Daniel says he'll start working a little tomorrow, but Barbara says she'll make sure he takes it easy."

"That's *gut*." She looked at his pants pocket. Maybe she should just ask him what was inside the envelope. Yet again, a part of her didn't want to know. She looked between the buggies and saw everyone gathering to eat. "We should get back to lunch." She looked at him, her next words completely serious. "We don't want anyone to get the wrong idea about us."

He leaned over, his mouth hovering so close to her ear she could feel the whisper of his breath, making a shiver travel through her even though it was warm and sultry outside. "Let them," he said, and then he pulled away, smiling.

• • •

That evening Roman went outside and sat on the chair on the patio. The day had been hot, but now a slightly cooler breeze rustled the leaves of the trees surrounding his brother's home. September would arrive in a little more than a week. He hadn't expected to be here this long. Hadn't expected to feel like he belonged here. Hadn't expected to fall in love.

Love. Something he knew so little about, yet he was becoming more and more sure of it when it came to Leanna. He'd arrived at church late, having overslept from working so many hours in the shop. Even though he'd wanted to go see Leanna during the week, the job had to come first.

When he walked into the barn, he'd been thinking about one particularly difficult motor that he might have to give to Leanna to fix, and he was so distracted he found himself on the women's side of the barn. He quickly left, but not until after he'd heard the two women talking. Then he heard the bishop's sermon, and it hadn't taken him long to put everything together. He'd spent the rest of the service angry that Leanna had to endure the consequences of gossip and that his brother's character was also being dragged into question. But by the time the service ended, he had settled down. Now he understood why Leanna was fired and why she'd been devastated. He also realized his brother's reasoning behind it. Daniel had no choice—or at least believed he hadn't had one.

Roman pulled the envelope from his pocket. He'd been surprised she had it. He hadn't given it a second thought since he'd made his decision. She must not have read the letter, since she hadn't asked him anything about it—although he suspected she was curious. He would have to explain it all to her soon. Maybe tomorrow after work. It would give him an excuse to see her.

He was smiling when Daniel came outside and sat down next to him. He didn't look at him, even though Roman waited for an acknowledgment. He held in a sigh. Ironically, the one reason he'd come to Birch Creek still hadn't materialized. He wasn't sure what else he could do to prove to Daniel that he was sincere in wanting to reconcile.

After a long silence Roman was about to go inside. But then Daniel said, "Right after the service today I asked Leanna to come back to work for me. In the shop."

Roman grinned, although he was surprised she hadn't said anything about it. "That's great. When is she coming back?"

"I don't know. I told her to think about it. She might turn me down, but I made sure she knows there's always a place for her." He paused. "I'll be working full-time this week too."

So much for Barbara making sure Daniel took it easy. "You don't have to. Leanna's picking up the slack, and I've caught us up on some of the jobs you were . . . that were running behind." He would never reach Daniel's skill level or have Leanna's innate talent, but with enough practice he could be an adequate mechanic.

He turned and looked at Roman. "You're not needed anymore."

Roman blinked. "What?"

"I don't need you here." His jaw tightened. "I can handle things from here on."

Roman jumped up from his chair. "I can't believe you just said that. You're still healing, Daniel. And there's enough work for three people." His eyes burned and his throat grew thick, and he felt like he was a kid again, not worthy enough for his parents' attention and a pest to Daniel.

Daniel looked straight ahead. "Leanna and I can handle it."

"So everything I've done has meant nothing?" Roman gaped at his brother, watching him for any sign of recognition. "I kept *yer* business afloat. I solved the problem with Leanna and brought her back on board. I went and found *yer* wife—"

"Don't bring her into this." Daniel's jaw clenched as he turned to Roman. "She has nothing to do with us." He rose and faced Roman, who was a couple of inches taller than him. "I'm being practical, Roman."

"You're being nonsensical." He fisted his hands at his sides. "Was *mei* work not *gut* enough for you?"

Daniel paused and then shook his head. "You did *gut* work. You always do."

Roman froze at the unexpected compliment. "Then I don't understand. You need me—"

"*Nee,*" Daniel said. "I don't. I got along fine without you when you left. I'll continue to get along fine."

Hurt punched at Roman, but also realization. "Is that what you think? That I'll leave again?"

"Won't you? You always do. You ran away when we were kids, and I'd have to come after you."

"You know why I did that. You know how hard it was living in that *haus.*"

"But I didn't run away."

Roman crossed his arms over his chest. "Apparently I'm not as strong as you." He saw his brother's shoulders wobble a bit at that. "I was never the perfect *sohn.*"

"Neither was I." Now Daniel's entire body was shaking. "Nothing I did was right, either. But I didn't run away from *mei* problems. I didn't leave without saying a word to anyone. I didn't break our *grossmammi*'s heart and leave the church."

Roman stood stock-still. "I . . ." What could he say? His brother was right. He had done those things. What he didn't know was how much he'd hurt Daniel by doing that. "I'm sorry," he said. "I didn't know . . ."

"Because you didn't ask. You didn't come to me and tell me you were planning to leave." Daniel slumped in the chair. "I woke up that morning and you were gone. *Nee* note. *Nee* call later to let me know you were all right. I had to find out from *Grossmammi* that you left the church." He looked up at Roman. "I can't trust you, Roman. That's what you've proven to me."

Roman sat down next to his brother again, pulling the chair closer. "I've changed," he said. "I know I made mistakes, mistakes that hurt and worried you. That was never *mei* intent. I just . . . I just couldn't stay in that *haus*, and when you married and settled in Birch Creek, I thought I would be okay here. That living and working with you would be the solution to everything."

"Obviously it wasn't."

"But living in the English world wasn't either." He looked down at the patio. "I was a failure there too."

"You've never been a failure, Roman."

He was surprised to hear the words from Daniel, but it didn't make him feel better. He explained about his struggles to go to college, leaving out the part about getting the grant letter. "I was on *mei* last leg when I came to you."

"I figured. Which was why I offered you the job. I hadn't expected you to stay as long as you did. I didn't even expect you to last a day. And if I hadn't had the accident, you'd be gone by now."

"That's not true. I think . . . I think I might be finding *mei* place here."

"Because of Leanna?"

Roman lifted a brow. "What about her?"

"You seem to be friendly with her. More than when you were here last time."

"We've grown close. And I'd be lying if I said she isn't a part of why I want to be here. But it feels right this time. It did when I first came back, even though I could see you didn't want me here." When Daniel didn't say anything, he added, "What do I have to do to earn *yer* trust? Whatever it is, I'll do it."

· · ·

Daniel looked at his little brother, hardly believing what he'd heard. It had been hard to tell Roman he wasn't wanted, because it wasn't true. Daniel had always wanted a good relationship with Roman, especially since their relationship with their parents was so sterile. But Roman hadn't made it easy. And although Daniel would never admit it, every time Roman ran off, every time he yelled about how he'd be better off in another family or somewhere else away from all of them, it hurt. When he left Birch Creek that day, Daniel had vowed not to let him back in his life. He was through getting hurt by him. Only their grandmother's letter had made him agree to give him any sort of last chance. That, and the desperation he saw in Roman's eyes.

Now his brother was saying he had changed, and Daniel could see it. But something inside kept him from believing it. He'd been down this road before and it always ended up in pain.

"What can I do, Daniel?" Roman repeated.

Barbara's words entered Daniel's mind. What had she been trying to tell him? *You don't have to do anything. You're always doing. Just be. Just accept that I love you no matter what.*

Remembering hit Daniel square in the chest. Barbara hadn't required Daniel to prove anything to her. She loved him, even though he made mistakes, this latest one affecting them both and putting his business at risk. And he had hurt her too. So why was he putting restrictions on Roman? Why did his brother have to beg for Daniel's love and acceptance? They'd both done that with their parents and had been rejected.

What right did he have to reject Roman?

Daniel's chest heaved, a lump in his throat. "I'm sorry," he said, unable to look at his brother.

"I see." Roman stood, pain evident even though he was standing as stiff as a rod. "I'll pack *mei* stuff, then."

"Nee." Daniel shot up from the chair, ignoring the pain in his legs. "I'm apologizing *to* you." He put his hands on Roman's shoulders. "You don't have to earn *mei* trust."

"I do," Roman said, his voice thick. "I've broken it so many times."

"You have. But I'm choosing to keep trusting you."

Roman's eyes widened. "You really mean that?"

"I do. And when I let you down, I hope you'll keep trusting me too."

"You won't let me down." Roman shook his head. "You never have."

"I will. Neither one of us is perfect. It's why we need so much divine help."

Roman nodded. "I'm starting to realize that, finally."

"So you'll stay? And you'll still work for me?"

Roman surprised Daniel by pulling him in for a big hug. "You don't have to ask twice."

CHAPTER 17

On Monday evening after work, Leanna stood at the pond, staring at the light ripples breaking the still water. Today she'd finally figured out the problem with the clock, but instead of feeling the satisfaction of solving the issue, she kept thinking about Roman and the letter. She didn't want him to leave. But she wouldn't stand in his way if he did. She was confident that whatever path he chose, he would keep his faith in God. It ran deep, and it was well tested. That was what truly mattered.

She picked up a stone and skipped it, only to have it sink to the bottom. "Really?" she said, staring at more ripples. This was the second stone she'd tried to skip, and the second time she failed. Was she losing her touch? She bent down and picked up another one. Third time was the charm. Third time she would—

Her breath caught as she was cradled from behind. "Here," Roman said, putting one hand on her waist and the other on the hand holding the stone. "You need to work on *yer* technique." Together they threw the stone and it skipped perfectly.

She turned to face him. "I could have done that myself."

"I know." He grinned. "But it's more fun this way, *ya*?"

His arms were now at her waist, and his eyes were tilted upward, gazing at her with such emotion that she nearly lost her balance. "What are you doing here?" she asked, sounding breathless.

"Looking for you." He took her hand and they sat down on the bank. "You forgot to tell me something at church yesterday."

"I did?"

"You forgot to tell me you were coming back to work for Daniel."

"Oh." She crossed her arms. "I haven't decided that yet."

"What if I sweetened the offer?"

Now she was intrigued. "How?"

"You can work for Daniel, but stay at *yer* own shop. The arrangement seems to be working out well, and you don't have to worry about any old biddies gossiping about you."

"It's not nice to call them biddies."

"It's not nice to gossip," he said, scowling. "They're lucky I'm just calling them biddies."

"Roman," she said, trying to sound stern, but failing. She grinned, only to have her grin slip away when she realized he hadn't said anything about him working at the shop. Once again she couldn't bring it up. She tugged on a piece of grass and started tearing it to pieces.

Finally he spoke. "Daniel and I have reconciled."

"That's wonderful," she said, meaning it.

"I didn't think it would ever happen," Roman admitted. "But *Grossmammi*—and God—had other ideas."

"So *yer* reason for coming here is complete."

"I suppose it is."

"Then . . ." She swallowed. "Then what are you going to do?"

"About what?" He put his forearms on his knees and whistled.

Did he really not understand what she was asking? "About *yer* future?"

"Oh, it's set. Set in stone." He started whistling again.

This was like pulling teeth. "Meaning?"

"Meaning I know what I'm going to do." He was grinning, his focus on the pond, not her. "It feels great, you know? Understanding exactly where I belong. There's freedom in that. True freedom."

"I'm sure there is." She waited for him to explain, but he started whistling again. Frustrated, she shoved his shoulder lightly. "Will you stop that?"

"Ow!" he said, his bottom lip poking out. "You're stronger than you look."

"And you're driving me crazy." She blew out a breath. "What have you decided about college?"

"So you read *mei* letter?"

"Of course not." She lifted her chin. "I don't do that anymore." At his puzzled look she waved him off. "But I saw the return address on the envelope. You applied to Dupree, didn't you?"

"*Ya.* Before I got to Birch Creek, actually. But I could never get the funding to *geh*." He told her about applying for government financial aid. "That was *mei* last resort. Until now. The engineering department awarded me a grant. Full tuition for the whole year."

"Oh." Her shoulders slumped. There was her answer, then. He had no reason to stay here, and every reason to leave. "That's . . . great."

"You think so? Because I don't."

Her head shot up. "What?"

"I thought college was what I wanted. That and adventure. Getting away from the rules and from *mei familye* and carving *mei* own path. Alone. And if I didn't get the grant money, I'd figure out how to do it another way. There's always a choice." He turned to her. "I'm choosing the right one. I'm staying here."

Her heart swelled with joy as she tackled him. He landed on his back with her on top of him. "Sorry," she said, her voice squeaking. She was about to move off of him when he pulled her closer, touched her face, and drew her down for a sweet kiss.

So perfect. Everything, including Roman, was perfect.

When he pulled away, he asked, "Was that okay?"

"Would I have kept kissing you if it wasn't?" she said with a smirk.

"Very funny."

They both got up and walked back to the *dawdi haus*. When they got to her front door, he said, "Now that I'm staying here, I want to make things official between us. Will you *geh* out with me? I can't promise I won't mess up this dating thing. I'm not an expert at it."

She leaned down slightly and touched her forehead to his. "I'm sure you're a fast learner."

. . .

Nearly a week later, Roman and Leanna finally went on their first date—which started as a scavenger hunt. Leanna found a note posted on the door of her house Saturday evening after she got home from work, and the clue led her and Jalon's horse and buggy on a hunt through parts of Birch Creek. Of all places, she ended up right back at her house, where she found Roman standing there, holding a picnic basket.

"You sent me all over creation for a picnic at *mei* own home?" she said, exasperated. Well, not completely. The scavenger hunt had been fun, and his clues were clever.

"Not here." He helped her with the horse and buggy and then took her hand and led her to the pond. When they arrived, he sat down with the basket, pulled out a blanket, and spread it on the ground. "I figured you'd like to have supper here one time."

"I've eaten here lots of times." But it had never been special, mostly a sandwich while she was fishing or a thermos of coffee and a cinnamon roll when she was ice-skating.

"Oh?" He started to pull up the blanket but she plopped down on it. He grinned and kept unpacking the picnic basket. "Barbara said these are some of *yer* favorites."

"They are." She looked at the spread and was impressed. He'd even brought a thermos of lemonade, one of her favorite drinks. When he sat down, he took her hand as they prayed over the food, and then he handed her a meat loaf sandwich.

She took a bite and savored it. "Barbara makes the best meat loaf," she said around a mouthful.

"True." He examined his own sandwich. "But I'd hoped *mei* attempt would be adequate."

"You made this?"

He nodded. "And the potato salad—*mei grossmammi*'s recipe, by the way—and the brownies."

"When did you find time to do this?"

"Daniel let me off work early." He smiled. "I hope this is okay," he said, gesturing to the food in front of him.

"It's more than okay. The scavenger hunt was fun too."

He smiled. "I thought you'd like that."

"We should do one together," she said.

"That's a *gut* idea."

They ate and talked a little about work, but Leanna noticed Roman was preoccupied. "There's something on *yer* mind," she said as she took a bite of fresh red-skinned potato salad.

He nodded, then reached into the pocket of his pants and pulled out a letter. "Barbara gave me this before I came over." He looked at the envelope. "It's from *mei grossmammi*."

Leanna could see the envelope was still sealed. "You haven't read it yet?"

He shook his head. "Daniel got one, too, and when I was leaving, he and Barbara were sitting at the kitchen table. I know Daniel was going to read it with her." He looked at Leanna. "I didn't want to read mine alone."

She didn't move. Remembering how she had read Daniel's letter without permission, she said, "Are you sure you want to read it in front of me? Maybe it's something private."

His eyes darkened. "Nothing is private between us, Leanna."

She got up from her side of the blanket and sat down next to him. After she gave him a little nod, he opened the envelope, pulled out the letter, and started to read aloud.

Dear Roman,

If you're reading this now, it's because you and Daniel have reconciled. Don't be upset with Barbara for withholding this letter from you. That was my last request of her—to give you and Daniel your letters only if you two had settled your differences. I wish I could be there to see the two of you, to hug you and tell you how happy you've made me. You've honored each other, and you've honored God by putting the past behind you and giving and accepting forgiveness.

I want to explain about your parents. I should have told you both this sooner, but I was afraid you wouldn't understand when you were younger. Then Daniel married and left, and then you left, and after that I didn't think it mattered. But facing death has given me a new perspective, and I don't feel like this is something I can keep to myself anymore. I wrote this letter at the last minute, after I wrote to you and Daniel about reconciling. I didn't want you to find out about this without you and Daniel being together. I wanted you to focus on the future, not on the past, and not on something that, without a miracle, will never change.

Your father has always been different. Even as a child, he never showed affection. It was difficult for both your grandfather and me, because we didn't understand why. Even though we showed all the love we could to your father, he could never reciprocate. We thought he would never marry. It was something he never talked about, never seemed to want. He was a loner, and seemed satisfied to be in his own world, a member of the church but not a part of it, following the rules but not embracing what his faith meant.

Then he met your mother at one of his cousin's weddings, and they started writing to each other. I didn't know much about her, other than she, like your father, was unusual. When your father announced they were getting married and she was moving to Draperville, I was overjoyed. Finally, someone understood my son. Loved my son. But from the moment they were married, I could see their union was not one born of love, but of convenience. They were expected to marry. It's the Amish way. So they fulfilled that expectation and had you and Daniel. But there was never any love there, at least that I could see. And when I saw how they treated you and Daniel, as though you were obligations instead of their sons, I knew I had to intervene. I wanted to give you both the love your parents couldn't. Only God knows if I succeeded.

Roman stopped, and Leanna felt him tense beside her. She reached for his hand and he squeezed it, and then he kept reading.

I don't know why your parents are the way they are. Only God knows that. I love my son as much as I always have. I love my daughter-in-law too. I've been frustrated with them, but that doesn't change my love for them. And they did give me you and Daniel. Especially with your grandfather gone, you two have given me all the love I need, and more.

Please don't let your parents affect your future. You and Daniel have so much love to give. Daniel has Barbara, and I know someone is out there for you. If you and Daniel can forgive each other and move forward, please, forgive your parents too. I promise you will feel free of the past if you do.

Love,

Grossmammi

Leanna looked at Roman. His eyes were misty. She turned and faced him. "Can you do what she asks?"

Roman looked at the letter and then at her. He chuckled despite the sorrow in his expression. "*Mei grossmammi* always knew what she was doing. If I'd read this before, I would have thought she was wrong. But now I can see how forgiveness changes people. How important it is." He cupped her cheek. "I can also see how love changes them." He took her hand and put it against his chest. "I love you, Leanna."

She felt the rapid beat of his heart against her palm. "I love you too."

"I know you're an independent woman," he said, a smirk on his face. "And you don't need a *mann*—"

"*Ya*. I'll marry you."

"I haven't asked you yet."

"But you're going to, right?"

"I was eventually," he muttered. "Just not this soon." He looked at her. "*Danki* for blowing *mei* future surprise."

She launched herself into his lap, and he hugged her close. "You've already surprised me a couple of times today," she said in his ear. "Isn't that enough?"

He kissed her. "*Nee*. When it comes to you, I'll never have enough."

She leaned her head against his shoulder, but then sat up. She scrambled off his lap, moving to her knees in front of him. "I can't cook," she said, unable to look him in the eye. What kind of Amish woman couldn't cook?

"That's fine. I'm not picky."

"*Nee*. I mean I can't cook, period. Not at all. I can't sew, and I'm fairly certain I ruined a few cans of Phoebe's tomatoes a few weeks ago when I was helping her put up the garden. I pray she'll forgive me for that." She glanced up and saw Roman's inscrutable expression. But she continued. He needed to know what kind of wife he was getting, and if he wanted her at all after he did. "I'm messy. Really messy. I can keep *mei* workstation tidy, but that's about it. I haven't made *mei* bed in a week. *Nee*, make that a week and a half."

"Are you finished?" he asked, still looking unreadable.

She wasn't, and this was the hardest thing for her to admit, but also the most honest. "I have *nee* idea how to be a mother. I can play with kids, but I don't know how to take care of them. I put Hannah's diaper on backward twice the other day. She wasn't too happy about that. She's turning out to be a little sensitive, by the way. Jalon is going to have his hands full." She looked at him again. "I never thought I'd have to learn any of those things. I never thought I'd be a wife . . . or a mother."

"Leanna." Roman knelt in front of her and held her hands. "I can cook, so don't worry about that. I'm also tidy, so let me worry about making the bed." He squeezed her hands. "But I don't know anything about being a husband or a father. I never thought I'd want those things." He gazed in her eyes. "Now I want them more than anything. And I want them with you."

"Are you sure?"

"Positive. We'll figure this out, Leanna. Together."

After their picnic, they headed back to the house. When they got there, she saw Tabitha and Melva standing on Jalon's front porch, talking to Malachi. He was holding Blue up to them. "See?" he said, thrusting the cat at the two women. "He's really friendly."

"Allergic," Tabitha said, turning to sneeze.

"Me too." Melva wiped her eyes.

"Malachi, what are you doing?" Leanna hurried to the front porch and took the cat from him. Blue scrambled out of her arms and ran off. Malachi scampered after him. "Sorry about that," she said, forcing a smile at the two women. What were they doing here?

"That's a big cat," Melva said, scrunching her nose.

"I hope he's had his shots," Tabitha added under her breath.

"Can I help you ladies with something?" Leanna fought for patience. It was one thing to impugn her character. Quite another to insult her and Malachi's cat.

Melva turned to her. "I understand our brother, Jedediah, brought you our grandfather's old clock."

"It hasn't worked for years," Tabitha said.

"At least thirty," Melva added.

"Thirty-five, I'm sure," Tabitha corrected.

"*Ya*, he brought me the clock. Believe it or not it was just missing a screw." A really tiny, almost microscopic screw. "That's all it needed."

"A screw," Melva said. "Well, I'll be."

"That's a surprise." Tabitha's graying brows lifted above her wire-rimmed glasses. "Something as simple as that."

"Oh, it wasn't that simple." Roman came up behind the women and stood next to Leanna. "She had to take apart the entire clock, examine each part, figure out what screw was missing and how to find a replacement, *geh* all the way to Barton to get it at a watch repair shop, and then put the whole thing back together. Not simple at all."

Leanna smiled at him, detecting the tiny note of pride in his voice.

"And you only charged Jedediah twenty-nine dollars? For all that work?" Melva asked.

"I enjoyed it. Figuring out what was wrong with it was like a puzzle. I can't charge for having fun."

"When Jedediah brought the clock home after you fixed it . . ." Melva wiped her eyes again, and Blue wasn't anywhere in sight.

"It brought back so many memories." Tabitha's smile deepened. "That was our favorite item of *Grossdaadi*'s. We thought it was permanently broken. *Danki* for fixing it for us."

"And we're . . . sorry," Melva said. "For causing you and Daniel any problems. We realized we made a mistake."

"*Ya.*" Tabitha lifted her chin. "We made a mistake."

Leanna exchanged a confused look with Roman. "Okay," she said, waiting for the other shoe to drop. Melva and Tabitha never apologized to anyone. She'd take it. "You're welcome."

As the women left, Leanna leaned against Roman. "That was a surprise," she said.

"More like a shock." He turned to her. "But like you said, God can change hearts."

Leanna chuckled. "Even Melva and Tabitha's."

EPILOGUE

Ivy Yoder stood to the side as she watched her sister and best friend marry the loves of their lives. She brushed away a tear, one of several she had shed over the past couple of weeks. It wasn't because she wasn't happy for Karen and Adam and Leanna and Roman. Or that she resented having to help with their double wedding. Because she was honored to do so. She was doubly honored to be the maid of honor for both women. But the same question entered her mind every time she attended a wedding, and she'd been to a lot of them. *When will it be my turn?*

The vows were spoken, the pronouncements made, and everyone gathered to congratulate the couples. Leanna beamed as she stood by Roman, holding the bouquet of dried sunflowers Ivy made for her. Karen's was filled with dried daisies, her favorite flower. Her sister kept looking down at her husband, who was holding her hand and beaming brighter than Ivy had ever seen him. No one had been surprised about Karen and Adam marrying. In fact, it was expected. The big surprise had been Leanna and Roman. Not only that they were getting married, but so quickly. Ivy was also taken aback. But she was truly happy for her friend. For all of them. They were her family.

She slipped away for a few moments, trying to gather herself before she pasted on a smile and went back to the festivities. She didn't want to be like this. When she and Leanna had agreed they would always be happy being single, she had spoken the truth. Or she thought she had. But all that changed in August, and not only when she returned home in early September and found out Leanna and Roman were dating. She'd given Leanna more than a few words for keeping her in the dark about that. But Ivy had her own secret. Something had happened to her in Michigan. Something exciting . . . or so she'd thought.

She pulled her sweater closer around her body as the fall breeze swirled the brightly colored leaves around her. She went to stand near Leanna's shop, which had a complete makeover last month courtesy of the Bontrager brothers. They had not only painted the wood, but they added extra space, which Leanna needed since she kept so busy. Roman had decided to split his time between his brother's shop and Leanna's. Everything was working out for the best.

Would it turn out that way for her, eventually? She thought it might when she returned to Birch Creek. She had believed his promise that he would write to her, that soon he would come out and visit, and that, of course, she was always welcome to come see him. She'd been so busy with the sudden wedding preparations that she couldn't get away. In the end it didn't matter since she never heard from him. Now, almost three months later, she didn't think she ever would.

"Hey, Ivy."

She turned around to see Noah Schlabach walking toward her. Tall, lanky, awkward Noah. Next to Joel Chupp, he was the tallest man she'd ever seen. He didn't live in Birch Creek, but a few times a year he visited his great-aunt Cevilla, who had moved to Birch Creek a few years ago. Ivy had sometimes chatted briefly with him when he was there.

Cevilla, who had never married, was a bit of an anomaly in the community, but Ivy liked her and always enjoyed their visits.

Ivy craned her neck at Noah. "Hi," she said, not really in the mood to talk to him. All she knew about him was that he was several years older than her and a sought-after auctioneer. He often traveled to Amish settlements to organize auctions. He was also friendly, at least he was in the few polite interactions she'd had with him.

"You got a minute?" he said. "I have a favor to ask." He frowned, his thick black eyebrows forming a V over hazel-green eyes.

"Sure. What can I help you with?"

He bent down slightly as he spoke. "It's about *Aenti* Cevilla."

"She's all right, isn't she?" Ivy had seen her at the wedding a few minutes before and she looked well. "Is something wrong?"

"She's fine. She's also full of surprises, that's for sure. Did you know her stepmother was English before she became Amish? She married an Amish man when she was in her thirties. Didn't have any kids of her own. She actually served in World War II as a nurse. She was also—" He gave Ivy a sheepish look. "I'm sure you don't want to know *mei familye* history."

She didn't respond, even though she was slightly intrigued. And more than a little puzzled. Why hadn't Cevilla brought any of that up before?

"Anyway, Glenda—Cevilla's stepmother—had a sister. She was the one who inherited all of Glenda's stuff. But her family has decided they don't want it, so they packed everything up and sent it over. Thirty boxes. Thirty *large* boxes."

"That sounds like a lot."

"That's just the first shipment. Apparently, Glenda was a pack rat."

Ivy peered past Noah's slim arm and saw the food was being served. "I need to get back to the reception," she said, looking up at him again.

"Oh. *Ya*, of course. I didn't mean to keep you. I just wanted to explain why I need you to help me *geh* through all the boxes."

"Me?" Ivy said in surprise.

"*Aenti* Cevilla is insisting on it. I don't know why." His finger twirled in a circle by his ear. "I think she's a little off her rocker."

Ivy chuckled. Cevilla Schlabach *was* unique, which was why Ivy liked her. "I can *geh* over there tomorrow and get started."

"No can do," he said in English. Then he switched back to *Dietsch*. "She wants both of us to *geh* through them. Together. But I'm booked up with auctions for the next six months."

"Does Cevilla know that?"

Noah nodded. "*Ya*, but she's still insisting we have to do this together. As soon as I'm free, I'll come back to Birch Creek and we can start."

"I'm sure she won't mind if I get a head start."

"You can try, but she'll say *nee*. Like I said"—Noah started to walk away, his finger circling his ear again— "Off her rocker."

Ivy shook her head and smiled. She suspected Cevilla wasn't the only one a little off-center in the Schlabach family. But it would be okay. She wouldn't mind sorting through boxes. She loved old things and antiques. Anything to do with history. The project might be fun, and Noah's aunt could always tell a good story.

Ivy was eager for the distraction too. If she was busy thinking about the past, she wouldn't have to worry about her future . . . or about the man she'd fallen in love with in Michigan.

ACKNOWLEDGMENTS

Many thanks to my editors, Becky Monds and Jean Bloom. You always keep me encouraged and on track. To my agent, Natasha Kern, whose support has been invaluable. And as always, thank you, dear reader, for coming with me on another adventure in Birch Creek.

DISCUSSION QUESTIONS

1. Leanna's life was turned upside down in an instant. Has this ever happened to you? How did you handle it?

2. Roman's grandmother never gave up hope that he would reconcile with Daniel. How does God sustain you while you have unanswered prayers?

3. Daniel's overprotectiveness of Barbara had dire consequences. What could he have done differently?

4. Tabitha and Melva's gossip caused huge problems for Leanna. How do you handle people who gossip?

5. Was Daniel fair in treating Roman the way he did when Roman first came back? Why or why not?

6. Roman thought he was following God's plan, but instead he was escaping from the pain in his life. Have you ever done this? How did God heal and redirect you?

7. Daniel realized he had to forgive Roman, but it took him a long time to do so. Why do you think he held on to his bitterness for so long?

8. At the end of the story, Roman's faith has been strengthened. How do you strengthen your faith?

AMISH BRIDES

— *of* —

BIRCH CREEK

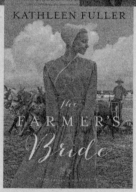

AVAILABLE IN PRINT
AND E-BOOK

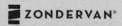

Read more from Kathleen Fuller
in her Amish Letters series!

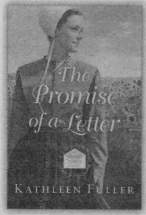

AVAILABLE IN PRINT AND E-BOOK.

DON'T MISS FOUR SWEET AND FUNNY AMISH LOVE STORIES.

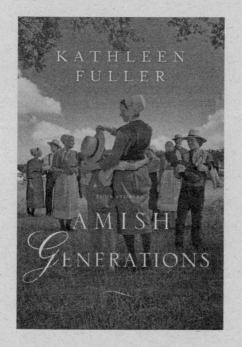

COMING JUNE 2020

About the Author

With over a million copies sold, Kathleen Fuller is the author of several bestselling novels, including the Hearts of Middlefield novels, the Middlefield Family novels, the Amish of Birch Creek series, and the Amish Letters series as well as a middle-grade Amish series, the Mysteries of Middlefield.

Visit her online at KathleenFuller.com
Instagram: kf_booksandhooks
Facebook: WriterKathleenFuller
Twitter: @TheKatJam